DEAD NEON

WEST WORD FICTION

DEAD NEON

Tales of Near-Future Las Vegas

EDITED BY

Todd James Pierce and Jarret Keene

UNIVERSITY OF NEVADA PRESS

RENO & LAS VEGAS

WEST WORD FICTION

University of Nevada Press, Reno, Nevada 89557 USA

Copyright © 2010 by University of Nevada Press

Manufactured in the United States of America

Design by Kathleen Szawiola

Library of Congress Cataloging-in-Publication Data

Dead neon : tales of near-future Las Vegas /
edited by Todd James Pierce and Jarret Keene.
p. cm. — (West word fiction)
ISBN 978-0-87417-828-9 (pbk. : alk. paper)
1. Las Vegas (Nev.)—Fiction.
I. Pierce, Todd James, 1965– II. Keene, Jarret, 1973–
PS572.L37D43 2010
813'.609358793135—dc22
2010014698

The paper used in this book is a recycled stock made from 30 percent post-consumer
waste materials, certified by FSC, and meets the requirements of American National
Standard for Information Sciences—Permanence of Paper for Printed Library Materials,
ANSI/NISO Z39.48-1992 (R2002). Binding materials were selected for
strength and durability.

FIRST PRINTING
19 18 17 16 15 14 13 12 11 10
5 4 3 2 1

to our children, who with any luck
will not inhabit a city of dark dreams

CONTENTS

PREFACE

To many visitors, Las Vegas is a din of dirty money, the sound of power and sex clanging together like a slot machine paying out a jackpot. It is the sound of taxicabs, hustlers on a street corner, and police sirens screaming in the distance. It is the sound of the American Dream struggling for its last breath, the sigh of desperation mixed with the faint staccato of hope. But if you listen closely, there is another sound in the mix: the quiet hum of technology, electricity whispering through circuits, and the murmur of neon illuminating the night.

Las Vegas is a hi-tech city founded on a powerful technological vision of the twentieth century: that millions of people from all over the planet might drive combustible-engine automobiles or fly in jets into the middle of a vast desert for pleasure and entertainment. The city founders foresaw that travelers could be lulled into machine dreams of sin and greed, most of which depended on ever-advancing technologies. From fresh food to water and energy, Las Vegas's existence is made possible by advances in transportation and aeronautics, surveillance systems and LCD screens, as well as humans' ability to manipulate the Colorado River.

Even in the early twentieth century, Las Vegas was a science-based vision of the future, one intimately connected to the Atomic Age. Not too long ago, guests could enjoy drinks on their hotel balconies and watch as a mushroom cloud billowed just beyond the valley. The Nevada Test Site is less than a hundred miles away, and it's where the instruments of the Cold War were tested and retested. Even though science and futurism are no longer part of the overt public-relations message of the city, hints of the apocalypse remain a part of the city's existence, like a bad memory or a bloodstain that simply won't go away.

Of course, science fiction isn't about stories of the past. Science fiction is about stories of the future—whether distant or near. In this town, though, the future has already arrived. Present-day Las Vegas already provides the technological sophistication and modernism necessary for a fabulous near-future science-fiction story. From facial-recognition software used by casinos to identify card counters to the cyborg-inspired mechanics of its shows, the people who work and play in Vegas are already immersed in next-generation wonders. Once you consider the simulated volcanic eruptions of the Mirage and the giant synchronized fountains of Bellagio and the massive glass-walled towers of City-Center, technology trumps humanity. No other city offers so many unique avenues for serious literary exploration of the end times; readers and writers of sci-fi know this.

Though early visions of Vegas valued spontaneous human experience and live entertainment, more recent visions have become burdened by technology, transforming the town into a sterile, electronic graveyard. What was once a boomtown is now a "doom town," especially if you live here. And if Vegas collapses, so does the United States, some say. So what would a collapsing, or collapsed, Vegas look and feel like? Who would live there, and why?

This collection explores the future of America by examining the near future of Las Vegas. Many legendary sci-fi, horror, and fantasy authors, including Stephen King, have already turned their literary attention to this city's myth and magic. But in this collection the most recent payout of Vegas-based and (inter)national writers presents a fascinating vision of Sin City. These imaginative artists will take you into the heart of America's most notorious metropolis, offering readers an insider's prediction, or maybe even prophecy, of the challenges that might one day be found there. These stories capture the sound of the slot machines and the taxicabs, the hustlers and the hustled, the whirr of a thousand circuits, and the trouble these noises portend.

Prepare yourself for the noise and the power, for stories streaked across the messy canvas of the near future, as you dip into this dark and delicious book.

ACKNOWLEDGMENTS

The editors wish to thank Avenger of Blood, Close to Modern, Curl Up and Die, Dreaming of Lions, Doom Snake Cult, Drainage X, Eleven Thousand, Goatlord, Guttural Secrete, Hallowed Butchery, Halloween Town, Hemlock, In the Flesh, Frank Klepacki, Las Vegas Club, Love Pentagon, Minor Suns, Mother McKenzie, Pancho Villa, Pigasus, Red State Soundsystem, Righteous Pigs, Romance Fantasy, Jacob Smigel, Sorcerer (Las Vegas), Spun in Darkness, Sutured Esophagus, the Vermin, and the Weirding Way for providing the soundtrack.

We are grateful for the visual artistry of Michael Baker, Elizabeth Blau, Rebekah Bogard, Catherine Borg, Diane Bush, Shan Michael Evans, Yo Fukui, Stephen Hendee, Dave Hickey, Angela Kallus, Wendy Kveck, and Jerry Misko, as they influenced the conceptual design of *Dead Neon*.

We especially appreciate the emotional support provided by Justin Chomintra, Michelle DiTondo, Vanessa Doleshal, Justin Hammond, and Douglas May during construction.

DEAD NEON

CHRIS NILES

> ## Sin's Last Stand

My name is Melissa Jane Gibson and I've just turned seventeen.

They've asked me to explain what happened. I'll do the best I can. Fact is, I don't know how I got from the person I was back then to the person I am today. If you had asked me before it started, I would have said that I wasn't capable of such things. Even though I'm a nongod, I know the difference between right and wrong.

My mother used to say that nongods were just as moral as forgods. But nobody else did. The forgods tell us that to be good it's necessary to have a personal relationship with the Lord Jesus Christ. Nongods by definition are immoral and bad. And they hate America.

There was a time when nongods were given a say in how the country was run. They were able to work as teachers, doctors, and scientists. They were able to hold public office. Apparently there was a time, too, when nongods made licentious feature-length movies that forgods were forced to go and watch and eat lots of bad food, which is how they all got so fat.

But most of the records of that time have vanished. Once the Onegod government was established, forgods said that the Onegod didn't like licentious feature-length movies, so they were destroyed, along with the rest of the evidence of that wicked time. You can understand it, I suppose: they are trying to help people to get to heaven and, if licentiousness stands in the way, then it's probably best to try and get rid of it.

My mother raised me to consider the other person's point of view. She called it open-mindedness—that's the word I remember. Although I never hear it spoken now in quite the way she used it. The language has changed quite a bit since my mother was a girl. According to the *Words of God* dictionary, open-mindedness now means the ability to choose quickly between two flavors of yogurt when standing in line at the lunch counter.

Perhaps I should just talk a little bit more about my mother, because it might explain how I got into this situation. Not that I am seeking to justify my actions. Forgods tell us that nongod science, developed by Jews at a time when they were allowed to live among the righteous, gives weak people an excuse to put the blame for their behavior where it doesn't belong—like on repressed thoughts and feelings—instead of on the wickedness of the first female. But I think if I tell exactly what happened, it might help.

Everybody knows about Sin's Last Stand, the battle for Vegas. I won't go over it again, except to explain how it made me an orphan.

♠ My mother had been a geologist, but her job went away after it became illegal to teach that anything was older than the Bible said.

She had not planned to move to Vegas, but because high principles had never had much traction there, it had become, almost by default, the last nongod refuge. Some of the best scientific brains in the country were working the tables, trying to make their living from gambling. "Numbers are numbers," as one theoretical physicist told me once when I asked her whether she minded.

Mom ran a roulette table at Bellagio, and most days I went to the casino with her because the schools had been closed. For years, forgods had been taking their children out of school and telling them things about Jesus at home. And even after forgods had control of the education curriculum, they still thought that schools were bad places where humanistic urges might spring up at any moment. Then forgods decided that nongods didn't need to be taught when all they did was clean forgod houses and ring up forgod groceries. And, as one forgod had explained on television, if nongods were given books, soon they'd be running the schools again, forcing forgod kids to learn some fool theory that contradicted the facts in the book of Genesis. No, it seemed safer all round to only allow the Bible—that way people wouldn't be tempted to learn.

♠ Sin's Last Stand. Sounds grand, doesn't it? Like General Custer, or Thermopylae? But, as the gambling professors once told me, the winners write history, and they usually fiddle with the facts.

Bellagio, like every other casino on the Strip, was home for nongods.

We had thought we were safe inside those walls with no clocks, no windows, no references to the outside world. We thought, too, that because forgod leaders were more often than not at the slot machines or checking into the honeymoon suite with women, or men, who were not their wives, that they would continue to describe the Strip as "a den of atheistic iniquity," but do nothing.

♠ The soldiers came before dawn. All the casinos were doing brisk business. Nongods usually stayed up all night because, since the Love Crime Act had made it legal for a forgod to kill a nongod if they thought their faith was being threatened, there was no sensible reason to be out on the streets during the day.

The troops wore goggles and had television cameras strapped to their helmets providing live network coverage. One carried a megaphone.

"Nongods, in the name of Brother John and the Onegod government, I order you to repent."

Nobody answered, nobody moved. The only sound was the clatter of a roulette wheel as it slowed.

"Step forward, nongods. Accept the Lord Jesus Christ as your personal savior."

Still nothing.

The man with the megaphone seemed agitated now. His hands shook; perhaps he was as frightened as we were. He cleared his throat before speaking.

"Christ died for your sins. Step forward, and repent!"

The roulette wheel stopped, the ball settling on red 14.

The soldiers fired. Round after round.

The lights went out. It got dark and dusty, and I could smell blood and fear. My mother was one of the first to be killed. She died right in front of me. I don't know how all those bullets missed me.

♠ Nongod orphans are usually sent to the Suffer the Children Home for the Ungodly. I'd heard that it was well named: kids do suffer there, and repentance is guaranteed after a short period of what's described as "godly persuasion."

But they didn't put me there, because it turned out that I have the same name as some old saint.

"Mel Gibson?" The woman at the front desk started when she saw it. "That's your name?"

I showed her my nongod papers, stamped with a pentacle.

"Goodness me, perhaps it's a sign," she muttered and reached for the phone.

There's something else I should mention. There are few children left. After the third repeal of the Clean Air, Water, and Mind Act, it was discovered that industrial pollutants—even when they're legal and blessed by God—permanently damage unborn children. Many of the forgods are sterile now, and nongods are forbidden to breed because, as the Onegod government says, "Acid rain falls on the just and the unjust alike."

So that was how I got to go and be the foster daughter of a forgod couple, Brian and Judy Lovely.

♠ Judy was fat. She ran a successful business that performed plastic surgery on forgods who wanted to look like their favorite biblical character. One had to credit her for spotting a gap in the market, she told me on the Super Enviro Hummer ride to their place north in the suburbs. She'd been looking through some old documents one day and had seen how years ago a piece of toast with a likeness of the Virgin Mary had sold for thousands at auction, and she wondered how much more people would pay to have their own face altered to look like that.

Judging by the size of their house, the answer was "a lot."

It was much larger than the motel room my mother and I had shared out in the Boulder corridor. It was in a gated community and surrounded by a high fence so nobody could see in. Like a castle within two walls.

They even had a swimming pool and a hot tub, which Judy said I was welcome to use any time I wanted. Just like a "real" daughter, I was to consider this my home. Those were her exact words.

Then she showed me my room and left me alone to unpack. I sat on the bed and thought about my mother and wondered when the forgods would try to convert me.

But they didn't. They went to church three times during the week and twice on Sundays. (Judy said she did some of her best business at prayer meetings.) They never asked me to join them. They almost never spoke to me about God.

Sometimes, usually at breakfast, when she was enjoying a large plate of blueberry muffins served by her indentured homosexual, Iglesias, Judy would say something like, "It must be such a help, dear, to know that your mother repented at the last minute and accepted the Lord Jesus Christ as her personal savior and is now smiling down from heaven.

What comfort to know that she's with the Redeemer at this very moment. And they're watching you, dear."

I don't mean to sound ungrateful, but, apart from the implication that my mother was now spying on me, I didn't like the way Judy called me dear. She didn't sound like she meant it. My mom had never called me dear. She had called me kiddo.

I missed my mom and my friends from the casino. I still couldn't believe I was the only one left, so one day I spent all the money I had left on a taxi to the Strip.

I wish now that I hadn't. Bulldozers were creeping over piles of rubble where the casinos had stood, and the air was smoky and smelled of death. A sign said the site was being transformed into the Jesus Conquers America Museum, which would feature a moving diorama, showing how the peaceful conversion of the last of the nongods had taken place.

When I got back to the house, I sat by the pool and cried.

♠ "Hey." The hand on my shoulder was light. I jumped. "Are you OK?" Brian sat down beside me.

"Come on," he said. "I'm going to show you something I think you'll like."

He led me to a part of the house that I'd never been to and pushed open a door.

It was a library. Row upon row of books. Floor to ceiling. Every book you could think of.

"You can read?"

"Yes." I was proud of that fact. It was an unusual skill.

"I'm sure you'll find something here," Brian said. "What are you interested in? Biographies? Science? Murder mysteries?"

I reached for *The Origin of Species*. My mother had told me about Charles Darwin, but I'd never seen the book. I liked how heavy it felt in my hands.

"It's OK," Brian said. "Take as many as you want." And he smiled. I realized how different he was from Judy. He seemed much younger and kinder. He wasn't fat, and he didn't call me dear.

Graham Greene, Charles Dickens, Charlotte Brontë, Aldous Huxley, Kurt Vonnegut. It was a huge illegal stash. The last passage of the Seditious Documents Act had got rid of all words that were contrary to forgod values. A person could be flogged for having even one of them.

"You're safe here in the house, but I wouldn't take them out," Brian said, his face serious.

I didn't want to go out. Now that the Strip was in ruins, there was nothing in Vegas for me. Seeing the wrecked casinos had brought home just how utterly alone I was.

"You don't know what this means to me."

Brian didn't say anything, but his smile was sad.

That big house seemed less like a prison after that. I still missed my mother and my friends, but I could escape.

In the morning I swam in the pool. Sometimes I'd go into the kitchen for a snack and a chat with Iglesias, who was very sweet, but because the homosexual aversion electrotherapy had been experimental, he was not very good with words.

After that, I'd go to my room and read until the heat became less intense, and then I'd sit out by the pool again in the shade with a glass of iced tea and something lighter, like a spy thriller.

Brian often joined me. I began to look forward to that. I began to like Brian. He treated me with respect. Judy was always nice, but I could never escape the feeling that it was only because she thought that was how forgods were supposed to behave. Brian laughed.

♠ You know where this is heading, don't you? I wish I didn't have to write it down.

I became infatuated with Brian, even though he was married.

I started to imagine things about him, late at night. I started to see us together. I started to think horrible thoughts about Judy. And I began to wonder if, as a nongod, I really was as wicked as the forgods said.

One day when I climbed out of the pool, he was there with a big white towel. He handed it to me.

I took the towel. His hand closed over mine.

"My god, you're beautiful."

And that was it.

♠ I knew that sleeping with Brian was wrong. I told myself that I loved him, but I'm not sure that was true. Perhaps I just wanted to be close to somebody because I felt so terribly alone.

Mealtimes became awkward, although Judy, who seemed to have a lot of not very nice things to say about people who went to her church, didn't appear to notice that Brian and I didn't speak to each other. Iglesias served our food and cleared our plates. Sometimes I caught him looking at me, but I couldn't read the expression in his eyes.

Then I started to vomit in the mornings.

♠ I knew I had to tell Brian, but I didn't know how. And I frantically reasoned that if my pregnancy remained unspoken, then it would go away.

I started praying, can you believe that? I tried to do a deal with God. My mother had told me that there was no convincing scientific proof that God existed, but in my more bitter moments I figured, "Hey, it's Vegas. You never know your luck."

But God didn't answer, and in the end Judy figured it out.

"More sausages, dear? Iglesias, make sure she eats more. Melissa, you're as thin as a stick, it's contrary to God's will." Judy gestured to Iglesias to fill up my plate.

The meat smelled sweet and, to my pregnant state, slightly off. I ran from the table with my hand over my mouth. Judy followed me to the bathroom and stood outside, fingernails tapping the door while I threw up.

♠ A life-sized oil painting of Jesus looked at me as I broke the news to Judy and Brian in the living room.

"Is this true?" Judy demanded of Brian.

He forced the word out: "Evidently."

"How far along?" Judy spat the words at me.

"What?"

"How pregnant are you?"

"I don't know."

"How long since your last period, you stupid little girl," Judy hissed.

I thought hard. "Three months."

Judy said nothing. Her lips were a thin, tight line. She didn't even look at Brian.

Then she hoisted herself out of her chair and walked out of the room. For the first time Brian met my gaze.

"I'm so sorry," he whispered. "So very sorry."

♠ I thought about running away. I had heard about underground networks that helped nongods escape to Mexico or Canada, but I didn't know how to contact them. Even getting out of the house would be a big problem. The walls were electrified and the gates were secured by an electronic code that I didn't have. And if I did manage to escape, as a pregnant nongod, I wouldn't get far.

There was nothing to do but stay put.

Iglesias fed me milk and meat and fresh vegetables, and fruit. I was always hungry. I ate everything. The baby grew. I began to feel it moving inside my body and, despite everything, suddenly I was happy.

One day a doctor came to the house. He was a friend of Brian and Judy's. He didn't speak to me. Even though he was examining me, he seemed to treat me as though I didn't exist.

"Looking good," he said to Judy when he had finished. "I can't foresee any problems. Congratulations."

It was an odd thing to say to her. I looked at Brian, but he wouldn't meet my eye. Judy's face was set in its usual expression of disapproval, but I fancied I saw something else there as well.

Three days later, I found out what it was.

♠ I got lost in the house and found myself in a corridor that I didn't recognize. I passed a door and heard a voice. I stopped outside. The door was open.

It was a nursery. Judy was talking on her cell phone, standing next to a baby's crib, her fat hand strumming the bars.

"Great," she said. "Yes, everything's going extremely well. We're so blessed. No, no, she hasn't got a clue, praise the Lord. Why would she? Yes, we'll soon have our ba—" Judy looked up and saw me standing at the door. She didn't even pause. "All right, talk to you later." She closed the phone.

And then I understood.

Judy and Brian had set the whole thing up. They had planned it.

♠ They didn't want me as their daughter. They wanted my child. And Brian hadn't loved me. He hadn't thought I was beautiful. He had said those things just so I would sleep with him and become pregnant.

Judy saw that I understood, and she smiled. It was one of the cruelest smiles I have ever seen.

I noticed then that the nursery wasn't new. There were scuffmarks on the paintwork.

"You don't think you were the first, do you?" Judy's voice was tight and cold. "There was Melody and Suzanne and Rachel. But they didn't work out.

"You really are quite blessed." Her tone was matter-of-fact. "Do you know who Brian is? He's a very important man. His father is Pastor John."

Onegod government leaders are known only by their first names. A casino professor had explained to me that, once the pretense of elections had been abandoned, the jobs went from father to son. The Onegod leader was like a king.

"Brian needs a child if he's going to be leader. There are lots of factions, all of them grasping for power. A baby makes him more powerful. It sets him apart."

"That explains the books," I said, impressed for a moment, despite myself. "He can have illegal books because of who his father is."

"The books were my idea. You silly nongod girls always fall for it. You think you can trust him because he reads lies." Judy's fat face was bright with pride.

"I hate you," I said. It was true.

Judy's laugh was pure delight. "If you have hate in your heart, you should ask Jesus to forgive you."

I didn't want Jesus to forgive me. I wanted to hit her. So I did.

♠ The Onegod government had outlawed science a long time ago. Evolutionary biology had been the first to go, followed by geology, mathematics (pure and applied), chemistry, and then physics. But as the professors in the casinos had said, outlawing science was like outlawing gravity. It worked whether you "believed" it or not.

According to Isaac Newton's law of inertia and mass, an object stays in motion unless it meets something that stops it. My punch shouldn't have toppled Judy, but as I swung, she stepped to avoid me. She lost her balance and went down like big game. The object that stopped her mass was the crib. It shattered like balsa wood, only it was much harder than that. As she fell backward, a vertical slat pierced her rib cage, drove through her heart.

She lay there. Her eyes were open. She looked surprised, like she might get up and tell me off for being so disrespectful. But that wasn't going to happen because she was dead.

I heard a noise at the door. I knew then that I was dead, too.

♠ It was Iglesias. He didn't look at me. He knelt beside Judy's body and felt for her pulse. His face showed no emotion.

"Ding dong," he said softly, almost to himself. Then: "Well, that's quite enough excitement for one day. I suggest we go." He grabbed me by the hand.

We half ran, half stumbled through the endless corridors of the big house.

I was in shock. All I could see was Judy lying on the floor, with a slat through her chest. I started to cry.

"Don't cry," Iglesias said, pulling me along. "I'm going to make sure you're safe. You can trust me."

I didn't believe him. My life had ended along with Judy's, I was quite sure of that.

"I didn't mean to kill her. It was an accident." I could feel panic choking me. I couldn't get enough oxygen into my lungs. I had taken a life. A forgod life. The wife of the future Onegod leader.

"It's done. It can't be undone. You can think about it later."

"Who are you?" Even through my panic, I noticed that Iglesias no longer appeared to be brain-damaged.

"Resistance. We heard a rumor that nongod girls were going here and disappearing."

We had reached the door to the garage. Iglesias breezed through the security codes, whistling under his breath. His calmness began to calm me. He seemed almost cheerful.

It's funny how your mind becomes sharpened in times of stress. I noticed for the first time that Judy's Super Enviro Hummer had a large Christian fish on the side, with racing stripes.

"The Godmobile. Best cover ever." Iglesias grabbed the keys and helped me into the car. It was a long way up.

"Melissa!" Brian had burst through the door. "I just saw Judy. What the hell is going on?"

He was holding what looked like a gun.

I got out of the car. I walked toward Brian.

"Mel," Iglesias hissed urgently. "What are you thinking? Are you insane?"

I saw that Brian's "weapon" was a phone. His finger was poised over the call button.

"A SWAT team will be here before you get to the end of the street."

I should have felt frightened, but I understood Brian. I realized he could have already made that call, but he hadn't.

"I'm sorry about Judy," I said. "It was an accident."

Brian laughed bitterly. "As you sow, so shall you reap."

I couldn't tell whether he was talking about me, or Judy.

"You know what they'll do to me, if you make that call," I said. "I won't survive and neither will the baby."

He said nothing.

"You like those books, don't you? You don't have them just to sleep with nongods. This plan, it was Judy's idea, not yours."

"Mel, for God's sake." Iglesias was walking toward us his arm outstretched. I held up my hand to stop him.

Brian's voice was rough and low.

"Stay here," he said. "Stay here with me. I don't want to be Pastor. I'll protect you and the baby. I can do that."

I knew that he meant it, but I also knew it wasn't true. He couldn't protect me. Nobody was that powerful.

"You know I can't."

"You'll be safe. We won't have to be . . ." His voice trailed off.

"Judy's dead, Brian. I killed her. You've seen the TV shows. Unless I go right now, I'll be stoned in Falwell Square and the baby ripped from my stomach."

Brian blinked and wiped away tears.

"Come with us," I said and heard a strangled sound from Iglesias who was now standing right behind me, so close I could hear his breathing.

Brian looked at me and laughed, a bitter sound. "You are extraordinary," he said. "You were never meant to survive. You know that, don't you? That wasn't part of the plan. We were going to take the baby and your body would have been found at the dump."

"I don't believe you're capable of that," I said firmly.

Iglesias put a hand on my arm. His grip was tight.

Brian appeared not to have heard me. He said nothing. I said nothing. Iglesias's grip was starting to pinch. For what seemed like eons nobody spoke.

Then phone clattered to the floor and broke. Brian stared at it as though he couldn't figure out how it had got there. He didn't look up.

For the longest time we stood there, heads bowed, almost like we were praying.

Brian drew a deep, ragged breath. He still didn't look up.

"You have no idea what I'm capable of. Now get the hell away before you find out."

♠ I live in Mexico now.

Because of what he did in Vegas, Iglesias is an important person in the nongod movement. We talk every day, and I'm starting to consider political work myself. Even though I'm a nongod, I don't hate America. I want my country back.

But it's going to take some years, I think. In the meantime I have another person to consider. My daughter was born a month ago. She has dark curly hair, like her grandmother, so I've called her Anna.

VU TRAN

Kubla Khan

I've arrived in Las Vegas. Where must you be now? It's half past midnight here, and raining as it always does nowadays. My hotel room feels as dank and empty as our house. By the time you read this email—tomorrow morning, or in the middle of the night if you can't sleep (though I doubt that), or maybe you'll avoid my emails for a few days—I'll hopefully be more clear-minded. Right now, I feel I'm inside some giant snow globe and from now on everything beyond that glass wall will be out of my reach, like I'll be trapped here inside this room, this hotel, and this city, forever. I know this sounds dramatic, and I know I can't blame you for everything. I just have no idea who else to blame.

On the way here from the airport, I rode in a taxi driven by a one-armed man. He looked Vietnamese, in his fifties, a round, forgiving face. His accent was kind. He was quiet at first, but then we got to chatting about poker, since he mentioned he played in town, and somehow I ended up telling him about you. He sympathized with me, told me these things happen to everyone, but it always feels like it's happened only to you. I couldn't help it, so I asked him about his missing arm. He said he lost it in the Fire. He said it melted off his shoulder. His parents and three sisters died that day, along with 90 percent of his neighborhood, *vanished into the ether.* And yet after twenty years (my God, has it already been that long?), the only thing he truly remembers is the sensation of his arm dissolving—in an instant—from his body. No pain at all. Just a hot submersion into sudden nothingness. And the smell, like burnt sugar. Sometimes, he said, tapping the empty sleeve of his jacket, he can still feel his arm there, bumping into furniture, its phantom hand making a phantom fist, a partial ghost of himself to remind him of everything he lost. Somehow I understand that feeling completely. When we arrived at the hotel and I handed him the cab fare, he took it and patted my arm. Stay dry, he said, the rain here can drown you.

I wonder what you and he are doing now. Yesterday. The day before. I've seen his photo and even heard his voice on your phone, but when I imagine you two together, he's faceless and bodiless to me. It's like he still doesn't exist, and so all I can visualize is you holding hands with some distorted shadow of me.

At the poker tables here, they say knowing a player, a person, is always more important than knowing their cards. But even so, it's always a gamble. As it is with everything.

I suppose I should try to get some sleep now. The conference panels begin at seven tomorrow morning. You have no idea, do you, how much you've hurt me.

♣ It's late again, the middle of the night and, my God, it's still storming outside. The rain sounds like someone drumming his fingers against the window, and what I think about is that look you used to give when you were impatient with me. I can see you reading this right now with that same face. But let me tell you why I'm still awake. It's not because of you.

After writing you last night, I fell into a deep sleep and woke up an hour late this morning. The day's first panel had already started, but I managed to slip in unnoticed. The discussion at hand was on the new architecture of the West, how messy and impractical it had become, how meretricious in spite of everything that's changed in the world. It amused me—their outrage. As if we architects were ever anything but superficial. Cut open any building—any man, for that matter—and tell me if the interior is any more real or substantial than the exterior. I was thinking this very thing when, sitting there, I started imagining the inside of a slaughterhouse and the cold, cleaned carcasses of cows and pigs, even humans, split open on stainless steel tables. I don't know why those images came over me so vividly, but I had to get up for a quick cigarette to clear my head.

After the afternoon panels, I went for a walk on the Strip. It's been more than fifteen years now, and the place is almost unrecognizable. A small forest now meanders across the entire Strip, wrapping its way around the new casinos and around the old damaged ones that have been rebuilt inside but left beautifully unchanged outside, like old European castles. A couple of the devastated casinos remain intact, no longer open for business, but still standing like ruins from an ancient civilization. They're monuments now, I guess, but to what, I'm not sure. I see tourists coming in and out of them with cameras and silly smiles. The city still has all the trappings of that glitzy sinful place we all once knew, but now there's a peacefulness to everything. It's like the city has been submerged underwater, swallowed up by nature and time. A prostitute propositioned me as she stood leaning beneath a willow tree, smoking and smiling as I passed.

It started raining again. I returned to my hotel and decided to kill some time gambling. I played a little blackjack and roulette but kept bumping into people from the conference who wanted to drag me here and there. So I finally gave up and headed for the private poker room. You know I'd eventually find my way there. It's been so long, but memories of my days playing here—before you and all my promises to you, before I'd ever considered a life without the all-night sessions, the chain-smoking, the protracted conversations with strangers I wanted to like and was sometimes loathe to beat, the exhilarating highs and devastating lows of gambling my days away—all these memories came home to me and settled like fine dust.

I bought in at a table with some touristy types, figuring at least half of them were dead money. It wasn't until I sat down that I realized my cabdriver from last night was sitting at the other end. He'd mentioned that he often came here to play on his days off, but I was still taken aback.

Our eyes met. I smiled and waved two fingers at him, but he returned it only with a glassy nod, like I was just another new player at the table. Perhaps he wanted to maintain an anonymous table image and was intentionally not acknowledging me. Or maybe he'd simply forgotten me. He was wearing the same chocolate Members Only jacket, the sleeve of his missing arm flattened at his side, which with his thin drooping moustache and dour demeanor made him look slightly sinister now at the poker table.

I bought in for three thousand dollars, all I had left from what I'd brought with me to Vegas. I know what you're thinking, but there's really no point anymore of lying to you about this, is there? So bear with me. Here's what happened.

For the next three hours, while I played no more than five or six hands, I watched the cabdriver methodically take money from everyone at the table without once losing a hand. Not once. He felted four players, two of whom bought back in and were felted a second time. Three players ended up leaving our table after losing a bundle to him, and when they were replaced, he'd start scouring the new players, too. What was most unsettling was how fast he played, often calling and betting instantly, hardly looking at his opponent, so that after a while a palpable silence descended upon the table every time he was in a hand. We obviously had some inferior players, but I'd never seen domination like this. He was seeing and controlling things that no one else at the table had access to, and I counted myself lucky to be getting bad cards that were easy to fold.

On my third smoke break, I chatted with a thin, dark-haired woman who'd recently joined the table and in one hand had lost about a grand to the cabdriver. We stood by the entrance to the poker room, watching the action at our table from a distance.

That guy's kinda incredible, I said to the woman, who was staring at him with a sad but admiring expression, like she was gazing at an old lover.

He's called Kubla Khan, she said matter-of-factly. Never drinks, never says a word at the table. Locals won't play with him, even the cocky ones won't. That's why you see only tourists at our table.

So why're you playing with him? I asked her.

To figure it out, she replied. She had not yet taken her eyes off of him. She was ghostly pale, with a long equine face and something stark yet intense about her, as if she'd come out of one of those old daguerreotype photos.

I said to her, Well, the Vietnamese have always been good at poker.

She shook her head and finally looked at me. It's got nothing to do with that. Or even with poker, really. She took a drag of her long thin cigarette and then poked the air with it. She said, Take this any way you want to, but people around here say he can read minds. Some weird fucking poker telepathy he's got.

She paused to see my reaction, then went on: He's been playing here twice a week for a year, and no one, not even a dealer, has once seen him have a losing session. Always bets and folds at the right time. Always makes those hero calls. And for some reason, no one can ever catch cards against him. It's like he can also will away other people's luck. She leaned into me, as if to lower her voice. They say it's got something to do with what happened to him in the Fire, when he lost his arm.

She was so keen on bestowing this secret information on me that I didn't tell her I'd met him last night. I said, What do you mean? What could have happened to him?

Who knows? All sorts of horrible things happened to all sorts of people that day. But apparently he was the only person to survive the Henderson storm. So maybe he was raped by a little lightning and now has the power to read all our thoughts. She laughed a little. I have no fucking idea. Probably nothing happened and we're just making up this mindreading thing because he beats us at cards. She shrugged and fell silent.

But you think it's true, I said to her.

Why not? Something's got to explain it. No one can be that good all the time, and definitely no one can be that lucky all the time. A player once asked the house to search him. Only thing they found was uncooked rice in his pockets. Did you know some Asians believe it's unlucky to throw away uncooked rice? The Chinese long ago used to fill the mouth of the dead with it. I have no idea what that means.

She put out her cigarette. Ask anyone here, she said. They'll tell you about him. We all wonder why he's still driving a cab when he's probably won enough money to buy this entire fucking hotel.

We both returned to our table. The cabdriver was out of the hand and riffling his chips, perpetually frozen in his poker face. At the beginning of our cab ride last night, while I was looking out the window, he had remarked that it rains every other day in Vegas, the very question I was asking myself. It seemed like something any cabdriver would tell a tourist, except that he had also gone on to say, apropos of nothing, that rain always feels like loss, doesn't it?

Half an hour passed before I finally started getting some good hands. I noticed him folding each time I raised. Then, on a whim, I decided to waste a little money on behalf of my curiosity. I raised big pre-flop with a very ugly three of spades and five of clubs. Everyone at the table folded except for him. He peeked again at his two hole cards, then called me without looking my way. The flop was a king, seven, and nine, all diamonds—missing me completely. I was first to act and bluffed at the pot with a $200 bet. He called instantly. I had no idea what I was trying to do, what I was trying to prove or how to prove it, but something about how the dark-haired woman was now staring at me—her look of intense pity and fascination—made me feel profoundly reckless, like if I just played crazy enough I might prove for her everything she'd said about this guy.

Another diamond, a two, came on the turn, further increasing his chances of a flush. I bet four hundred this time. Again, he called without hesitation. He was staring at the board, his face calm, his one arm wrapped around his mountainous stacks of chips like he was embracing them. The river was a meaningless four of clubs. I had absolutely nothing, and I figured, since he'd only called me twice, that he might have been playing cautiously with top pair, or maybe two pair, or most likely a medium flush. But there was also a real chance that he was trying to reel me in with the nut flush. I said fuck it to myself and pushed in the rest of my chips, betting everything I had left, nearly $2,500 more. It was crazy, but I didn't care about the money anymore. It struck me then that if I could get away with this bluff, if I could fool him and disprove all that mumbo jumbo the woman had talked about, that I would also be punishing him for forgetting me. And maybe then he would remember.

He continued staring at the board, the longest he'd taken all session to consider a hand. He told me last night that sometimes, inexplicably, he would feel his phantom hand aching, and he'd have to squeeze his right hand to ease the pain. Right now, his right hand was a wound fist.

He looked up at me. There was recognition this time, a chosen recognition. He thought for another moment, then finally folded, but not before pushing his cards to the dealer with a hundred-dollar chip on top. He pointed at me, neither kindly nor unkindly, and said, Just him. The dealer looked confused for a second, but then slid the hand over to me. At this point, everyone at the table was staring at me. As the cabdriver stood up and started stacking his chips onto trays, I quickly peeked at his hand. It was an ace and queen of diamonds. He had gotten an ace-high diamond flush on the flop, an absolutely unbeatable hand for this board, and he had just folded it to my nothing hand—in effect, giving up what would have been a $6,500 pot. I tried to slide the two cards nonchalantly back to the dealer. When a couple of players asked me what they were, I just shook my head. Then they started complaining that, if I could see the hand, then everyone should see it, too, but the dealer explained that house rules didn't require it. The dark-haired woman had been watching me the entire time, and, as she glanced at the cabdriver walking out the poker room, she threw me a dark grin.

I played a few more hands but felt a quiet animosity toward me at the table, like they were suspecting something shady between the cabdriver and me. It was the only hand they'd seen him lose all night—and it was a monster pot. So after another half hour, I stood up and cashed out.

I immediately went looking for him, hoping he was still close by somewhere. I had proven nothing about him. He obviously knew there was no way my hand could beat his, but any competent poker player would have known that. The question now was why he had folded it to me. Out of pity? Generosity? He had remembered me, after all, but beyond my face what else exactly had he recognized?

I circled the crowded roulette and craps tables, then wandered around the walls of slot machines. He was nowhere in sight. I finally found a seat at the bar, ordered a drink, then another and another, and let my eyes roam the casino floor. I kept imagining him alone in his cab, staring out his windshield into the dark rainy night, waiting for the next stranger to step into and out of his life like just so many passing shadows. Maybe that was easier than actually trying to know anyone. Maybe he'd always been alone, ever since he lost his family and his arm, and had found comfort in that aloneness, and that made him not necessarily mean or cold or unmoved by others, but just unwilling—a creature at peace in the anonymity of night, of a cab, of a casino, driving or playing cards, not for money, but for a chance to be among humans without having to do anything but know them long enough to take their money and then walk away.

It occurred to me that the dark-haired woman might have been lying. The idea of reading someone else's mind was ridiculous. Inconceivable, really. Even if you could have access to someone's thoughts, how would you organize them? How would you make any sense out the jumble of thoughts that run through people's heads every single second of the day? How could they possibly be understandable to anyone but the person who owns them and, more importantly, feels them?

I thought of you, then. Of the day my mother died fifteen years ago and we had just started dating and how, after the funeral, I had remarked to you that I was finally an orphan. And the look you gave me was not sympathy, but rather a cold faraway pity. I couldn't tell then what you truly thought of me, and I guess I've never been able to. It was the same face you gave me last week when I asked if you loved him and all you did was drink your coffee and look at me.

I finished my drink and was about to leave the bar when I spotted the dark-haired woman at the other end. She was looking at me with a bored expression. I took my empty glass and slowly walked to her.

Are you down or up? I asked.

She sipped her cocktail and showed me a thumbs-down. She was not pretty, but in the dim light of the bar, her narrow eyes and long face had a kind of sad elegance. She said, He had the nut flush, didn't he?

I nodded. How did you know?

I can read your mind. And his, too. She grinned and lit a cigarette. You've been looking for him.

I glanced around the bar and shrugged. I just want to know why he did it.

Does it matter? You won the pot. He gave it to you. What else matters but that?

You wouldn't want to know? A player voluntarily gives up a $6,500 pot to you, and you wouldn't want to know why? Didn't you say you were here to figure him out?

Yes, she replied, but I could care less what he thinks of me. She glanced at my hands. What do you do for a living?

I'm an architect. I design houses.

Of course you do, she chuckled. Order, form, and function. Everything in its rightful place. Of course you're a fucking architect. Have you ever designed a building for the soul?

Are you making fun of me?

She looked at me standing there beside her at the bar. Are you going to sit down? She drew deeply at her cigarette. Or do you want to come back to my room?

I leaned against the bar and noticed a long pale scar that ran down the left side of her thin neck and dipped into her collarbone. I said, I thought you were a local. What are you doing with a room here?

She emptied her cocktail glass and replied, You ask stupid questions.

♣ We rode the elevator to the fifth floor in total silence, and I followed a few steps behind her, watching her thin figure stroll down the hallway. It was not until we reached her room that I realized where we were.

She opened her door. I did not move. Who are you? I said. What are you trying to do?

She turned around to look at me. What do you mean?

I pointed at the room next door, which was my room. Seriously, what are you doing here?

Is that where you're staying? she asked. How funny. She turned and walked into her room.

I hesitated, but then followed her inside. Why is your room next to mine?

You don't believe in coincidences? I live here. I should ask you why your room is next to mine. Now please shut the door.

You live here? I said. Who the hell lives in a hotel?

I do. Now do you want to stay or go?

I watched her take a bottle of whiskey from atop the dresser and pour out two shots. I shut the door. She left my shot on the dresser and I downed it.

The room looked nothing like a hotel room. It was lived in. The closet was open and jammed full of clothes. Mismatched shoes were strewn across the floor. Stacks of books and magazines and newspapers lay everywhere—on the dresser, on the couch and the nightstand—and tacked across the walls were countless postcards and personal photographs. Most of the photos were self-portraits of her in this very room, taken by her own hand.

In my silence, she went to turn off the lamps, leaving on only the small one on the nightstand. Then she said, The house I grew up in was destroyed in the Fire and I decided never to own a home again. I've been living in hotel rooms for twenty years. I move to a new hotel every six months or so.

It must be expensive, I said, as she started picking up her clothes from the floor and tossing them on the dolphin chair.

Not if you're a good poker player, she said.

Then it must be lonely.

Not if you prefer the company of strangers.

I allowed myself a smile. I picked up a single leather glove on the floor and tried to put it on. It was too small. I said to her, You were in the Fire? What else was destroyed?

It doesn't matter, she replied, and turned to face me and casually took off her blouse, her bra, her jeans and panties, until she was standing perfectly still and naked across the room from me, as if to wait for what I would do next. I took a step forward, then came within a few feet of her, close enough that I could clearly see, even in the dim light, the thin pale scar on her neck running all the way down to her left breast, where it disappeared into the pinkish rippling map of a burn scar that covered half her chest and wrapped its way around her left shoulder and bicep. The rest of her body was normal, beautiful and porcelain white.

She was watching me, and I didn't know how to react. I came to her and put a hand on her shoulder and felt the soft plastic terrain of the scar. I caressed it with an open hand and traced it to her chest, then her breast, as she watched me intently and began unbuttoning my shirt. Then I kissed her scarred breast and she pushed me onto the bed and fell on me, mouth and body, so much heavier and warmer than I had imagined.

But then, in the middle of all this, I suddenly asked her what her name was. She laughed quietly, brushed her lips against my ear, and then whispered your name. I must have frozen or pushed her away from me, because she stopped and sat up on top of me. I could tell from the child-ishly playful, satisfied way she was looking at me that this was no coin-cidence, that her real name was something else completely and that she knew she had said yours. How she knew it was beyond me. I was still a bit drunk and didn't know whether to be angry or utterly confused or amused.

She stood from the bed and walked to the bathroom and shut the door. I heard it lock, and then I heard the shower turn on. And that was the last thing I remembered.

If this part was difficult or awkward for you to read, it was not my intention. I'm only telling you so that you can imagine how I felt when thunder woke me in the middle of the night, still lying naked in her bed, and she was gone.

I checked the bathroom. For some reason, I even checked under the bed. Then I picked up my pants and felt for my wallet. It was untouched, but out of my front pockets fell grains of uncooked rice. It all seemed like an elaborate and inexplicable joke that she had played on me, and yet I was more intrigued than angry.

As I emptied my pockets of all the rice and got dressed, I finally noticed the door that connected our two rooms. There was light beneath it. It opened and I stepped back into my room. As far as I could tell, all my belongings were still there. The connecting door crept shut behind me, and when I went to open it I found that I could not. I walked out into the hallway and tried her front door. It, too, was locked. I knocked despite knowing no one was there. I finally went back inside my room and sat on my bed, staring at the connecting door for what felt like hours. And finally I went to the computer to write you.

I'm not sure what any of this means right now. I only know that this is the last thing I will write you. I promise. You don't have to write a single word back. I say this, knowing you won't anyway. Because when you read this—if you ever do—you'll think that I've made it all up. But I don't care. It no longer matters to me. Tomorrow I will find her. And if I can't, I'll stay in this hotel room, wait by this connecting door, until she returns.

♣ I woke up this morning and, for the first time in almost two weeks, I opened my eyes and did not think of you.

I dreamt last night that I was walking up a flight of stairs. In fact, there were many flights of stairs, ascending and descending around mine, amid the red velvet walls of some grand mansion. And there were people passing me up and down the stairs. Strangers at first. Until suddenly I realized that their faces were familiar, though I could not place their names, none of them, except finally two people standing on the landing far above me, my parents, long dead, and I found myself weeping uncontrollably as they started descending the staircase toward me, and then passed me without seeming, whatsoever, to recognize me.

LORI KOZLOWSKI

> ## Nuclear Wasted Love Song

Under my feet, I could feel the club below me. I locked the door. I knew they couldn't hear me, and I wanted to stay inside forever. I could hear the thumping through the walls—the nonstop taps of trip-hop, strange record scratching, and strong drum and bass. The room shook little earthquakes, and I just sat on the floor. This was the only place I felt safe.

I scraped notches into a dirty windowsill. With small tally marks, I kept track of the days since I had last seen him. So far I counted ninety-three. There were no clocks in the room, so I had to try to keep the date in my head.

Hiding wasn't something I was used to. As a dancer, you were so exposed on stage, showing off, as you performed. But life inside this theater was different. I was a prisoner. I looked out the only window, but I couldn't see very far. Just a few red lights in the far distance. The rest was dry land, tiny dust devils swirling through, and sharp metal pieces of old hotel signs jutting out of sand.

My life before this was hard to remember sometimes. Growing up in this strange town was something that was peculiar to others, but not to me. All I ever wanted was to be with a boy named Vin.

The last time I saw him, we were at a house party. We hardly spoke because we were fighting. I poured him a drink over crushed ice cubes, and we stared at each other from across a bright kitchen.

Now, lying down, curled up in this shadowy corner, I tried to remember his voice, but I couldn't hear it anymore. I tried to scream, but nothing came out.

♥   The bees were all dead, and there was no honey. Spring's sticky amber juice had left the planet long ago. Funny how no one seemed to think this was a sign that there was something wrong. The little yellow jackets were the first to go. And after that, many other life forms became extinct, many of them a thousand times bigger than the bees. Polar bears, blue whales, walruses. They all succumbed to the global collapse. While the outside world suffered, too, ours was just the last city to see real desolation. Since the desert always had limited flora and fauna anyway, no one even noticed the despair until it got completely dark.

The Big Boom ruined everything. All the mass implosions caused the caliche to give way. As difficult as digging could be in a town of constant construction, the Boom left a cavernous hole in the middle of the city where the Strip once had been. All of Las Vegas imploded. Not just one hotel, here or there. But all of them. In one big cave-in, the entire city fell. Shards of glass from a million hotel windows blanketed the landscape. Dried-out shrubbery became ensconced in metal scraps. It left the town a wasteland, a place where listless life forms wandered alone. The drifters and chemically altered characters roamed around, seeking signs of other life. It was quiet, and we were all plagued by a deep loneliness that would not go away.

For years, all the magic of Vegas had been piling up. The wizardry, the gluttony, the lust. We went from everything all the time—wild sex, designer drugs, food and drink, flash and cash—to nothing. What was once life on an accelerated track came to a complete stop. A town that once shined with so much light not a star could be seen in the desert sky. A city with enough neon gas to light up the whole world. Now we sat in darkness.

I wanted to go home, only I didn't know where home was anymore. The desert valley I had once known was no longer a pearl string of fancy casinos and bright lights. Instead it was a no-man's-land. A hole.

How the Huntridge remained standing, no one knew. Its walls weren't particularly strong like the newest hotels. It wasn't retrofitted, remodeled, or remade. It was just itself. An old art deco movie house that became alternative music's finest grunge palace. In the ruins of the Huntridge, it's almost as if we went back to where we started. The place became a simple theater again for small vaudeville acts to entertain the sad crowds. Deformed once-humans, androids, freakish animals—all of us trying to exist in a lightless world. Struggling to create a tiny romantic biosphere, singing and making bad music to bring back the happiness we once enjoyed.

The last entertainment hub and our only shelter, the Huntridge also became a fortress and a control center. It was a place for the pigs to run their show.

♥ After the Big Boom, not much survived. Those that lived were morphed in odd ways. One species that lived on past all the others was the pig. While almost all the animals died off, pigs just multiplied and mutated until they were army generals that ruled the desert.

The pigs had unusual tastes. They wore platinum pocket watches, even though they couldn't tell time. They donned little pin-striped jackets, wore bad cologne to cover their horrible smell, and listened to sad opera arias. They acted as both the government and the mob.

Sometimes the pigs had evil urges. While they listened to lengthy dirges about days gone by, they dreamed up new ways to use the dancers as sex toys and playthings for their own personal release. In their midst, I thought of that one novel we all had to read in seventh grade. When I saw them walking around on two legs, conversing and carrying on, I wondered if what I saw was real. It was as if they had climbed out of a storybook, gotten high and drunk, and then started plotting their own brand of evil.

I was once a ballerina. Not a showgirl or a stripper, but a real-life, formally trained dancer. I had taken ballet classes since I was three, and I knew how to sweep myself across the floor, appearing weightless. How to make my sinewy limbs stretch out and flow, entrancing those who watched me. Tiny pas de bourrée, strict sous-sus, and a million dizzying pirouettes—these steps were my natural rhythm, but my skill did not matter inside the Huntridge. Within its walls, the pigs controlled everything—from what we wore on stage to how we danced. All of us were told what numbers to perform and when. The show consisted mostly of stripteases and company numbers that involved four or five of us grinding on poles or on each other.

All the other ballerinas were schizophrenic. The Boom made them that way. They talked to themselves and to their tutus. They danced to imaginary music that no one else could hear, ripping and scratching at their tights. Their craziness made them better strippers. Allowed them to unhinge in a way I never could.

When they weren't talking crazy, they acted like robotic droids. They danced in a trance state, moving not with grace, but with a dominant formality that lacked feeling. When they danced this way, it was almost as if they were a marching army, smiling only because it was part of their duty. Their faces were glittery, but cold. That's the way the pigs liked it.

The schizo-robo-ballerina strippers were just obedient pets, never showing warmth, only taking in what the pigs gave them. Which wasn't much—food, shelter. As long as they were showered with the littlest bit of luxe at the end of their day, they cared not if they danced until their feet bled. In fact, I once heard some of them talking about how they preferred being taken care of in this way. Seeing the pigs as generous bosses. They understood light was limited, as was food and clean drinking water. They appreciated what little they got. Most of them didn't eat. Their preferred form of payment was the shiny plastic purple beads left over from the Orleans Hotel. They loved holding the faux jewels, pretending to be wealthy heiresses, talking to themselves about shopping excursions that never happened.

More than anything, I wanted out of there. Wanted to find Vin. I thought that maybe, if I could get out and I could see him, he would realize that we were supposed to be together. Vin always thought I was a sap. Someone who couldn't accept the reality of things, a silly heart. And he was right.

I was getting thinner by the day, losing the breasts and hips that Vin so loved and my ballet teachers always hated. I could feel my cheekbones, jutting out more than ever. My lips were dry, and my long brown hair was full of split ends and sticky from hairspray. From all the costumes I wore on stage, I had tiny scratches from tight elastic and misplaced sequins.

Except for the Huntridge, everything else in town had been decimated. Only the worst of the area lived on—the roaches and the pawnshops. Because we had nothing, the smallest things became glamorous.

At the pawnshops, they leased luxury items, renting out things of various values—tattered library books, a Bonanza High School letterman jacket that someone had lost long ago, one heart-shaped earring, a love note with very crinkled edges and the words "My Baby" written in big pink letters on the outside. I could see our memories rented out to others, and I wondered if they enjoyed them as much as we did when we lived them. I wished I could reclaim all the stuff I recognized as mine. But things were pretty desperate. I once saw someone trade his brain for a nightlight.

♥ I still had to dance for money. Of the things that changed in Vegas, that wasn't one of them. All the life forms still loved to look at something pretty. To watch a curvy, coquettish thing twist and spin herself into the samba of simulated sex.

Desire wasn't gone. Though we all felt the loneliness of this desolate place, just knowing that desire still existed was some strange comfort.

I was just a girl in a skirt using my body for cash. This was nothing new. Las Vegas had thrived on this for years—stripping, shadow dancing, bar and tabletop two-steps, showgirl extravaganzas, and even prostitution. It began and ended with the body of a woman.

And while the pigs watched me dance, I thought of Vin. Wondered where he was. I was using an old ballet move to arabesque my way into a pole dance, when I remembered our last movie together. He was mad at me. The ache to lay my head on his shoulder was so strong that my neck tilted to one side. It craned without my noticing, leaning as far as it could go before touching down on his plaid sleeve. In between my legs, I felt the dull ache of a space missing its object. I wanted that human touch back so badly.

Without Vin around, I felt colder. Not just temperature-wise, but hardened in ways I hadn't been before. We grew up together, so he was my family. The person I told everything to. As kids, we ran around town like it was our playground. Ignoring slot machines and casinos, we reveled in our own ideas of fun and danger. We once stole his parents' car to see if we could get it up to a hundred miles per hour. Along a curvy desert road that was still under construction, we crashed into a large ditch. Big boulders popped up all around us, but somehow we came out untouched. And I never got over the time his father walked in on us. We were both sixteen. I was wearing only a lemon yellow tank top.

Even before everything changed, we often acted like we were the only two people that existed. We slow danced in empty white living rooms when no was looking. And pleasured each other in the courtyards of church gardens while everyone else was eating doughnuts.

My images of this town were so wrapped up in him. I wanted to be wherever he was.

♥ "Again!" he yelled from the front row. He liked to watch us from close up, showing us that he was the spectator, the director, the owner, and the one who later in the night got to watch us change. Josef was a merciless keeper. He was a pig.

He made us practice three hours a day, and, when we weren't practicing, we were supposed to do "favors" for his pig friends.

Josef was fond of me. I could feel him watching me, sometimes while I performed and other times when I wasn't expecting it—while I walked down a hallway, while I was tying my pink toe shoes. His creepy blue eyes followed me around, his stern brow making the staring more intense.

"I like how you're always singing all that jazz about love and how you wanted to be together forever with what's his name."

I smiled, pretending to be polite.

"What you need, Mel, is a good once-over. You know what I mean?" he said, nuzzling his pig nose next to my neck.

"What you need is right here," he said, touching me more. "Learn to appreciate. Not every girl gets the attention I give to you."

I pulled away and ran down the hall. Sometimes I would hide to get away from the smokiness and the raw lust and the pulsating techno beats that seemed to never end.

In 1945, a cry room was built into the Huntridge, back when it was still a movie theater. The space was intended to be a soundproof room where mothers could take their babies and not disturb other moviegoers. It was ironic and crazy and perfect. I'd sneak into the cry room to hide and weep. The carpet was dark green and scratchy, and the walls were just concrete. It wasn't a pretty place, but it was somewhere I could be alone.

I had so many dreams that never came true. I had so much built up inside that imploded, too. When the pigs took over the city, it was as if everything ended. I wanted to resurrect all that I could. I wanted the Stardust and the Dunes and the Frontier to come back, like beings back from the dead. I wanted the Mirage's volcano to rise up out of the ground and flood the land with lava love. A true baptism by fire to renew this godless land.

The pulsing beat of the industrial music downstairs was taking over my thoughts, and I knew it was time to make a plan.

♥   The only way out was to make one. So I decided that after the late show I would climb out the cry-room window, jump onto the roof next door that held the busted air conditioner, and just run. It wasn't an elaborate plan, but it was one that got me out of the theater and away from the pigs. Before I was afraid to defy them, but now I didn't care. If I had to dance one more dance, do one more favor, or just smell Josef's cologne on me again, I would become just as crazy as the other ballerinas.

That night, I broke the window and ran into darkness. I couldn't quite see where I was going, and I tasted the dusty breeze blow into my mouth. Spitting out the dry granules, I closed my eyes and walked against hot wind.

For what felt like days, I wandered into what seemed like outer space. It was how I imagined deep space to be—sometimes blazing hot, other times freezing cold, and all the time just blank and black. Time stretched out into longer, more painful pieces. I stumbled toward what I thought was the Strip. I had to find him.

I thought of all we had done together. Back when we were kissing in a theater, wearing 3-D glasses. When he was a wallflower and I was a mosh-pit queen. When we made out in the dark and later he held my hand up to the light, looking at my small fingers. I touched one of those fingers to the dimple in his chin, and after he'd bent to kiss my freckled thighs.

A plastic bag blew by my face, and I somehow remembered that Vin had three earrings in his left ear and a pet named Alice in Chains. Alice in Chains was a gray tabby cat that was abandoned as a small kitten. He had found her on his balcony one night, whimpering, sounding like she was a cat on repeat, mewing like she was strapped to railroad tracks, crying out for an epic rescue.

I thought of his white T-shirts and how I was obsessed with that smell for about two years.

I had no shame. I wanted to slip my tongue underneath the doors of hotel rooms. I wanted to dig through the ruin, excavate the bodies to find his. I wanted to know everything. If he brushed his teeth in the dark. If he still prayed. If he still loved Neil Young.

There was nothing else left to live for. The pigs spoiled everything good with their own disgusting nature. The pawnshops barely stayed open. And the land. The land gave me no hope. Everywhere I looked I saw the same thing: miles of dusty vistas and Joshua trees that once reached up to the heavens, now drooping down, sad and alone, just like us. A planted reminder of our charred hearts. I shivered for Vin. I wanted him to find me, save me, take me from this place.

My head became a little clearer the farther I got from the theater. I tried to remember how things got this bad. This town wasn't new to things being blown up. Our city was one of experiment and renewal. Atomic testing had happened in the area for years. With sugary sweet names like Operation Teapot and Operation Sunbeam, during the 1950s, the military tested nuclear weapons out in the open land, sending puffs of smoke high into the air.

In the 1980s, the Kidd Marshmallow Factory exploded—shaking the entire desert valley. White, pasty goo covered the houses of Henderson. I was in fourth grade, hiding under my desk. Vin was the fat kid who sat next to me. He was crying, and when I looked at his face I cried, too.

Somewhere between then and now, our town grew sick of the outward bursts. Instead, we wanted things to crush themselves. An implosion is the reverse of an explosion—when things cave in on themselves. In the 1990s and for years after, one by one, old hotels in town were conquered by their makers. The ultimate form of control—to be able to destroy what you create. Build it up, then watch it all fall down. People liked to watch the implosions—sometimes the events were filmed and made into New Year's Eve specials on TV. Beside fireworks bursting in the sky, tourists were treated to the crushing of an aging edifice. The sad crumbles, mixing in with the desert rock.

Even the Huntridge had seen its own trouble—its roof once caved in before a punk concert. I remembered that often, whenever I was dancing on that rickety stage.

When Nevada finally became the home to the nation's radioactive waste, no one could have predicted that dying bees would be one of the first signs of massive danger. Right inside Yucca Mountain, our fate was tucked away. The nuclear leftovers came out after the Boom. A poison stream floated out of the super-volcanic mountain and infected all of the things that it touched.

♥   Strange things crossed my path. Mostly trash, but certain items somehow made my heart excited. A broken compact disc provided hope. The half-empty mini shampoo bottle told me cleaner hair and a better future were coming. Red poker chips seared on the edges let me know I was getting closer.

The rubbish brightened my day. Almost anything I recognized made me grateful.

After a while though, the little things stopped appearing. As I pushed on farther, there were fewer and fewer tokens, and that is when it struck me. Vin wasn't coming back. In that moment, I stopped walking and I just stood there, wondering what to do.

The night of the Boom, I was at the university performance center and

Vin was helping his father on a small construction job, near the Strip. His father's firm was only a handful of guys who worked hard, sweating in the sun all day to help build new hotels. The humble crew specialized in the minor details of highrise work.

I pictured his smile, waving to me from a big tower.

Wherever he was buried, I wanted to be there, too.

♥ I treaded along for days, trying to get to what I thought was the Strip. I was getting delirious along the way, feeling weaker as I moved.

Fission and fusion. Feast and famine. Fleeting and forever. It was all becoming the same. Sometimes I prayed to the moon. I begged the pale satellite to save me. It seemed like the only thing I recognized. The only sweet light.

But in its white face, I didn't see an answer.

Although everything was gone, my memories—they lingered like something still floating in the air. Like the yellow smoke sliding along the ground.

After climbing over broken palm trees and taking shelter inside the beams of dismantled hotels, I reached a giant opening in the ground. A gorge that looked like a sinkhole that had swallowed the Strip whole. I peered down inside of it. An abyss in the desert.

Vin was down there. His body at least, somewhere in this huge well.

At first I stood there, teetering on the edge. Letting my feet slip a little, I stared out toward the moon again. Feeling that milky light shine down on me, I felt encouraged.

I closed my eyes and bent my knees. There was nothing left to do but jump.

GAIL TRAVIS REGIER

Glonze

Gloriana stepped carefully through the warehouse office, avoiding the pressure alarms in the floor. Kison, her partner, had hacked the system diagram from the files of the security company that installed it, and Gloriana had memorized the pattern. There was a motion detector in the wall, but her enhanced hearing let her beat it. The detector scanned for a ten-second period randomly selected out of each minute. She could hear its motor when it came on, and froze until the mechanical humming stopped.

The safe had an old-fashioned digital lock. She jacked into the lock and closed her eyes, letting the binary combinations flow across her vision. Then one of the chips in her skull clicked on and began deciphering the patterns.

It took longer than she expected—too long. By the time the safe opened, she was past her safety margin. She had slipped in through Glonze, dematerializing outside, then using a ring she wore to guide her through the protective maze that bordered the Glonze matrix. Some human, scanning randomly, would have spotted her by now.

She switched on the desk video, flipped through channels. Guards milled in the lobby. Her no-eye function might get her past them, but there were two knights in the warehouse itself, making their way toward the office. She felt a surge of fear as she watched them, striding confidently in their armor. These were military clones, three meters tall, with four arms stretching from their long torsos, and psych-conditioned for brutality.

The interior of the safe was not a storage chamber, but a simple cyberjack. She unwound cabling from her pocket and connected the jack to the neural tap in her right wrist. The data flow that appeared to her inner eye was garbage until she recited the codes Kison had given her. One by one the barriers evaporated, until she was in the secret executive files. She sent another code, and the data stream blurred as the files were downloaded into one of the chips in her skull.

She left the safe open, since she was blown already. Lights and sirens came on as she raced across the pressure alarms in the floors. The drop tubes had been shut off by an automatic circuit, so she used her jump vest to slow her fall as she dropped forty meters down the tube shaft. Nevertheless she went to all fours, and might have broken her ankles if her reinforced boots had not protected them. The tube opened onto a cargo space several kilometers long. She hid behind some packing crates and engaged another chip in her skull, trying to monitor the knights' bodyphones, but all she got was scramble. These were serious types. Professionals. She would have to kill them.

They wore military armor without insignia. Light blurred slightly around the edges of the black metal, telling Gloriana they were protected by personal shields. She didn't waste a shot on them, but holstered her pistol and drew her second weapon from her belt. This was two meters of thin chain, attached at one end to a pair of brass knuckles and at the other to a small oval of metal. She slipped the knuckles securely onto her left hand, then dangled the chain through her right hand, ready to swing and fling the metal ball. The ball was superdense titanium, with a nuclear device at its core; it generated jamming fields that would let it penetrate the knight's shields, and when it struck something solid, it let out a meson zap that would rip armor apart.

Of course she would have to tag them, and they had meson rods two meters long. The odds were impossible. She was dead. But Gloriana had one equalizer they couldn't know about, and she was counting on that.

As they thudded her way, Gloriana took three deep breaths, charging her blood with oxygen, then triggered the neural impulse that actuated the rings she wore under her Kevlar gloves. As the no-eye function kicked in, she seemed to herself to become a psychedelic swirl of shades of blue, and the armored men appeared to move more slowly. To anyone else she was invisible, both to normal sight and wide-spectrum lenses, and inaudible also, even to enhanced hearing. The effect was a Glonze function, and though it lasted only three seconds at a time, the temporal dilation made those seconds seem like a dozen to her.

Neither knight had drawn his laser; they were expecting their enemies to be armored and shielded also. Gloriana wouldn't have minded armor, but it would have triggered alarms the moment she materialized out of Glonze. The knights walked with their meson rods raised like quarterstaves. Their faceplates clicked red as they scanned the warehouse's dark bays, oblivious of Gloriana rushing toward them. She was counting the seconds in slow cadence, keeping track of her three real-time seconds of invisibility.

As the third second was about to expire, she spun her chain and leaped high over the soldier's head. He never saw her, but she saw him stagger from slo-mo into normal motion as her body became visible. She lashed the chain down toward him, feeling it wrap around his neck, turning her head away at the right instant to protect her eyes. The flash of the meson charge was silent, but metal screamed as the armor ripped and his helmet flew into the air, blood spurting and chunks of flesh bursting from the suddenly headless armor. She didn't wait to watch him fall, but jerked the chain to reel it back in.

She twisted in the air so that as her boot toes touched the ground she had the chain in motion again, its slashing menace keeping the samurai at bay. He slashed at her twelve times, shifting the stave elaborately between his four hands, probing her defense. Gloriana sidestepped the strokes or leaped above them, the jump vest letting her rise and fall quickly, so that she was never in the air long enough for him to catch her on the backswing. Her ankles ached from the shock of her landings, but she focused on the movements of her enemy's weapon and pushed the pain to the back of her mind. Pain was for later.

They circled, Gloriana holding her chain spread in loose hands, keeping the end with the throwing ball spinning. The knight had seen her use the weapon, and knew that if he overreached with his stave she would send the ball past his guard like a cobra.

Unarmored, Gloriana was faster, but his four arms gave him an advantage, and the staff moved too unpredictably for her to risk a throw. He could have killed her that way, driven her against the wall where her superior mobility was useless, or else simply waited for her to tire, while his armor gave him strength. But he was impatient and galled by his inability to dispose of an unarmored opponent and worried that she might turn invisible again. Flexing his exoskeletal leg muscles, he leaped high over her head. She slashed the chain at his ass, but he was already settling into the metal rafters and fumbling for his pistol.

Gloriana rattled a fog capsule out of her sleeve, and with a whoosh the hyperpressure filled the room with darkness. With her enhanced vision, she could see, but only for a few meters. She knew the soldier's vision would be about the same, and she ducked about in the billowing black mist, shifting her position. A laser bolt flashed briefly in the darkness, and a packing crate behind her burst into white-hot fragments. But Gloriana had been counting seconds. Enough time had elapsed that she could trigger the cloaking function again. She went no-eye and ran toward the exit in a jagged weave, not looking back.

But around her now she heard the buzz of lasers building up power, too loud for just one weapon. Then beams began to crisscross the area, slicing like diamond blades through the mist, and she knew she was in the middle of a firefight. Ahead of her, armored figures leaped high into the air, battling each other with staves and lances, the meson flashes bursting almost too quickly for the eye to register. She hurdled a pallet stacked with heavy machinery, only to land in the middle of a half-dozen security guards as she became visible.

The fog was thinner here, but they were all too knotted together for the guards to use their guns. She slashed and whirled with her chain until they were all dead, then went no-eye again as another knight came at her with a mace. This time she stayed blank for only a second, long enough to dodge behind him, spin her chain, and strike his arm from the shoulder. Blood, steaming hot from the meson flash, sprayed her. She drew her pistol and took cover behind one of the laser-reflective structural beams that kept the roof from coming down.

It was over. Uniformed bodies were strewn about the room, charred by laser fire. Pieces of armor lay here and there, blood oozing from the severed joints. Troops in federal armor strode through the lifting fog, with pistols in two hands and a meson lance gripped in the others.

One of the knights, who had a marshal's badge on his helmet, opened his faceplate. It was Col, who was really with the secret police. "So then, Gloriana," he said. "Get what you came for?"

"I don't know what you're talking about," she said. "These guys shanghaied me."

"Uh-huh. That cloaking function you've got—must be expensive. I thought we were the only ones who had personal invisibility."

"I don't know what you're talking about."

"You need the medico?"

"What makes you say that? Just because I'm covered in blood?" The crisis adrenaline was draining from her, and she felt like laughing hysterically. "I'm not wounded." She shut her eyes for a moment, glancing at the green-glowing pips of her medchips to make sure. Someone gave her a carafe of coffee, but she passed it on. She didn't want Col to see how her hands were shaking.

Col's eyes narrowed. He glanced around at his knights, then said loudly, "Somebody hacked our net and ordered us to hit this place. You wouldn't know anything about that?"

"If somebody did that, you owe them a favor." She glanced at the crates the other knights were opening. There were armor components, tactical nukes, fuel cells, semiportable lasers. "There's half a revolution in those crates."

"I guess you didn't see that stuff," he said.

"I didn't see anything."

"I guess you were never here."

"Right." She headed for the doors to the outside, hearing the crackle in her skull as Col phoned ahead for the troops to let her pass. She had been prepared to go no-eye if she had to, but Kison must have squared things already with Col.

♦ "Yes, I did," Kison said, stroking his long gray beard. "I sent in the first raid, then messaged Col that we had a score he could take credit for if he asked no questions. He knows we're interested in the industrial side, not the political."

He sat behind his desk in the office they shared, letting the transgrav circuits of his special chair support his gross bulk. Their office was fashionable, as it had to be to impress the big corporate clients they had begun to work for. The room was a replica of a picturesque rock grotto, with a waterfall and a pool full of real fish. Gloriana hated the expense of the fish; live things were pesky and always dying.

"This other job—" Kison started to say.

"No way," Gloriana said. "Me for a hot tub and some time in a honeycomb."

"You deserve it," her partner said. "On the other hand, there's a lot of money involved. They want you bad enough to bring you in outsystem. They want you bad enough to pay the price of a tachyon message."

"What's the scam?"

"It's a Glonze world, with lots of tourists they don't want to scare away."

"OK."

"And they've got a serial killer in their matrix."

"Oh my god," Gloriana said. Kison was right. It meant a lot of money.

◆ Gloriana woke in cold and darkness, woke to terror. Her hands scrabbled against the coffin lid above her. Her nails broke on the hard plastic. She did not know what had happened, but she knew she had been dead, dead, and now she was alive, and she had to hope someone would hear . . . someone would save her.

The lid opened, as it always did. She heard the whoosh of hydraulic pumps and her memory came back, as it always did. She remembered going into no-life when she boarded the starship, recalled the languor as the narcotics flooded her system and the temperature in the coffin dropped. She lay trembling while the tech detached her IVs and oxygen and catheter and helped her out of the coffin.

"Ya were scared, huh? I saw the dials," the tech said.

"I hate cold sleep." Gloriana took the robe handed her and wrapped it around her nakedness. The steel floor under her feet felt ice cold.

"Message for ya," the tech said, nodding to a blinking light on the console before she went on to the next coffin.

Gloriana dropped her head between her knees for a minute, fighting nausea, then straightened and slipped the phone jack into the neural tap in her wrist. Ideograms flowed across the lids of her closed eyes.

gloriana deltawine spycop private 33337551833202 greetings—limo waiting—meeting at 9200 standard—Daniel Daniel magistrate corporate 90222945792

Screw life, she thought. Her stomach rolled and her head pounded. But in ten minutes she was dressed and a porter was loading her bags into the limo. Gloriana settled into a belted hammock while the rocket engines warmed up. Then the big doors opened and the space station fell away.

From orbit the planet appeared all ocean. The limo dropped into the atmosphere, then opened wings and flew west over roiled seas. Gloriana stared tiredly out the window at giant waves and leaping fins, putting flesh on the data she had scanned before the trip. Nu-Vegas was an ocean planet, with settlement limited to a few islands of bare rock. The ocean could not be economically farmed or mined, because of constant storms.

Gloriana thumbed the intercom switch. "Do you fish here?"

"Dunno," the limo said. "Fish, what is they, lady?" She could barely make out the computer's accent.

"Aquatic organisms. To eat."

"Some they washes up on the cliffs. The old timers eats 'em. But the tourists, they wants food like they gets at home."

"Is everything here imported?"

"Pretty near, lady."

"So you live off the tourists. And they come here for Glonze."

"Some looks at the ocean. Some plays the casino, some go the honeycombs. But it's Glonze they comes for. My people, we live off tourists since forever. Come up space from Old Terra, desert city there, Las Vegas. Sin City, they called it. In the First Testament, they say Babylon."

Gloriana didn't know what he was talking about, his religion maybe. Surely Nu-Vegas must have been settled from the Vega system? But everybody liked to claim some kind of descent from Old Terra. Whatever, it didn't matter.

Gloriana leaned back. After taking this case she had pulled up Intertour's bank rating, and let out a low whistle at the figures. Only a handful of worlds had Glonze networks, but the other ones were on prosperous worlds, rich in land and resources. Here, there was nothing but the Glonze trade. Why the Mandarins would have built a matrix here was a mystery, but then who really understood those prehistoric starcrossers? Gloriana had scanned enough galactic archaeology to know how much slack and humbug there was in every theory about the Mandarins.

The hotel was a spire among others on a rocky mote. Two protocol flunkies met her in the lobby and escorted her though the maze. She placed a box of rings in the hotel vault (*this* safe was uncrackable, because it extended into Glonze). Her room was a fashionable open-plan suite, with areas on three levels. The floors were dotted with cushions and the walls crawled with kinamik displays of marine life. She strolled about the suite, raising her left hand to suspicious fixtures until her ring tingled at the presence of the management's Eye-&-Ear. She got out her tools and disconnected it, taking care not to damage the mechanism.

An hour later she lay on a futon watching the ceiling display, a circular design showing a stylized pair of oriental lovers. She pressed a key; soft music sounded and the display began moving in slow motion. Then she plugged into the phone and impulsed Bendex's number.

"You," Bendex said. The pale green face of Intertour's planetary security chief floated against her closed eyelids. "Good. Give me a minute to connect everybody." Other faces began to appear, until there was a cluster of twelve and she had to roll her eyeballs back and about to focus on them.

One of the faces, Daniel, began the presentation. "First let me welcome our distinguished guest, Gloriana Delta-wine. As you can see from your files, she's one of the most highly recommended spycops, with a unique expertise in Glonze surveillance—"

Gloriana yawned. "Daniel, can we cut to the chase here? I've got a coffin hangover."

"Ya, mmmm. As you know, about six standard weeks ago, we began finding mutilated bodies in Glonze. At first we thought some nutcase tourist had gotten into the system, and we began screening everybody in and out. Then some survivors got glimpses of it, and we knew we had a doppelganger. They're pretty distinctive: blue-shadowed features, green sparks dripping from the hands." An artist's reconstruction of a doppelganger filled the screen. "And of course they can survive in Glonze indefinitely."

"The doppelganger can't exist outside of Glonze," Gloriana said. "It's purely a creature of the matrix. Just astral energy, like we are when we're in Glonze."

"Yes, well. Conventional methods failed to trap the doppelganger, so we've called in an expert." He nodded toward a spot that must be where he saw Gloriana's face.

A face asked, "How long can we keep the lid on this?"

"It's costing us a lot in compensation, but Legal thinks . . ."

"I don't understand," Gloriana said. "Isn't the web shut down?"

Some of the faces looked embarrassed. "The cost . . ." one began.

"You're shitting me," Gloriana said. "You know that thing's in Glonze, but you're still letting tourists in?"

"Gloriana dear," Bendex whispered on a private circuit, "we need to remember that we're all employees here, even the board—"

"Oh yes," she whispered. "Your people have crunched the numbers, right? The revenue exceeds the legal damages."

Daniel was going on with the briefing. "Investigation uncovered members of a mystery cult, the Stss. They believe—"

"I know about the Stss. They worship the Mandarins."

"Mmmmm, ya." Daniel looked peeved that Gloriana kept breaking up his presentation. "We raided the cult's cellar church. Found a member who fits the, mmmm, doppelganger's description."

"Then why haven't you caught it? It's just a duplicate. It'll come to its master."

"The master was killed in the raid."

"That was stupid."

"OK," Bendex said, not offended. "But we've never dealt with this kind of problem before. We didn't think about it."

"Just answer me one question," Gloriana said. "How many soldiers have you lost already, trying to nail this doppelganger?"

"I don't have that figure," Bendex lied. "Does it matter? Aren't you the expert?"

"Right," she said. "I'm the expert who's on the next ship out of here, if you don't give me information."

"We lost some troops. Couldn't catch him."

"It," she said. "Not him. All right, you have to close down the matrix. I can't work with bystanders around."

"Impossible," a voice said. "When you do surveillance in Glonze, aren't there others present?"

"Yes, but this is different."

"It's impossible," Daniel said.

"Of course, I'm sure all of *you* are traveling by limo these days . . ."

"Give it up," Bendex whispered privately. "These are hard guys, Gloriana. You'll blow your fee."

Gloriana opened her eyes. In the display over the desk, one of the figures was reaching orgasm. Gloriana watched the woman's delicate mouth grow slowly into a round while the other woman arched and smiled beneath her. Gloriana shut off the music, freezing the display.

"All right," she said. "I need all your data on the encounters."

"There's a lot of stuff," Bendex said. "You'll need to come physically to Government Island."

"Sure," Gloriana said, smiling coldly. "I'll come by Glonze." She savored an instant of their blanched faces, then cut the circuit.

♦ Before the human diaspora, the mysterious race we now call the Mandarins had spread through the terrestrial worlds of our arm of the galaxy. Everyone has seen the ruins of their cities, those strange serpentine wheels of stone. But on their capital worlds, the Mandarins built machines to bend space itself, then warped the machines right out of normal pace into a null-entropy continuum where the machines could never wear out.

When humans first settled on these worlds, they found that when they fell asleep their astral forms tended to slip off into an eldritch realm. The hallmark of this alternative dimension was the unique texture objects took on, at once both crystalline and metallic. ("It's like I'm made of glass," one of the first explorers reported joyfully. "Or bronze." So scientists on the project nicknamed the void Glonze.) Everyone who went into Glonze was too entranced to want to leave, but there was a time limit on it. After an hour in Glonze the body-form broke down into fragments, shattering like a crystal goblet flung against a wall.

After the first explorations, methods were developed for moving safely through Glonze. Time within the continuum flowed unevenly, and sometimes seemed to run backward. An hour might seem like a week in Glonze, or only a few minutes. Small bioclocks that fitted into one's neural tap were designed, though it took physicists a century to work out the equations that were used to set the clocks.

Only a few score of the thousands of human-settled worlds had Glonze networks. On those worlds, transportation cost effectively nothing, and this economic edge made those worlds rich. Then crowds of off-worlders came to sample the delights of the enchanted realm, and the worlds became richer. When it was discovered that time spent in Glonze sometimes cured diseases, and in many cases prolonged youth, the super-rich of the galaxy shouldered ordinary tourists aside.

The Mandarin cults regarded a visit to Glonze as a sacred pilgrimage, and tried to stop the secular invasion of it. They bombed hotels and villas. Although the price of living on Glonze worlds kept spiraling up, the tourists kept coming.

♦ Gloriana lay down on her futon and closed her eyes. She took deep yoga breaths, for about twenty minutes, breathing from deep in her body, slipping into a drowsy numbness. Then, suddenly, she seemed to be looking down at her own body, as her astral form separated. She waited a couple of minutes while the body on the bed gradually faded and then disappeared. In the corner of her eye she could glimpse the mirrorlike sheen of Glonze, and she leaned herself into the realm in the way she had been taught.

In Glonze, Gloriana's astral body drifted with inhuman lightness among the shards of metallic glass (or glasslike metal) that flowed in all directions. In Glonze, four senses—taste, smell, touch, and hearing—disappeared, yet her vision was so enriched and extended that it seemed like several senses. Her sight was almost infinitely variable; she could study the texture of a surface in microscopic detail, or extend her sight to the farthest horizon. Motion left a trace in the air and the gravity field that the eye could follow; temperatures and pressures could be seen directly. Unnameable colors gleamed, and vision became as sensual and intimate as the sense of touch. To gaze on something was to embrace that thing, almost to become it.

In Glonze, Gloriana moved through cathedrals of light. Colors became indescribably rich and sparking; the sea was sapphire, the sun a colossal diamond. At some points, the Endless Corridors followed the landscape of the planet; elsewhere they wandered off into radiant vistas of their own.

Gloriana moved through the holy silence of Glonze, marveling as always. Could this be the *real* world, she wondered? Is everything *really* like *this,* pure and shining? Is that the truth the Mandarins meant to show us? Or is this the illusion, and the reality our own universe of muddle and sludge. Labyrinthine walls sparkled like gems, and their colors caressed her like a lover's hands. She "walked" without lifting her feet, with the inhumanly light gliding motion that seemed so natural in Glonze. Soon everything began to move with liquid slowness and she knew that, in the outside world, she was traversing the ocean floor. The water didn't get her wet, but it tingled all through her like a euphoric drug, and her headache disappeared. Then a mountain of filigreed silver and white jade loomed before her and, still "walking," she slid slowly up its glittering slope.

Far off, her keen sight discerned two men, crouched in a garden of starlike flowers, laughing in sheer pleasure. She took a deep breath and held it for a day or so, keeping an eye on the outside time her watch showed. When she could delay no longer, she closed her eyes and let herself slip from Glonze back into the light of common day. She did this slowly, savoring the last moments of ecstasy before her astral form filled with flesh. As always, she felt a sudden revulsion for her physical body. She felt heavy and greasy, a sack of festering meat. She shook her head back and forth, letting her hair fly, to root herself in her body again.

Two minutes of real-time had passed while she was in Glonze. Here, it was dusk, and the lights were coming on in towers all around her. She had awakened on the suspension bridge that straddled the urban chasm. Advertising hols—celebrities and mythological figures a hundred meters tall—squatted or sprawled on the tops of the towers, postured and preened. Below, limos crawled the aerial and ground lanes of the Strip, like beetles scurrying beneath the holiday lights of the hotel-casinos. The wind snapped at her short skirt, and she gathered her deep-violet cape around her as she walked. Tourists were everywhere, gawking at the ocean, babbling loud inanities about the beauties of Glonze. The dominants, male and female, turned their heads to watch Gloriana's flashing legs, and the submissives in their trains darted her poisonous looks.

The café was a nautilus shell of spiral galleries. Bendex was waiting in a private room. He clicked his heels and bowed, and she flicked her skirt in a curtsy. He was taller and somehow rougher than he looked on holo. Gloriana made him for a gunslinger. His gestures were quick and precise and the two pistols in his belt looked restless.

◆ "I came off the famine worlds after the war," Gloriana said as they dabbled at fondue. "Don't ask me about my childhood. Then I worked security on industrial freighters."

"Rough job."

"Union busting, that's what it was. I hated it." Bendex raised his eyebrows, acknowledging her candor. "When I had some money saved, I found a partner with connections on Tau Ceti IV, and we opened an office together."

Bendex nodded. "There's a matrix there." He nudged a dish of Cetian eyeballs toward her. She spooned one out.

"People that are on the run, they duck in and out of Glonze. The Endless Corridors really *are,* you know, but the gates aren't; you have to come out sometime, or you fade away. But I noticed something else. Lovers used them for rendezvous, so there was divorce work."

"Is that true? That you can have sex in Glonze?"

"I've seen it. But it's pretty tricky. You can accidentally destroy each other."

"Just like regular sex."

Gloriana looked down to hide her smile, forked a baby carrot out of plum sauce. "But then I figured, wouldn't bootleggers of all kinds meet there? Industrial spies? Politicals? All of a sudden there was lots of work."

"Dangerous."

"Making real money always is."

"Would you describe yourself as materialistic?"

"Not me, I'm a romantic," she said. "But the universe we live in: yes."

Tough babe, Bendex was thinking. He liked her, though. She kept glancing up from under her eyelashes, then dropping her gaze. Jade eyes blinked on the hint of an ecopanthic fold. Her hair was natural forest green, her complexion the ancient terranic manila.

♦ As they followed the footman through the main dining hall, a needle of purple light suddenly crisscrossed the room, searing and crushing everything it touched to slag and rubble. Screams rose above the wasp buzz of the laser. Gloriana dived into a forward roll that carried her behind a table, kicked and rolled again, trying to keep the crowd between her and that flickering death. Boot toes bruised her ribs; broken glass licked at her face. As she rolled, she fetched a derringer laser from the hidden pocket in her skirt. But a boot thumped against her hand and the gun went flying.

She came up behind a portable bar. The shooting was coming from a service door to one of the kitchens. Gloriana's head swayed with the screaming and stench of burning flesh. She peeled a bracelet from her wrist, yanked the silver crab from its chain, and flung the bracelet at the door. It skittered across the threshold into the unholy glare.

Gloriana risked a look and spotted Bendex, lying on his side behind a knot of charred bodies, shooting energetically with both hands.

"Bendex!" she yelled. "Fire in the hole!"

He heard and began rolling toward her. Gloriana had been counting seconds. She put her face to the floor and covered her head with her hands. Then the explosion drowned out all sound, and the walls came down.

♦ Gloriana waited impatiently while a medico taped her sprained arm. It would heal as soon as she entered Glonze again, but she let him go ahead. Bendex's men were everywhere, questioning the survivors and running nano detectors like busy mice through the rubble. They had a portable workstation set up, integrating the nano data. A tech sat in the folding chair, jacked in, eyes closed.

Bendex was unhurt. He had a badge pinned to his gunbelt. "They must be really scared of you," he said, "to set up this ambush."

Gloriana said nothing.

"We've traced the guns they used," he said.

"That fast," she said.

He shrugged. "These people aren't professionals. We think the guns were supplied by one Nakayama Rike, a suspected associate of the Stss. We're running a go-find on him now."

The tech unjacked and whispered to Bendex.

"We'll find him soon," Bendex said to Gloriana. "Feel like arresting somebody?"

"You can," she said. "But I want to go with."

There were three types of establishment that Gloriana, for good reasons based on harsh childhood memories, loathed. These were bars, hospitals, and police stations. Unfortunately, her profession required that she spend a lot of time in such places. At a downtown trauma center, she followed Bendex down long corridors past alcoves curtained with stasis fields of opaque air. Medicos came and went through the alcoves, briefly disturbing the fields, and Gloriana glimpsed charred limbs and gaunt faces jutting out of the surgical units.

"One perpetrator's still alive," Bendex said. "Wasn't hurt much. In here."

A sentry in half-armor stood guard outside an alcove at the end of the corridor. They stepped through the shimmering indigo field and into a recovery room. The machines were mostly concealed behind wall hangings and cabinets so that the room looked much like an ordinary bedroom, decorated in a classic oriental style. A naked man lay strapped down on the bed, surrounded by more machines. Here and there on his body, patches of new synthetic skin gleamed pinkly. He was wriggling his body this way and that, struggling against the unbreakable straps. At the sight of Bendex and Gloriana he lay still.

"Our shooter," said Bendex, glancing at the readouts. "Minor burns and a greenstick fracture in his left hand." He spoke to the man: "You're here for observation overnight. Tomorrow we take you to jail."

"I have the right to call a lawyer," the man said. "Your fucking medicos disconnected my phone implant."

"This is a company planet," Bendex said, "not a republic." Then he leaned casually against a bank of machinery. "You got no rights here, bub."

"Corporate law has to respect my rights under interstellar criminal law."

"That's right," Bendex said, "*in theory*. In practice . . ." he let his voice trail off. He was studying one of the hangings, which showed a bird with mountains and waterfalls in the background. It was rendered in red and black, simple, complete.

"At least give me a fucking sheet," the man demanded. "You guys get me naked, then bring a woman in here."

"See, that's an example," Bendex said. "We do what we want. I'll bet you can imagine some other examples, 'ey?"

Gloriana waited. She didn't expect much to come of this. The man on the bed looked unshakable as a rock. A true believer. Bendex started asking questions, but the man remained stubbornly silent. Once he barked, "You are all filthy defilers of a sacred realm. He-Who-Kills will drive you from it."

"Tell us about He-Who-Kills," Bendex invited.

But the man would not speak again.

"OK, be that way," Bendex said. "Tomorrow we take you over to HQ and interrogate you in a VR lab. Think about it." He turned to Gloriana. "If you want to talk to this guy, I'll wait outside."

"That's OK."

"Are you sure?"

"Sure."

A limo took Gloriana and Bendex above the city traffic, then arrowed swiftly out across the ocean. Bendex explained that they were going to another island, to arrest the supplier of the guns.

"Rike's a shyster," Bendex said, "makes connections for small-time thieves and smugglers. We don't usually bother them; not worth the trouble."

Gloriana nodded, knowing what this probably meant: the corporation was taking its percentage. "But we've had an eye on him for a while as a suspected Stss," Bendex continued. He leaned back, his eyes unfocusing for a second as he listened to a message on his implant. "We've tracked him to a honeycomb palace on another island. My lads have it staked out. We'll go in and make the arrest. I have backup in armor waiting in a van just up the block, in case there's trouble."

Bendex hesitated. Then decided to go ahead and speak. "Back at the hospital, I thought you might want to hang around. The guy tried to kill you. I thought you might want to pay him back a little."

Gloriana shrugged. "I'm not into revenge. If something threatens me, I attack it. When it no longer threatens me, I don't have any feelings about it."

She wondered why she was explaining so much to this man. It wasn't like her. She looked away, then looked back and met his clear blue eyes.

"You're a very moral person," he said.

She shook her head. "I don't think so," she said. "I think I'm a pretty *numb* person. Desensitized." Oh my god, Gloriana thought. Why did I say that?

Bendex leaned back in his chair and looked at her, smiling slightly, saying nothing.

♦ Shortly before the Age of Space, a group of terrorists on Old Terra secretly released a bacterial agent stolen from military labs into the human population. For some reason, the terrorists wanted to eradicate homosexuals and individuals classed as "black" (one of the old mythical "racial" categories). But the epidemic soon spread beyond these target populations. The agent was a virus that spread through sexual contact, destroyed immune systems, and mutated rapidly in the ensuing decades. By the middle of the twentieth century, scientists determined that there was no way to eradicate the agent, barring some entirely new discovery in microbiology. The agent mutated more rapidly than any naturally occurring virus, endlessly adapting to changes in its environment. It was a sword in a stone-age world, and human medicine was helpless against it.

And still is, after all these centuries. Humans went out to the stars and settled the worlds, bringing the viral parasite with them in their blood. Medicine advanced. Genetic screening eliminated many diseases; cloned organs became available for transplant; metabolism treatments retarded aging; cancer could be cured by time spent in Glonze. The average life span reached a century, then two. But the virus remained in the population, mutating, dormant and undetectable at times but flaring up every few generations.

Many people forswore genital intercourse altogether and used bottle labs for reproduction, despite the disapproval of eugenics boards. Some cloned themselves, despite the expense and the hazard of criminal penalties for that anti-evolutionary practice. But sexual intercourse and natural procreation were deeply rooted in human instinct. On most worlds, monogamy became customary, and multiple or serial partnerships became as taboo as incest or bestiality (which does not mean, of course, that they did not occur). But the restrictions of monogamy applied only to intercourse and childbearing, and alternatives to intercourse became increasingly popular among all ages, encouraged by law and custom.

Of the many alternatives, the most popular was the honeycomb palace.

♦   Caesera Casa was the most famous and luxurious of the honey-comb palaces. The anteroom looked like the lobby of a nineteenth-century grand hotel. Tourists loitered all day there, sipping drinks, chatting with strangers, then retiring to the honeycomb cells when their mood was ripe. Gloriana and Bendex went straight to the cloakroom, checked their clothes, and selected masks. Bendex's mask was a traditional African type, twice as tall as his head and tapering at top and bottom, so that the lower tip grazed his breastbone. The mask was scarlet striped with green, with round ghost eyes and a fleshy mouth outlined in white. Glori-ana chose the first mask to come to hand, a goblin face with a thrusting snout, all sharp edges and mottled colors.

"It's you, dearie," Bendex said in faux falsetto.

Gloriana laughed merrily.

They walked on through the doors of the honeycomb, avoiding look-ing at each other's bodies. They had left their guns in the limo. But Bendex was in contact with his men through his phone implant and Glo-riana stuck close to him. Normally, they would have waited for the sus-pect to exit the palace, then arrested him at the door. But people some-times spent days in the cells. The Stss had made Gloriana an assassin's target and there was no time to waste.

Gloriana whispered in Bendex's ear. "How do we make him?"

"They're tracking his implants by satellite," Bendex said, "and echo-ing it back to me." He blinked to check the display inside his eyelids. "I've got a hum that gets louder as we approach."

They moved along the catwalk, going deeper into the palace. The honey-comb was an intricate structure of six-sided faux-glass cells. The cells were mounted on rotating gimbals so that they constantly slid past each other like elevators, but in all the different directions their hexagonal shapes allowed. The possible combinations were almost infinite, so that the cells were always rearranging themselves, like the shapes in a kaleidoscope.

Inside each occupied cell, nude masked figures strutted, displayed, or fondled themselves. Each cell circulated past other cells, exposing the occupants to ever-changing views of each other. Most cells held a single occupant, but often two and occasionally three people would squeeze into a single cell. Some occupants played coy, acting as if they did not know they were observed; others masturbated ostentatiously or flattened their bodies aggressively against the glass. Transparent pillows allowed the occupants to arrange their bodies in outrageous postures. Some used vibrators or handcuffs or orchids.

None removed their masks.

Gloriana and Bendex paced the catwalks, looking like a couple reluctant to take the plunge. Masked figures gestured to them as they floated past. Empty cells, their glass hatches open, passed below, slowly enough to climb down into them. But Bendex loitered until a certain cell moved closer. In it was a tall man with waist-length red hair; moreover, he was obviously a member of one of those rare subspecies that still retained facial and body hair. He flaunted and stroked his well-thatched torso and bush-decked hefty penis. His face was obscured by a traditional opera mask, a black-and-white Dick Nixon. Gloriana tensed as Bendex swung his body out over the cell, unlatched the glass lid, and scrambled inside. The man inside turned, startled, as Bendex dropped down beside him. His hands came up and shoved Bendex in the chest, but Bendex laid a hand on the man's arm, and the hirsute form collapsed into his arms like a sleepy drunk.

Palm implant, Gloriana thought. Some kind of neuroshock. She stared at her own palm, thinking she should have something similar installed. There are times when you can't carry a weapon.

On the catwalks, armored men with security insignia took the man into custody. Not samurai; the corporation didn't want to scare the tourists. Still, cops spoil a party. Masked nude figures began climbing from cells and streaming for the lobby, grumbling.

"Bendex." Gloriana took his arm, pulled him aside. "Let me speak frankly. We're wasting our time dicking around with all this. It's a routine investigation."

"They tried to kill you."

"And failed. Let's not let ourselves get distracted. It's the doppelganger we want, and it's in Glonze. I want to get a good night's sleep, then enter the matrix tomorrow and hunt it down."

"I'll go with you."

"You don't have to."

"I know."

Gloriana shook her head gently. "You'll be in much more danger than I would."

"Still, you need someone to watch your back, don't you?"

Gloriana had always worked alone. Still. "It would be useful," she admitted.

"Then we'll go," he said.

"Rules," she said. "You follow my lead. And you stay behind me."

"All right."

"All right," she said. "Then we both should go get some sleep."

♦ Back in her suite, Gloriana bathed and collapsed on the futon. She knew she must sleep, but she tossed and turned restlessly. She thought of the bodies in the honeycomb, the endless rhythmic circulation, like the design inside a kaleidoscope. Bodies entering, bodies leaving, the pattern always changing, always the same. She began to masturbate, thinking about Bendex's smooth emerald flesh and muscular thighs.

She kept on with it, but nothing was working. Gloriana plugged into the phone. She let her awareness drift through the VR circuits, feeling the shadowy presence of other nightwalkers, men and women plugged in all over the planet. Anonymous flesh grappled her, and she gave herself up to rough caresses. The thighs were muscular enough. It was easy to imagine that green skin, those blue eyes. That smile.

Opening her eyes, Gloriana watched her writhing body in the mirror, leaving her tactile sense still in the circuit. What a fine game, she thought, as her lashes fluttered and the crimson flush spread down her throat to her breasts. Fucking the invisible man. When she finally came, the sheets were drenched with sweat. She yanked the plug roughly from her neck and lay trembling and filled with shame.

♦ In her high chamber, Gloriana armed herself for Glonze.

She had fetched her case from the hotel vault, and opened its digital locks. She lifted the lid to reveal a dozen metallic rings, their flat faces etched with ideograms. As she lifted each piece, it gleamed with the metal of its making: beryllium-iron, titanium, cobalt, nickel-osmium, white gold. She slipped the rings onto her fingers, each in its prescribed position. As she did so, the flexon in the metal stretched to accommodate each knuckle, then contracted to fit snugly in place.

"Are those what I think they are?" Bendex asked.

"Uh-huh. Rings of power." The rings were filled with microchips and cold-fusion power cells. A master craftsman had forged them, one by one, over a period of years. Together they cost the price of a starship.

"What do they do?"

"Here, nothing." No reason to tell him about the no-eye function. "But in Glonze they magnify certain brain centers."

"Psi?"

"Sort of. More like magic."

She checked each ring's fit, then tugged on long white gloves.

Bendex had a weapon, a two-handed sword with a blade well over a meter long. "That's the only way to kill it, right? Cut off its head?"

"Mmm-hmm," she said. "You have to completely sever the spinal column."

They lay down on the futon, the naked sword between them. Bendex's hand gripped the hilt of the sword. Gloriana slipped her hand down and wound her fingers in his. Then they closed their eyes and began to breathe deeply. The Glonze state was not regular sleep; even the brain waves were different. But it was a kind of half-sleep. Gloriana slid quickly into the meditative state, then waited a little for Bendex to catch up and cross over with her into the astral realm. For a moment, they had the sensation that they were floating above their bodies. Then the awefull radiance welled up and wiped away the mundane universe.

They were in Glonze.

For the first few moments, they just looked around, breathing deeply, smiling uncontrollably. Their hands were still linked, though they could not feel them. The sky gleamed like sheet metal; water tumbled like a cascade of gems. Gloriana checked the islands she saw in the distance, lumps of hematite and brass. There was no danger visible, though she spotted tourists on the islands. She looked down into the ocean, depth and depth of gemlike radiance. People walked on the sea floor, smiling and pointing. She closed her eyes and could still see them. Light upon light pounded at Gloriana, made her head swim. The beauty ached in her like pain.

Bendex looked like a being made all of jade and polished bronze. Colors rippled across his body, flashed and sang at his joints. Gloriana looked down at herself, something she usually avoided, and saw herself as she might be, an hourglass of grace and shining.

They walked, without taking steps. The surface they walked on was bronze sharp with glittering scales, was glass stained a million colors. Gloriana walked with her hands raised, groping uncertainly like a sleepwalker, letting the rings show her the way. Bendex came behind, poised sideways like a crab, rotating his head slowly, shifting his vision to scan the horizons. He carried the sword propped across his shoulder like a workman carrying lumber. In Glonze it had no weight and he could not tire.

By the power of her rings Gloriana was able to move herself and Bendex much more rapidly, in short bursts, than was otherwise possible. They traveled above and below the water, following the land. They traveled out of the faerie landscape altogether and into corridors of light that were their own place, unrelated to the terrain of the planet. Several times Gloriana felt the presence of the doppelganger, an unmistakable tugging of her rings. She was sure it was watching them somehow, lurking just beyond horizons, just behind crystal spires. But they did not see it, and then her internal clock told her it was time to leave Glonze.

They made their way back, and slowly wakened on the narrow futon. Bendex opened his eyes slowly, stirred his sluggish limbs.

"I felt it," Gloriana said. She was angry with herself. "I felt the damn thing, but I couldn't find it."

"Tomorrow we'll find it," Bendex said. He lifted the sword, careful with its razor edge, and seated it in its long scabbard.

That night they went to a tiny island, one just big enough for a café and a strip of beach. The roof of the café was crowded with limos. Inside, the servers were real-life people, stark naked and obsequious. Most of the tourists were in the beer garden watching a real-time holo of two executions being performed elsewhere on the planet. The condemned, an arsonist and an adulterer, were turned loose on a rocky islet with hungry neo-pards. The tourists keyed in running bets on which would die first. Gloriana looked at the hole with interest, but noticed Bendex turn from it with distaste. They made their way to a green marble table with wrought-iron legs, mere meters from the waves crashing at the foot of a shelf of rock. As they ate, Bendex described the peculiarities of the local Glonze matrix. Gloriana nodded, memorizing each item of data.

"I'd spend all my time in Glonze if I could," Gloriana said. "It feels so good there."

"I love it," Bendex agreed. "The euphoria . . ."

"It's like everything's all right," she said. "Tell me something, Bendex. Do you ever think about the builders?"

"Who, the Mandarins?"

"Yes."

"Actually, I do. I'm not a philosopher. But they had all this," he gestured to include the planet, Glonze, outer space. "And where are they now?"

"Where are the snows of yesteryear?" she quoted.

"It makes me feel like the human species is just a dot in time. A flash on the monitor. On the scale of galaxies, we're nothing."

"And we waste it," Gloriana said. "Think about how it must have been back on Old Terra, when space travel was just getting started. People must have thought, we have all this technology, our lives are going to be perfect. Now we're on all these worlds, and what do we have? All the violence, all the grubbing for money. I think people were happier in the ancient days. They lived in communities. They made love with whoever they wanted."

"Life's always been harsh," Bendex said. "Our species must want it that way. There's something self-destructive in us, when all's said and done. We don't love ourselves."

"Maybe the Mandarins aren't extinct," she said. "They made Glonze. Maybe there's a place somewhere beyond it, where they still live. Maybe it's a perfect world. Maybe they live forever."

"There's no forever," Bendex said. "There's no perfect world."

"I know," Gloriana said, meeting his eye. So blue. She laid her hand beside his on the table, a couple of centimeters away. It was the socially acceptable signal for permission to touch her hand. He looked in her eyes a second, at her faint clear smile. Then he covered her hand with his and held it lightly. They sat like that for a while, not speaking, just smiling at each other, listening to the waves tumble below their feet.

Then he let her hand go. His head tilted slightly as he listened to an incoming message.

"They just brought two more bodies out of Glonze," he said. "Tourists. A woman and a child."

"Mutilated?"

"Yes." His fingers drummed restlessly on the table. "It's time to go to work."

Gloriana stood and straightened her skirt. "I know."

♦ They lay down again, their hands wreathed around the sword that lay between them.

Deep breathing, increased flow of oxygen to the brain. Metabolism shifting, brain waves changing. Mysterious machines, beyond the dimensional gates, clicked and turned.

They woke in glory.

Gloriana's rings sent them skating along the surface of the water, ducking recklessly among the crystal waves. They crisscrossed the seas, following the vague hints the rings gave her. They came to a beach of cut glass, topped by a mountain of brass and platinum. With a thought, she conveyed them to the top of the peak. They crossed an uneven plateau, agate and bloodstone and tigereye, and reached what seemed like the crater of a volcano. Gouts of light fountained from the crater like fireworks, and a seepage of many-hued molten glass flowed around their feet like lava. None of it harmed them; where touch is hot, there is no pain. But Bendex saw how the molten glass turned his legs white hot and clung to them as it cooled. He peeled away strips of it with his sword, and they whirled off like wisps of burnt paper into the luminous sky.

Her hand on his arm. She tried to touch him, to make him look at something. He saw the hand and followed her gaze, then saw it and stood ready. Gloriana shifted deliberately, setting her body squarely between Bendex and the crater. She was staring down into it, holding her palms out in front of her like a blind woman feeling her way. He followed her gaze down into the crater and saw nothing strange. He saw only the fountain of color, like light from a mirror, beauty indescribable. But then slowly against the vortex of light a black speck took shape. It rose slowly and steadily through the gusts of radiance, settling finally on the opposite lip of the crater, only a kilometer from Gloriana.

It had the shape of a man, but was sooty black, indistinct, so that the eye had trouble allowing the lines of its figure. There was a hint of a face, blue shadowed, and green sparks dripped from the claws of its raised hands.

It did not glitter. Like nothing else in Glonze, it soaked up the light and did not give it back.

Bendex stood ready, left knee cocked, sword raised. Gloriana stared at her adversary, then raised her hands over her head. She seemed to grow larger, until she was as tall as two women, then three. Across the crater, the sooty black figure grew, too. Sparks popped from its hands, which began to glow. Then the hands reached out, jagged claws immense against the sky. Space seemed to tilt, so that at shoulder level Gloriana and the doppelganger were close together, though at ground level their feet were still a kilometer apart.

Hands clasped throats, and they began trying to strangle each other.

Bendex ran, loping around the rim of the crater. Everything seemed to move with dreamlike slowness, but then suddenly he was there, near the doppelganger. His vision seemed to disappear into its inky blackness, as though he might be drawn into it. With an internal bellow of rage he swung the sword. Sunlight flared on the blade as it moved, a rainbow of color more lovely than any our many skies have made. His secondary visual senses watched the air forced away by the blade, saw the silvery motion of it through the gravity field. The blade sheared into the doppelganger's calf and droplets of blood beaded out slowly, like rubies sinking in olive oil. But when he yanked the sword free, the blood ceased and the wound closed almost instantly, like a film run backwards.

Bendex looked up. Gloriana had broken the stranglehold. She straight-armed the creature in the chest, then stepped away. She looked wary and disinclined to match strength with the doppelganger. Bendex fled back along the lip of the crater. High above him, he saw fangs glint in the face of shadow, and believed the doppelganger laughed.

Suddenly everything was normal-sized again, both her and the dop-pelganger, and Bendex saw how far he was from both of them, out along the crater's edge. He rushed to get back and take up a position behind her. She had told him to stay behind her. Gloriana bent and reached into the crater, thrusting her arms in up to the elbows. She gathered pure light like molten steel into her hands, turning and turning her palms, elon-gating her fingers, so that light dripped from them in sticky clumps and strings. Then her hands moved like a potter's, shaping the light quickly. She flung the blobs of light up into the sky, where they hovered and grew and took on definition, congealed, crystallized into shapes of fiery gold and milky glass. Bendex saw knights in armor, their warhorses rearing and plunging, their swords and maces raised. He saw lions, their great maned heads held high, and a dragon, winged and coiled, and a mino-taur. They were icy, crystalline shapes, like figures carved from gigantic diamonds. Yet they moved and were alive.

The figures plunged down onto the sooty demon, slashing and flail-ing, surrounding him on the lip of the crater. Soon he could not be seen for the battling figures that covered him. Yet he fought back, raking this way and that with his claws, ripping the diamond bodies apart. Entrails like strings of gems, and blood like liquid garnets, burst from the armored men and their spirited mounts. Knights and lions, dragon and minotaur, fell back before his claws.

One by one they died.

But Gloriana had grown tall again, standing aloof from the battle and pouring ring-energy into her own body. Now she grasped the sooty figure about the head and shoulders and bore down upon it steadily like a wres-tler, forcing it to its knees. It was weak from battling her phantoms, and though it struggled in her grip, she kept the viselike hold clamped tight.

Bendex moved into position.

Gloriana increased the pressure on the head, bending it farther for-ward. The deep curve of the neck stood bare, and the knob of the spinal cord bulged outward. Bendex raised the sword, brought it down with shimmering force, and effortlessly sheared head from shoulders. As the sword cleared the neck, the blade exploded in his hands, into a billion crystal fragments. But the doppelganger's head was rolling along the lip of the crater, and the body slumped in Gloriana's arms. She opened her shining metallic hands and let it crumble.

Bit by bit, then, the sooty figure began to come apart. The wind carried it away into the light-flooded air, like funeral ashes.

♦　Gloriana and Bendex sat at a wrought-iron table. On the rocks below their feet, waves crashed. "It's lovely here," she said. "I don't want to go back."

"Do you have to leave right away?"

Gloriana met his gaze, then dropped her own. "Well," she said, smiling slightly. "I could stay on for a few days, if the company eats the tab."

"I can swing that."

Gloriana shuffled her feet, looked around at the ocean. She said, "It was good working with you, Bendex. If you hadn't been there with that sword, I don't know what might have happened."

He sensed the white lie there, let it slide. "It's been fascinating working with you, Gloriana," he said. "I learned a lot." He smiled again, then waited politely. It was the woman's place to make the first move, if there was going to be one.

"I suppose you can tell," she said, "that I'm attracted to you."

He took her hand. "We could do something before you leave," he said. "Like what?"

He shrugged. "We could go to a honeycomb."

"I'd like that," she said, and kissed him, on the lips, slowly, just once. "I'd like that very much."

KIM IDOL

$\diamond$

Coyotes

$\diamond$

Tara didn't remember hearing the explosions, but just before the firestorms came every shadow in her yard disappeared. After the attacks, in the absence of a plan, she headed back to Vegas where she could at least spend her end days with people she knew. By the time she arrived, the city was defined by shifting dust devils and a ceaseless wind.

When she'd had a future, she had abandoned her family, but no matter what she felt about them she couldn't face the end of the world alone. Returning home she found that only her brother and sister had survived. But she also discovered that, if you hate the ones you should love, loneliness grows. She couldn't forget failed apologies and old fights. The three siblings made an agreement of sorts and found a way to live together in the final days of a dimming world. But Tara's anger was a thing that lived inside her, something she couldn't shape or kill. It grew. She took her pain out on strangers. Violence became her new creed. She tried to channel her impulses. Whenever stragglers passed by, Tara shot them down. Expressions of the darkening sadness unfolding within, the killings gave her momentary relief from her demons and could be excused as necessary.

Today she saw a man trying to make his way in the land behind their yard. Aiming the long-barreled .44 above the windowsill, Tara studied the stranger. Sagebrush volleys marked his passage. The wind whirled around him in turgid gasps. His movements were hobbled by flying rock bits and trash. She sympathized with his plight. She knew what it was like to struggle.

She squeezed the trigger. Dust kicked up at the traveler's feet when she missed.

The stranger wheeled around and tripped.

When the stranger tried to regain his balance, she shot him. Then she put the gun down and shut the window. Fists of air pounded the windowpanes.

She buried him in the fried remains of her parents' yard, at the base of three hunching pepper trees. It took her longer to dig the grave than it used to. She was definitely growing weaker.

She liked sitting by the trees and remained in place for a while. Eventually, her brother Sandy tapped her shoulder and brought her back from her daydreams. Tara judged his form. While disaster seemed to have whittled her to a hardened essence, it had made her brother buckle.

"You look like a faded photograph," she said. All Sandy's colors had dulled, and a lazy eye that had never been corrected now constantly pulled to the left.

The wind pelted them both with a dusty spray, and Tara realized that her face was coated with grit. Sandy shielded himself from the sandstorm behind Tara's body. She instinctively turned to take the brunt. Stepping inside would have sheltered them both, but the stultifying decay within drove them outside now and again.

"He was probably just looking for food," Sandy said. The newly dug grave had become a cockroach highway. A piece of pink chintz flitted across it and danced off.

"I buried him decently," Tara said, spitting out a strand of graying hair. Both she and Sandy wore their hair bound up in frazzled braids that framed stressed angular features.

"Course, not right to let decent folk rot, but OK to shoot them," Sandy said.

"Ask Sarah how she feels about strangers. If you ever see her again," Tara replied.

A roving patrol had taken their sister two days previously. Local militia seeking volunteers for cleanup crews. They followed regular routes but worked slowly, without ambition.

"Wouldn't have thought she'd be so careless," Sandy said. He reached out and pulled a handful of crispy leaves off a tree. Tara and Sandy stood in the somewhat shade of Sarah's pepper trees. Her final efforts had been dedicated to saving the garden, but fallout had poisoned the soil too deeply. Eventually even the saltbush died.

Sandy raised his hand and let the leaves fly. They whirled away lightly, like ash.

"Just you and me left now," Tara said.

She'd been standing in a doorway in Barstow when heat and mushroom clouds had claimed the view. If the powers that be hadn't closed Nellis, she supposed Nevada would have taken a direct hit, too. Then gale-force winds turned ground-bound objects into angels, and ash fell until the ground seemed covered in snow. Afterward a dirty veil rose and covered the sun, which now existed as a cool dimming glow. Then temperatures dropped. The towers of the Strip went dark. The bastards that ran them took off. On clear days Tara could stand in her yard and still see the Strip on one side and the ragged peaks of Red Rock on the other.

"Leaving now," Sandy said. Tara examined his pack to ensure that he only had enough water for the day.

Sandy clenched a scarred fist, but he didn't stop her.

"We're running low," Tara said, setting his water bottle back in place. She fingered a scar on the back of his hand before he could withdraw it. He held one of Sarah's old brown hats in his other hand. A girlish shape that no one but Tara could see crossed between the pepper trees. Tara shook off the vision. She'd been entering a dreamy state more and more often lately. The farther away the past got, the more it haunted her in person. Because love and hate were interchangeable in Tara, she was both sorry Sarah was gone and relieved. One way or another, there was one less person in the world who knew her.

"I'll make lunch when you bring it home," she said to her brother.

"I used to run a restaurant," he said. "Now I forage for crap even a dog wouldn't eat. Why, again, do I go out while you stay?"

"Maybe because you can't shoot people down like dogs when you need to. You want to stay and defend?" The offer wasn't genuine. Their parents' home was now Tara's by default—her guns, her house, her rules.

Instead of answering, Sandy fumbled for his glasses.

"Is it so bad with just us?" Tara asked. "You can't stand to be alone anymore than I can."

"When I was stronger, you couldn't stand to be near me," Sandy replied. He found his glasses. Ski goggles, one hundred percent UV protection. Like her, he was fair and freckled, but now his complexion was blotched.

"Please shut up." Tara watched the chintz patch that had crossed the grave run the length of the fence line, as if it were seeking an escape.

"I used to tell people that you tried to kill me. Now I can say you are all I have. How sick is that?" Sandy asked.

Tara opened her own water bottle and sipped. "Why are you dragging this story out now? Don't you have other things to worry about than unchecked sibling rivalry?"

"You attacked me." He brandished his scarred hand. A number 2 lead pencil had done the trick.

"So you say," Tara replied. "Put your hand away and go."

"This is all coming to an end," Sandy said. "But I will play along for a little while longer." He put on his hat, straightened the brim, and headed out. Tara stood at the front door and watched him work his way down the drive. It occurred to her, not for the first time, that though her brother was all she had left, two was not enough company. She wondered if living in solitary fear was better.

Sandy scaled the gate, secured with a lock that had no key, and dropped to the other side. Tara watched until he disappeared from view, then closed the door and tried to think. A sense of urgency compelled her to set goals. Her brother was right: an end was near and she resolved to control it. If he were going to leave, she would decide how. Her house, her rules. To keep her mind from spinning, she cleaned house. Neither Tara nor her siblings had kept the place up. Grit was pressed through every crack. The floor was as sandy as the desert. Wallpaper rolled to the base of walls in stripped piles. Curling wood slats had pulled away from seams. The dining table was shabby and sagging. The chairs were pulled apart at the joints and leaned in at odd angles like drunks stumbling down an alley.

She started in the great living room, a large oaken space with a battered teak floor, and found herself steeped in family history. The broom lay on the floor underneath a great mirror that her mother had loved. The furniture was inherited from her grandmother. Sweeping with care around the table legs, Tara bumped the table and the Lazy Susan tottered. The spinner, bowed from the time Sarah winged it at her brother, no longer rotated. An arcing stain on an opposite wall reflected Sandy's rejoinder. The hamburger had come in high and missed Sarah altogether. The stain spanned the door to the china closet that remained open because the latch wouldn't catch. Tara shut it whenever she passed by.

When a piece of tin foil batted against a cracked pane, Tara stared through the badly boarded windows and was greeted with a view of plastic bags skipping across the sand. Looking more closely at the glass, Tara saw where the panes had been spackled. As teenagers, they all broke in whenever they forgot their keys. Following an urge to track echoes of her history further, Tara dropped her broom and picked up the trail.

Sandy's room was the nearest. Green carpet, green walls, brown bed sheets.

♠ "You're so like one another," their mother had said once. She'd been trying to force apologies after another fight.

"I don't need a twin," Tara had replied.

"He'll grow up bigger than you."

"Then I'll need to beat him as much as possible while I still can." Their mother stopped speaking to Tara for the rest of the day after that. Sandy and Tara had always been antithetical energies constantly seeking dominion. He sold her stereo for a fix. She put a brick on his doorjamb. He hit her. She punched back. No one could explain the hostility; it simply existed, like nature.

"Oldest child sets the example," their mother had said. Tara had disagreed. The last fight left her with stitches and a story for the cops that her family denied. She left for college earlier than expected and rarely visited afterward, but never fully cut ties because they were family.

By the time she returned home for good, Tara's parents were dead. Neither, it turned out, was the type to soldier on after the death of civilization. Neither had waited to say good-bye. But her siblings had welcomed her in their fashion.

♠ Still seeking shelter in the past, Tara headed down the hallway. She peeked into other rooms, remembering this dent or that, not all of it ugly, but all of it tainted. Glancing in her sister's old room, she remembered the figure of a girl with a bat slung over her shoulder, coming through the door. There was a mashed tarantula at the end of that bat. Sarah the Spider Killer. The room had been decorated with pink and white chintz, doilies, and lace curtains. The spider had taken refuge in a pillow sham and had scared Tara so badly that she'd asked her sister to kill it.

Entering her parents' bedroom, Tara stopped to stare at a figure, fully formed, in the closet mirror reflecting from a sliding glass panel. Then she saw that the left door of the closet was open, stuck an inch from complete closure. When something blocked her effort to close the door, she stuck her finger in, to force the object back. This failed. So she muscled the door open in order to address the offending object: a backpack, filled to the brim.

"Asshole." She checked the contents. Sandy truly planned on leaving. An ugly heat rose in her. She picked up the pack and returned to the living room and raged at the memories the room held. Then, still not too tired to be angry, she bolted through the front door and ran down the drive to the gate. Like her brother before her, she climbed the fence but stopped just outside the gate. Fear and heartache stopped her from going further. She hadn't the nerve to face the world alone or the desire to start over. Looking down the driveway, she remembered a figure running down the drive, its form sliced up by the rails that made up the fence.

"Sarah?"

The imagined spirit calmed her. She climbed back into her safety zone, then squatted in the dirt to consider Sandy's impending desertion and the need to counter it. Whatever her intentions toward her brother, today was the last day to express them.

"It should seem like a celebration," she said to herself. "Today lunch should be a special occasion."

So she returned to the house and located her mother's best dishes. She also found place settings that were stained but serviceable, replaced the table spinner with two bottles of red wine, and threw a clean tablecloth over the table.

She dressed in her mother's bathroom because it reminded her of a time when she had trusted her mother. Once lined with silver and green wallpaper, it had a tropical look that had made the room seem bigger. Because the windows were small and set high, there were no views of the world outside to frighten Tara. A row of dried atomizers on the counter reminded her that her mother always smelled like honeysuckle.

A wave of nausea hit while she prepared. She threw up into the toilet and wiped her face clean while staring into the mirror at herself, the ghost to be, and tried to will her illness away.

"We'll need candles," she said, trying to inch her mind forward. Memories of stone-cold faces sitting on the tub behind her came to mind. As kids, Tara and her siblings would perch on the rim of the tub and talk to their mother while she dressed. The last time Tara and Sandy fought, her mother and her sister bathed her in that tub and used perfume as a means of wiping away the tragedy. Tara hurled the empty bottles at the shadow children until a memory of bright flashes and railing sirens stopped her. She knew that she would be forever soldered here to her family by the piece of bad history. History that had also driven her away.

"Someone owes me an apology before they go," she said. "Or they can't go."

♠ Sandy arrived shortly after one.

"High times," he said, surprised that the table was set but willing to play along with the notion of a holiday. He hung his jacket up and began unpacking the goods.

"I wished the stove still worked," Tara said. The food, whatever it was, would be served cold.

While they were setting up, a broken piece of palm started scratching against the front windows. Sandy startled at the sound and went outside to cut the branch back. Tara watched him through the window. Middle age had been mean to Sandy before the wars, and now, with the end days torturing his features, he was speedily aging. She pitied him a little, but not enough.

"Do you find you're more sensitive to sounds now?" Tara asked.

"I hate the way the wind whines," he replied. "I dreamed of being hunted by coyotes last night because the wind won't stop."

"What about things that happened before the war?"

He shrugged. "The past is not my problem." Tara gestured toward their seats, and he filled their cups with wine that she could no longer keep down. So he consumed both portions and set the bottle on his side of the table, finishing several glassfuls before he talked again.

"I'm going," he said, slurring a little. His face slackened, as if a wave of intoxication had just rolled across his cortex.

"What about me?" Tara asked. "Who buries me in the yard when you go? Who remembers what I've endured?"

"God, the sound of your complaints will never die," Sandy said, as he suddenly seemed to see the living room in detail. "What the hell happened in here?" he asked.

Tara was sitting with her back to the room but didn't turn around. She knew without looking that shards of glass were sprinkled everywhere. When their parents died, there had been no reason to divide their belongings, so it had all been ready for throwing. She had even used her father's forty-four caliber Smith and Wesson on the great mirror before she put the gun on the seat beside her.

She surmised that her brother hadn't noticed the mess earlier because he felt as shitty as she did. When he finally located the backpack pieces, he shook his head.

"It's over," he said.

The statement was all-inclusive. The fights, the conversation, the living.

"Forget about it, all of it," he said surveying the damage. Then he shivered and slipped into his jacket. "I don't want to die here with you. I'd rather die with the coyotes tearing at my bones than die here with you."

The statement touched the edges of the building rage within her. "I can't leave here. I can't get much past the gate," Tara said. "You come and go every day, but I can't. I have to stay."

Her brother tried to sympathize: "Too many memories?"

"Why do you come home at all? Everyday you leave and come home."

"You're my sister. You should stand by your family."

"No matter what."

"Don't be an idiot." He seemed amused. "You've gotten what you wanted. I don't owe you a thing. Maybe even gave you something you needed for free."

"Until you apologize"—she was too tired to find the right words—"I will always be carrying your fucking sin."

"Which is probably really why you came home. Couldn't die without grinding me one more time. Could have lived forever with it, but the end of the world meant that you had to come home. Game's not over for you until everyone knows you're still angry. Well, we don't care. We all moved on."

Tara reached for the gun.

"You got your baggage," Sandy said. "You kill people. I guess that Sarah tried to leave, too. That was her right."

"Patrols took her," Tara said.

"No troops out here for months," Sandy replied. "Bet she's buried out in the yard, too." He finished the bottle and threw it. It ricocheted off the sideboard and fell without breaking. "You scare the hell out of me, but I want to die somewhere else. And I want to die with anyone but you by my side."

"If you go, I'll stop breathing. It'll be just me," Tara said. "You have to stay."

"So you can keep punishing me? Bullshit."

"You owe me." As she raised the gun, a flash of the stubborn little girl who would not apologize to her mother haunted her for a second. In the pieces of broken glass scattered about the room she saw slivers of herself, visions of a disintegrating core. She fired from her seat and hit him in the chest.

He slumped over, but did not die instantly. "Fuck! You're really ruled by your ghosts, aren't you?" The question startled her.

"Say you're sorry," Tara said. "Say you're sorry."

Instead, Sandy sighed and stopped moving.

His body was heavy. Heaving him from the house to the yard was a bitch. Tara closed his eyes and knew he was dead but thought that she could see his chest rise and fall when she dumped him into a cardboard box and closed the lid. She had no tape. She had to fold the tabs carefully so they would stay closed.

She held an old-fashioned funeral, just Tara and her memories standing in the dirt on a cold, dull day. She knew that without someone else to talk to the size of her worries would only grow, but at least her brother had been punished. He'd been right: if the world had not ended, retribution wouldn't have become vital. For a while, she remained in the skimpy shadow of her sister's pepper trees, imagining an end to the wind and thinking about a day when the trees would again cast proper shadows. That dream was overrun by the notion of rows of unburied cardboard boxes.

Eventually this thought drove Tara back inside.

ANDREW KIRALY

Your Recent Acquisitions in the Neonesque (Microfables)

A Legendary Casino

For seven years, the Highgate was an enigma wrapped in scaffolding and silver tarpaulins. Naturally, its concealment fed a growing speculation about what would present itself on the day of unveiling. There were rumors of a central spire constructed of gold-veined jade; its point would hook passing clouds and hail the march of constellations. There was excited talk of a water feature in which patrons, giddy with their winnings, would slide into fizzing pools of nutritive champagne; a grand hall lined with Byzantine statuary; gleaming mosaic floors whose autumn coolness whispered of empire and mythic conquest. One gossip columnist, insistent in his claim that he had been allowed an exclusive preview tour, wrote of floors rippling with purple damask, so soft and comforting it recalled the subsea pleasures of the womb, and he wept as his journey came to an end.

A clan of devotees formed, anticipating what was assuredly to be the world's most opulent casino. The clan was so zealous, in fact, it could better be called a cult. Its members were known on sight for their distinct dress: sacklike cowls made of silver tarpaulins, which they would wear to their solemn nightly vigils in front of the shrouded casino. Skeptics, meanwhile, claimed the cultists were in the hire of the Highgate's owner, Penetrus (you will perhaps remember him for his failed, but well-publicized, hot-air balloon excursion to Toulouse), who was notorious for elaborate promotional stunts. It became fashionable to ridicule the cult, and unbelievers took pride in seeing beyond what was surely a ruse to generate enthusiasm for the Highgate, accreting silently beneath its misshapen chrysalis of silver and steel. Yet it took only a tantalizing glimpse of silver fabric flapping in the wind to stoke anew even the diminished imagination of skeptics. And despite their dismissals in public, competitors secretly grew nervous, because they sensed about the Highgate a discernible rhythm of growth that hinted at something momentous.

The day for the unveiling arrived, and there was Penetrus at the podium with his tricorn hat and inimitable grin, standing in front of what had become in the public's mind a pastiche of so many dreams, rumors, hopes, and fascinations. When the winch tugged the last yard of tarp away, what stood before them was a skeleton of rust-flaked scaffolding that enclosed nothing but air. Penetrus, whose grin now seemed to have something pained and truculent in it, was laughed off the stage. That laughter followed him all the way out of town and, some historians argue, was responsible for chasing him right into a Texas sanitarium.

The Highgate cultists claim the last word in calling this grand antic of Penetrus's a heartbreaking act of charity, and leave the rest to cryptic silence. Perhaps their reasoning is revealed in the fact that, long after the skeleton was pulled down by rioters and picked clean by junkmen, the Highgate is still remembered for all its jade towers, broadways, secret fields of heather, and golden doors. Its seven years robed in that tarp were seven years of the most delicate construction, as well as a staggering efficiency. Who can even number the casinos that Penetrus built?

You have bought the Highgate, but you cannot own it.

A Themed Casino

The historic event of the city of Paris's spectacular annihilation at the hands of an accidentally launched Deathspitter ultranuke in 2127 has among its numerous side effects a nourishing irony.

Perhaps you remember the burning derision with which both the press and the public treated the Neonesque's Paris casino: dubious, third-rate, uninspired, "the blandest baguette this side of the Champs-Élysées," muttered those officious wags of Fodor's. Paris casino workers themselves seemed to absorb and embody those views. Their eyes were as expressionless as dough, indifference ran through their limbs like some syrupy humor, and every conversation seemed stillborn in the retiring sigh of the uninterested menial. The Paris had much else to warrant the criticism: a plastic, life-size replica of the Eiffel Tower that teased the senses maddeningly with the impression that it leaned, almost imperceptibly, to the west in an unwitting tribute to American indolence; a cabaret revue in tortured textbook French whose leading woman was a shrill, insufferable diva, ready to hurl her glass of Bordeaux across the dressing room at the slightest provocation; a surfeit of amateur mimes. Critics said that if the city of Paris were cast in a magic mirror that turned its reflections into gibbering grotesqueries, it would look like this.

That was prior to the Embarrassing/Deadly Nuclear Fumble of 2127, courtesy of a faulty missile-tracking system and a not inconsequential language barrier between Portugal and Lebanon. Now with the original Paris destroyed, the Paris casino has experienced a renewed life few could have predicted. In fact, it has since become a small city in itself, drawing Parisians by boat and plane who have transplanted their surviving art and culture to the site, from their wine to their penchant for worrisome trysts to their tailored sense of aggravated hauteur. Parisians embraced this contemptible façade an ocean away, and filled it with themselves until the casino began to pulse with indisputable life: tattered paintings from the Louvre, broken cups from sidewalk cafes, steak frites, and badly burned and slightly radioactive but nonetheless wonderfully fashionable shoes. Once a ridiculous distortion, the Paris casino has been newly authorized through tragedy, resignation, and will. Today the baguettes are real, as are the Eiffel Tower and the mimes. In fact, they are incomparable.

A Legendary Casino

If you stand still in the failing light at the eastern edge of the Neon-esque and rest a hand on your bosom to calm your heart, gaze up at the Medulla. Steady yourself. You might see what others claim to have seen. That the casino breathes.

The Medulla has become the repository of such numerous fears, desires, myths, and stories that it is difficult to separate fantasy from fact. But I have been able to confirm a few. Others, I suspect, will have to remain categorized as rumors that have been planted by rivals, or Medulla management itself. It is true the Medulla was effectively founded by renegade Bavarian botanists, whose willingness to break their country's bioethics accord and consequent alignment with certain nascent rightist groups earned them the questionable privilege of fleeing their home continent on a Japanese fishing trawler. It is also true that sympathetic media coverage of the Bavarians led to a lucrative private grant from construction magnate Toby Weller Trask of Phoenix. It is finally, and sadly, true that this connection guided the Bavarians' experimentation with stretching chlorophyllic cells to create "living walls" to the ends of commercial application rather than pure science, though it is yet unconfirmed that Trask had the visas revoked of certain scientists among them who were especially vocal in their criticism of his meddling. (However, I have been able to dismiss as outrageous fiction the reports that Trask punished these more vocal dissident scientists by using their blood to feed and fortify the inchoate plant walls, inspiriting them with a lifelong taste for blood.) And while it is true the Medulla was biomechanically engineered to photosynthesize its own energy with chlorophyllic cells stretched to the proportions of wall panels that convert sunlight into food, it is not demonstrably true that the casino is actually *aware,* despite the excited chatter of many who claim that if you carefully watch the Medulla's spiny silhouette and succulent leaf structures outstretched to the sunlight, not only will you see the building breathe, but you will feel acknowledged doing so by some type of eyeless sentience not yet understood by man.

But all of this might as well be true, because the Medulla thrives on such rumor. The importance of the truth has dissolved in the face of a durable enthusiasm that sets its own terms: whatever excites is true.

People flock here as if in pilgrimage, to grin or grimace in front of the mutant aloe with keno machines and roulette wheels secreted amid its cool, verdant folds. They have fertilized the Medulla with their apprehensions and secret terrors, and the casino's management has responded in kind when pressured by journalists, curiosity seekers, and surveyors such as me: it denies nothing.

A Floating Casino

Those who ask why the Transluce is made from the same thin membrane that goes into the manufacture of drinking straws and form-fitting codpieces for fetishists soon realize the reason for the construction material: the casino was never intended to last. Owner Agrippa Miff was no amateur among the dukes, dandies, and CEOs of the Neonesque desiring to write their names on history's brow. He was, instead, aiming to pique the interest of land speculators, and prove that a casino could in fact be built on a plot of real estate no bigger than an oddly shaped beach blanket disturbed by a fickle zephyr. Until your purchase, however, his model had convinced no one.

When a strong wind churns up red dust in the Neonesque, the Transluce trembles like a frightened priest. In fact, with the help of friends, you can grasp one of its eggshell corners and, pulling upward, peek at its foundation of dried grass and cedar shavings. And though it has yet to be tested by a pioneering soul fortified with enough strong drink, the rumor persists that a sufficient amount of inebriated velocity can take you (with only mild discomfort) right through one of the casino walls, leaving your outline as a signature of your speed and determination. Also, when the various heats of the desert converge to create a fist that pummels the land, the Transluce sags, teasing the jurisdiction between solid and liquid. Calculations suggest the Transluce will meet its end by either blowing away in a particularly strong wind or breaking down into some sort of plasmic muck in a brutal summer.

At the risk of presumptuousness, however, I predict the casino will perish from another cause. As a delicate and temporary model, it is particularly dear to those pained by their awareness of the Transluce's limited future. They visit not as tourists but as greedy curators—that is to say, bandits—plucking a plastic beam here, a joist there, souvenirs of a fated demise. The casino will not blow away or melt, but succumb to these grasping hands that kill with their aggressive form of early remembrance, the vice of nostalgics who lack patience. Their worry about its fleeting nature fulfills itself, and is what truly makes the Transluce fleeting.

Rival Casinos

Twin fangs rising from the valley's edge, Nux and Scylla are entwined in a rivalry that has inspired poets and confounded philosophers. Conventional history tells us that Nux was built first, with its main tower of red marble, finned and twisted like a birthday candle. The construction of Scylla commenced not a week later, and the last red stones of its structure were heaved into place by the same cranes that had put the final touches on what would turn out to be its reluctant twin.

Nux strung itself in crepe paper and fringed banners proclaiming its Buffet of Hypersatisfaction; Scylla followed suit in a matter of mere hours. When Nux, unannounced, wrapped its tower in the steel spine of a rollercoaster it dubbed the Eternal Return, Scylla followed, garlanding itself in an identical thrill ride that, too, would faithfully deliver to riders rattling concussions to inspire stories for years to come. Nux dug a leafy bingo pit; Scylla dug one as well. In a fit of gimmickry, Nux manned its roulette tables with disgraced Swiss royal guards; Scylla did, too. Sometimes in as little as minutes, Scylla mirrored Nux in theme, promotion, and architecture, in a competitive reflex honed to its sharpest, most absurd point: a commitment to complete imitation, senseless and mechanical.

And why, the toters of briefcases wondered, didn't Nux challenge Scylla in the courts to air this outrage? Instead, Nux continued without fuss, accreting to the pace of smug, measured success. To this day, so does Scylla, its unwanted twin, rival and reflection. The majority opinion is that Nux, in its refusal to counterattack or even lodge a protest, has all but surrendered to its hated relationship.

However, a different view has taken hold in recent years. Some observers look upon the identical Nux and Scylla not with peevishness or contempt, but awe. They utter the names with a catch in the throat that suggests reverence, because they see the facts in a new way. Perhaps Scylla is not imitating Nux in every window, vault, and courtyard, every fountain, column, and thrill ride, driven by the impulse to duplicate. The new thinking holds that Nux, rather, is the culprit in a crime much more sinister and elaborate: wretched foreknowledge. Like an obsessed lover or a true enemy, Nux anticipates Scylla's every move and makes it first, having mastered at least one art of disquieting a rival: becoming a mirror of what was thought to be hidden intent.

A Forgotten Casino

How could I ever forget the name of the band that performs at the casino whose name I cannot remember? Kelsey Radiant and the Blazing Footlights rampage like drunken lynxes on a night prowl, itch like a loving disease; they are sideways-walkers, they are pope-tamers and king-biters. Their repertoire draws the romantically murderous cannibal women; religious wearers of black; raving, blind seers; and children born with badger teeth. One critic perhaps said it best when he wrote, "The ferocious introspection they inspire rattles my soul's very hair; I hereby publicly tender my resignation and subsequent suicide." Since seeing Kelsey Radiant and the Blazing Footlights, I, too, have been transported to new, barbaric planes of savage grace. This accounts for my queer limp.

The superlative quality of the band has plunged into a quandary the casino that hosts it, the casino whose name I cannot remember. The Footlights attract riotous crowds, who thrill, drink, and spend like flagrant caravaners. This excitement has the effect of rendering the casino forgettable. It must be maddening, akin to being known only for one's expressive green eyes or conqueror's nose, but only that and nothing else. (It is the casino with the finned portico and the emerald lights on top, near the gravel pit jurisdiction on the eastern outlands. It is not particularly hard to find.)

The casino whose name I cannot remember, in fact, despises the band for its glorious infamy. But it must also concede that the band is the only reason anyone visits this casino whose name no one can remember. In the thrall of their jealousy, executives have often considered ejecting Kelsey Radiant and the Blazing Footlights, but they know not a day would pass before a rival would immediately snatch them up. (Then it, too, would chew on a bitter jealousy in its new, popular yet forgotten state.) The band is forever menaced by this jealousy, but also forever jealously guarded, and daily the forgettable casino makes the wrenching decision to keep the unforgettable band. It thrives, but without a face.

But the casino does derive a mincing, cruel pleasure in pretending to possess that which eclipses it. (It is the casino with the three minarets flying yellow flags.)

An Abandoned Casino

The Dominux is surrounded by husks, shells, empty carapaces of old structures. Ducts, curls of wallpaper, and knobless doors lie in great heaps; tumbled archways and bridge supports are stacked like felled forests. There are painted glass displays of poker machines gone dim, the hollow ovoid eyes of blackjack robots, chairs disgorging feathers, cracked roulette tables consigned to the timeless gnawing of sand bugs. Whole wings of buildings have been lopped off and deserted, their rooms hosting only grainy sunlight. Parlors lie in the dirt like ships run aground, their chandeliers trembling in the gritty breeze of the Neonesque, their drapes gone brittle from the heat, the frames of paintings turned to bones.

Venture closer, and the detritus of abandonment becomes more recent. Here, the paint and carpet of these empty rooms are not so faded. The wallpaper still smells like lavender. These outdated poker machines claw the air with wires that still might contain electric life. The ball crawl echoes, it seems, with the terrified laughter of smelly children. Moving on, you will find the desertion taking place before your eyes: laborers in masks and jumpsuits pilot work elephants; cranes and dozers remove halls, porticoes, patios; they dump banquet tables still laden with meats and pudding. Monogrammed towels grow in great piles. Expansions are sawed off by giant, insectlike machines, and crumple like cakes, whistling dust from the keyholes.

This is not destruction, but refinement. The Dominux sheds itself like a reptile, but its renewed form is always more streamlined, more thoroughly dedicated to purpose. With each sloughing off, it hones its effectiveness with the spirit of perfecting a weapon. Yesterday rots in the sun: the outdated styles, methods, and gambling odds; the exhausted gimmicks and cloying comforts; the fashion the Dominux has quite correctly turned its back on; the means, techniques, tricks, and ruses it has quite correctly determined have inefficiencies that cannot be rectified, but must be abandoned immediately. Beneath them is newness: new promotion schemes, more effective machines, richer pudding.

The Dominux knows its essential function. It cleaves off its own limbs as a devotee of ruthlessness and efficiency, and the unfortunate gambler who enters here suffers for the sacrifice, being enchanted, induced, and flattened to poverty faster than the flutter of a moth's wings. The next day, this occurs even faster.

Thus with each new mode of being, the Dominux reduces its own clientele. Its journey toward perfection, an ultimate refinement of method, leaves fewer clients to eliminate. It exhausts its fuel in its mission to more quickly and efficiently exhaust its fuel. With each sheaf that peels away in the shatter of glass, the splintering of wood, the Dominux moves toward a vital mode that can only be expressed with a definitive means in which if patrons so much as rest their gaze on the grim obelisk pulsing at the center of the debris——

Where will it turn when there is no more fuel?

No one, including your surveyor, pretends to know toward what end the Dominux journeys, undressing itself to reveal leisure as an act of warfare.

(Another school of thought that has developed around the Dominux anticipates a more peaceful end: that on the day it becomes a perfect version of itself, it will disappear, having achieved a state of holy abstraction.)

A Themed Casino

The poker machines clatter with manifest vigor at the Motif, the deep ocean light seems weighted, lurid. The rouge on the cheeks of the barmaids is so thick as to suggest something wanton. The orange carpet confesses to a hopelessness in human striving to beauty, the scent of stale mint lingers, the heavily pomaded hair of the lounge musicians gleams, complacent in its own excess. And what is it in the bellow of the stickmen that sounds like cheap theater, inflated with too much rehearsal? The Motif lolls, thick and saturated.

The air is humid with another smell you cannot quite place. It seems to recall apricots from Georgia plantations, or apple blossoms on the Amalfi Coast, or the sensation of a stifling hug from an Old World aunt who wears too much lavender oil. In the rooms, the furniture appears to be arranged so as to direct a sustained but delicate assault on your senses: the dreary flatness of the pillows, the thin teal sheets, how the bed creaks like a midwestern hotel bed should, the remote control that feels as though it has just been touched by the hand of a stranger with unsavory habits. The window looks out on a postcard view of the Neonesque's sleepy neon lagoon, a portrait that is trying in its precision.

At the machines, there is the blue-haired old woman, Montana vintage, encased in a nest of oxygen tubes, mechanically feeding coins to the machine. At the table there is the fat conventioneer, filled with Idaho grain, accompanied by a younger woman whose red lipstick seems applied with a hand moved by desperation. And you can never walk too far inside the Motif without falling behind a herd of waddling tourists in sandals, visors, and horrid, shapeless clothes. Your muffled frustrations surface only as a grumble, themselves muffled, of how typical this is. But it is more than typical. The carefulness of this picture betrays a suspicious intent.

Many say the Motif casino does not have a theme, but that is not true. The Motif is a casino that has taken itself on as a theme. It is a reflexive charade, a gesture to something authentic but lethally immediate. It is a recollection superimposed.

The consequences of referring to itself have proven irreversible and deadly. Thus, your unmistakable realization upon leaving and looking back on the casino steeped in its own emblems: the Motif will someday collapse under the sultry weight of its own self-consciousness. It would be its first genuine act.

Rival Casinos

A glittering skyrise banded by its famous aqueducts of immaculate stone, the Spirato makes of simplicity a form of opulence. Rotary slot machines and mechanical poker robots are spaced like trees among fluted pillars, and its broad marble floors echo with the feet of tourists, impressing upon newcomers the idea of a train station attached to a mortuary: the patrons of Spirato will, at most, succumb to a decorous stimulation. The butlers and cocktail servers are so understated and genteel they seem to flirt with invisibility itself; little wonder they are said to take two-year courses in the arts of being unseen. And to enter the Spirato's private par-

lors is to find yourself among elite company, from Portuguese trade patri-
archs to queens of ancient Malaysian lines. They need not bring luggage.
Their clothes are sewn by hand in Spirato's lower chambers, which are
discreetly hidden from view. However, there is one spectacle available to
all the clients of Spirato. When dusk flows over the Gloaming Range, twi-
light shifts through the deep windows of the casino, and it is as though a
solemn procession of soldiers with shields of light marches through for
some martial inspection.

The procession ends at the casino's twin, slouching next to Spirato
proper like a wastrel brother with deplorable posture. It is the tower of
refuse that contains the castoffs of Spirato's construction: fabric scraps,
stone dust, onion tops, opera glasses, wagon wheels, casements and carv-
ers' tools, crossbeams, and wedges of marble. This sagging tower is a
night-casino whose hazardous warrens host their own clientele of crick-
ets and junkmen, Neonesque rats and coyotes, unwashed fugitives who
feel safe only under cover of darkfall.

Philosophically, at least, the owners of the real Spirato embrace this
negative space. They consider the Spirato the Neonesque's only complete
casino; the others are but halves, and mere masks, and sheaths. The Spirato is complete because it accepts its history, its unsightly parentheti-
cals. However, when pressed (which, I admit, sometimes required a few
encouraging jabs with a dagger), the owners will betray a conception of
their fetid sibling as but a shadow, a contingency rather than an equal.
Their pride in their relation is, in fact, a form of wicked condescension.
The prejudice is all the more sharp because of its subtlety.

The denizens of the slouching night-Spirato are not innocent of prejudice, either, but theirs is not difficult to tease out. The scrap hunters,
bandits, and furtive dogs who play with castoff dice see the night-Spirato
as the true casino of the two. After all, its cousin next door is just one
possible casino that could have risen from these necessary source materials piled up in sclerotic grandeur in the shadow of the Gloaming Range.
The Spirato proper could have been built with onion tops and tattered
drapes, and could have served hewn stones at meals, and covered the
windows with marble; the night-Spirato is a bibliography of its potential.
If you ingratiate yourself to these shifty-eyed residents and press them for
details (I surmised the use of sharp objects would be unwise here), they
only shrug and utter their favorite phrase: we necessarily exist. The Spirato could have been otherwise.

An Unfinished Casino

The Hierophant may appear to be complete, with its painstakingly crafted roundels supporting a series of broad windows that turn the place into a sort of greenhouse for wakening impulses, or the capitals that top the supporting columns with a flourish of stylized laurels. But the constant presence of work elephants and flattening machines betrays a quaint compulsion: in a constant state of dissatisfaction, the executives of Hierophant openly admit the Hierophant's form does not correspond with the image they harbor in their minds. This explains the architects walking around with blueprints, and it explains the machines adding columns, erecting a tower, or crumpling an arcade. For more than twenty years, the Hierophant, at the ruthless direction of president Petronel Danforth, has been making revisions to itself, striking you with the impression of an entity with a need to constantly itch, preen, and adjust. Petronel Danforth takes a certain pride in this frenzy of self-improvement that wreaths the Hierophant in an ever-present cloud of work dust. When talking of the Hierophant, he talks of two: the one of brick and plaster he is constantly refining, and the ideal Hierophant that lives, unadulterated and whole, in his mind. He gallantly avers his goal of matching the real with the ideal. When the two Hierophants merge in this cracked plane of the Neonesque, only then will the Hierophant have attained its true nature. Danforth goes so far as to publicly refuse to speak its name until the building, by some baffling standard known only to him and his men, truly partakes of its proper form.

The irony is bitter for being so obvious. For all his vaunted talk, he is the only one who does not understand the casino's true nature. Neighbors, foes, and even casual observers know the Hierophant better than itself. When Danforth talks about his relentless pursuit of the Hierophant's true nature, beyond any conception of his curiously damaged soul, the whole notion is a laughingstock. The Hierophant attained its ideal self long ago: vain, obsessed with self-correction, and known to fatally confuse means and ends.

An Abandoned Casino

Ashlyn Quinby, heiress and socialite renowned for bewildering her father with her outrageous acts of philanthropy—most recently buying Calcutta and turning its administration over to private firm—also has on her vast resume a little-known achievement: the building of a most exceptional casino in the Neonesque. Its obscurity is due to an entrenched confusion over whether it is, in fact, even a casino. Careful interpretation of her acts reveals she is not some creature given to caprice, as so loudly proclaimed by the tabloids. I recite here not my own opinion, though I disclose, at the risk of death by flattening, that I happen to also endorse it.

Ashlyn Quinby's building of the Coronis was deceptively routine. She raised investors, purchased the land—a considerable parcel in the quarter of Rival Casinos—and announced her intentions at a press event that was less a media briefing than a sort of dignified bacchanal, whose centerpiece was a marvelous life-size hologram of the Coronis itself, a lattice of graceful, parabolic arches; the effect of fashioning ovoid rings into a larger curve made it appear as though the building itself was rapt in a languid dance of mourning. The casino opened on schedule two years later, and press and patrons were one in their praise of its beauty. Architects as well marveled at the aching poise of the pillars, arcades, and estuaries, the oculus that resembled the eye of a sleepy child, the banisters that took the turn of dancers' elbows and bent knees.

What occurred within a year of its opening still baffles: the casino began to empty. Vidpoke machines gradually disappeared, never to be replaced. Or one day, a chanteuse imported from the Left Bank would be bringing listeners to tears in the lounge; the next, a cavernous void had replaced the scene. Restaurants vanished in the space of a day, table by table, sous-chef by muttering sous-chef. Talk of financial trouble had long since sent Coronis stock into a permanent decline, and it was delisted with somewhat doleful ceremony. The payroll department ceased issuing checks, and employees emptied their lockers, leaving behind aprons and cravats. The brief life of the Coronis is considered an object lesson in the frequently underestimated perils of this business. Analysts note with sneering satisfaction that neither celebrity nor a dynastic fortune guarantees success in this thorny business of building casinos. The towering Coronis, vacant and quiet as a churchyard, testifies to this.

But the conclusion that Coronis is dead is possibly flawed. Ashlyn Quinby has since bought a voting percentage of the stock, and has written into the purchase agreement her quiet, steadfast refusal to raze or condemn the property. This refusal holds the key to what is Coronis's success: some speculate the building was meant to be empty and quiet. The clamor was simply a dutiful preparation for cultivating the proper content for the building's form.

Now form and content perfectly coincide. The Coronis has achieved its function: the manufacture of silence.

Rival Casinos

You'll be forgiven if you cause confusion when you say the name of this casino. Streed actually refers to three casinos of sundry merits. Streed boasts a grand canal that snakes through the property, meandering beneath bridges and piers, past women carrying clamshell parasols under a generally convincing painted sky. Streed, on the other hand, has made its name with lounge singers and midway barkers of famously filthy, sarcastic demeanor; grown men have been known to weep from the insults the barkers fling from their bearded faces. Finally, the third Streed distinguishes itself with its vast, mazelike fern gardens, in which a few confused men and women are said to have been wandering since childhood. (Plates of curry provided daily by unknown persons seem to support this theory.) When you say you plan to visit Streed for the first time, it's considered wise to specify.

In different ways, each Streed claims that it is the whole and correct embodiment of Streed, that it alone attains Streedness. How can an arbitrary form perfectly embody an arbitrary word? It is not a question of semantics but of correct behavior. While two of the Streeds loudly proclaim their legitimacy on banners, pamphlets, and poorhouse residents induced to wear sandwich boards, the third is content to be a casino with a wide bridge made of brass, and a mischievous panda that escapes from the menagerie at least once a month, and a neon sign that resembles a clown's mouth opened in unpleasant surprise, and a glass dome that turns sunrise into a torrid waking dream. It does not strive to embody its name, but shapes the word to fit its form. When tourists say they plan to return to Streed, they don't need to specify.

A Reverse Casino

The Limpid casino was built next to the Neonesque's only lake, a broad disc of spring-fed water near the valley's edge, where the ruins of a goatherd's village still inspire stories of wraiths and monsters. Its far-flung location was curious, as monorail service to the Neonesque's edge was and remains peevishly intermittent. But that curiosity was quickly overtaken by another. After the proper officials were bribed and permits obtained through legally questionable means, mogul Scalper Thirry arranged to have his castlelike Limpid, made of yellow porcelain that rings musically when struck, submerged in the lake, using cranes and laborers paid in imported cheese. It was not simply the vain gesture of a madman. Advised by court scientists, Thirry foresaw the day when the whole Neonesque would dry up and leave the casinos humming in the gritty, desolate winds. Presumably, the lake would prove the final stronghold. When the drought arrived and the water dropped, the Limpid would finally rise.

Thirry's anticipation of a drought that will someday savage the Neonesque is not completely unfounded, but his preparations are considered by many to be comical and premature. Until that baleful time of the predicted drought, you can technically visit the underwater resort, but only for a few minutes at a time. Otherwise, the Limpid draws an elite company of divers and avid swimmers. For now, it is largely a silent museum, tickled by strands of shimmering kelp, watched over by fat, glum carp, a museum whose life of riot and pleasure is not behind it, but far ahead of it. Its current life as an artifact—its watery, static, murmuring readiness, a kind of death—is a prologue.

BLISS ESPOSITO

Kirby and the Portal to Hell

When they discovered that the portal to Hell actually was in Las Vegas, no one in town really was all that surprised. "I mean," said a local in one newscast, "where else would it be? I just hope it doesn't hurt the housing market too much." And in fact it didn't. After years of a steadily declining economy, entire neighborhoods going into foreclosure, banks closing left and right, major casinos laying off anyone who wasn't locked into a union, Hell was exactly what Las Vegas needed.

As soon as the portal was discovered, behind a vending machine at the dilapidated Silver Angel Motel, Gene Banks promptly bought the property and started erecting Inferno, a Hell-themed casino with the portal at its heart. Oh, it would be glorious, the papers boasted, showing sketches of the harpy uniforms the cocktail waitresses would wear on the front page of the Sunday edition. The hotel promised more than five thousand new jobs, a spectacular buffet, and an opportunity to view the portal itself. As soon as it was announced, tourism exploded once again. Empty rooms were booked, and property was being claimed. Hell was the answer. Everyone in Vegas was happy.

Kirby wasn't happy.

Kirby had been trying to hide the portal for years. He'd found it while searching for coins to buy a candy bar. Kirby always searched for coins behind this particular vending machine because there was always exact change back there. If he needed fifty cents for a candy bar, he would find it. If he needed $1.25 for some chips and a can of soda, it would be waiting. Kirby had learned in life not to question things. Things often left him confused.

Then one day he noticed something on the wall. He was huddled in the corner unwrapping the 3 Musketeers he'd just bought. He liked 3 Musketeers because he could slide his finger inside and wiggle it around in the creamy nougat. But just before he broke the seal of chocolate on the bar with the broad tip of his finger, something else caught his attention. It was on the wall behind the vending machine, about chest level. It was the size of a pin, and gave the impression of blue and red. Most people probably would have missed it, but Kirby knew the back of this machine like the back of his hand: the linoleum turning up with potato chip edges along the wall, the brown and yellow water stain, the family of cockroaches that waved their antennas at him every morning.

And now this strange dot right in the middle of everything.

He reached out to touch it, he liked touching things with his finger, but he knew somehow that now was not the time, and he pulled his arm slowly back.

Kirby began spending the majority of his days hanging around the corridor staring at the slit of space between the wall and the vending machine, where the hole grew a little each day. Once in a while, the manager of the Silver Angel would come around and shoo him away but other than that pretty much left him alone. Kirby didn't cause trouble like the others and never kicked or punched the vending machine to get something for free.

Then one day, after many months of gazing, he realized that the impression of blue and red, swirling together like Easter egg dyes before they mixed, had become actual colors. Suddenly he wanted to touch it, like nothing else he had ever touched. Pressing the side of his head against the wall as hard as he could, he could tell that the hole was bigger, maybe big enough to get his finger into. He had to see what this lack of space, concentration of energy, hole in the wall, felt like.

He looked up and down the motel corridor. An icy desert breeze cut the warmth of the machine. He jostled the vending machine, once, twice. Then he slammed the side with all of his ninety-eight pounds. He did it again. He just needed an inch or two. He pushed and pushed until the vending machine squealed against the concrete floor. He tried his arm to discover that he had enough room to reach the hole.

Kirby licked his dry lips and reached his hand behind the humming machine. He was right—there was just enough room for his arm, and he was able to reach the colors. He tapped the outside with the tip of his finger and tapped it again. It was like melted chocolate, but better than even a 3 Musketeers. He worked his finger in a little more deeply—to the first joint, then to the second. He felt euphoric entering this hole. Putting his finger into things always made him happy, but he knew vaguely that this was a bad habit. He remembered doing it to the mouth of a sleeping girl at school once, but while savoring the ecstasy of sliding his stiff finger slowly inside her warm, wet mouth, he was scolded by a pretty young nurse and punished. After that, he learned not to put his finger into people's mouths. Instead he put it into things: candy bars, pudding cups, melted tar in the cracks in the street.

But nothing, not even mouths, came close to this hole he'd found.

His connection with this something was almost unbearable as color webbed itself up his finger and across his hand. Kirby felt every part of his body reacting to the sensation: his eyes strained, his lips stretched across his teeth, everything came alive.

Suddenly something sharp bit into him and pain shot through his finger and up his arm. It was miraculous pain, eclipsing even the pain of the sparks he would get at the school. He retracted his arm instantaneously, cracking his elbow on the back of the vending machine. He looked at his finger, but instead of blood, Kirby saw something written. It said simply, *hi.*

Kirby couldn't read. But he knew instinctively what the markings meant. He stared at his finger, then watched as the symbols slowly faded. He thought fast about how he could respond. For a moment he panicked. He had no pen, and even if he had, well, he couldn't really use it. Instead he stuck his finger in his mouth and chewed on it a few times, fusing his thoughts with the extended piece of flesh. When he retracted it, he was pleased to see the odd cipher, which he somehow knew to mean, *Hi. I'm Kirby. Who are you?*

Kirby squeezed behind the machine again and poised his finger. He worried for a moment about the pain again, but of all the things Kirby had been called in his life, *coward* wasn't one of them. In an instant, his finger was back in the hole. His knees went weak at the sensation, and he felt a sheen of saliva form on his lips. After a few moments, his finger was gently pushed out, no pain. He looked. It read: *I'm Bruce.*

Kirby waited and the writing disappeared. Then he jammed his finger back into his mouth and wrote, *Where are you?*

Don't freak out, it said. *We're in Hell.* Then: *We saw your finger.*

What are you doing?

Playing cards.

Why is this thing on the wall?

I knocked a lamp over and it kinda split the dimension a little. Hey, Kirby, can you do me a favor?

Sure.

Keep hiding it, OK? For as long as possible.

Sure thing. Kirby felt a seed of pride bloom inside of him.

We don't want anything to, you know, "break loose." Hahahaha.

Hahahaha, Kirby responded, but he didn't really get it.

♥ That had been years earlier, and now, as Kirby watched the groundbreaking of the hotel, he worried that he'd ruined everything. No more conversations with his friend Bruce. No more vending machine and chips. No more having the magnificent hole all to himself to dip his finger into when he felt like it. But the portal had gotten too big, and the iridescent glow was almost noticeable from the side of the vending machine. Trying to slide the vending machine over to cover the glow, he'd tipped it, and it smashed on the ground in a heap of glass and metal and corn chips. When the manager of the Silver Angel came round the corner to see what had happened, the hole was completely naked and swirling and hypnotic before him. That was the second pair of eyes to see the portal, and everything that happened between that moment and this one, in which Kirby's feet were sucked into the powdery dirt that had once lay silently under the Silver Angel, blew up like a volcano.

Kirby stood at the far edge of the crowd, just close enough to see Gene Banks donning a construction helmet and posing for a photo with a golden shovel in his hands. Kirby looked through the crowd: all excited faces, happy to have Hell as part of their town.

Then he noticed someone looking back at him.

She was a pretty black woman wrapped in a pink shawl. She gave him a slow, warm smile. Kirby immediately wanted to put his finger into that radiant smile. The thought overcame him and he looked down at his feet. He wondered if maybe she worked at the mission, but he would have remembered her, and if she knew him, she probably wouldn't have smiled. People learned not to smile at Kirby quickly. He dared once more to look at her beatific face, but couldn't find her smile again. Instead, he saw Gene Banks grinning his plastic face as he dinked the golden shovel into the ground.

"Caliche." Gene shook his head. "What the . . . *hell*?" The crowd laughed and flashbulbs popped. The portal was behind him, with two heavily armed security guards at the entrance. It was bigger now, about the size of a basketball, still swirling on the same chunk of wall, the only remnant from the Silver Angel. No longer the little tight gap that had been uncovered by a bum. Now it was open and waiting, vibrant and throbbing, a thrill even to a town like Vegas.

Gene Banks shuddered with glee. People always saw Las Vegas as a dirty little den of sin, a place where you could get a cheap buffet and put your cigarette out on the ass of a hooker any night of the week. But that wasn't Vegas at all. Sure, years ago it was different, dangerous, but now Vegas was more regulated than Washington DC. Thanks to men like Gene, their money and corporate power, the "good old days" of comps and juice were over. Maybe now comps were based on a point system and the majority of people dropping their paychecks were on fixed salaries. But the world needed to think that the vein of danger and spontaneity in which Vegas was born was still there in order for them to keep coming back.

But after years of ridiculous profit margins, Vegas started to lose its edge. With the economy in ruins, rooms were being left empty and fewer and fewer were putting it all on black. Then the jobs started to wane and stocks started to plummet. Gene needed the people to come back, to fill his casinos and eat his gourmet food and watch his shows. At night, looking out from the balcony of his Lake Las Vegas home over the glistening lights of the city and feeling the settled heat bake his plastic cheeks like a chicken, he worried that all had been lost. He'd made this town what it was today, goddammit. They were his visions, his towering, golden hotel-casinos that changed the Strip, upping the ante for all the other places. He'd crushed the old-school joints like the Dunes, the Sands, and the Aladdin, and even made a spectacle out of their deaths. Letting them breathe their final breaths of hot air and dust onto the street, while the people went absolutely wild. He was a modern-day caesar, promising blood and spectacle to keep his subjects happy.

And now he had found his answer. He would do it right so the people would give him the freedom he needed. He'd fund student research of the portal. He'd provide buses for field trips. He'd make a glass-floor club right on top of it. He'd charge $25 a person ($17.50 for kids) to see it. He had never booked a loser in Vegas, and he didn't plan to start now.

"Oh, Harvey," Gene said to his bodyguard as they walked behind the tarps to his black Bentley. The two men, black suited for the ground-breaking, approached the car. Gene was so elated he didn't even care that his Italian leather shoes were covered in thick desert dust. "I want it to be spectacular. Everyone in the world will come to see it. We're already booked through March of 2013, and we haven't even put a stick in the ground yet."

They could still hear clapping and laughter from the crowd as the building operations manager gave a more detailed explanation of how the construction would run. Harvey was reaching out to open the car door when they noticed a lump of gray approaching them. It was a small man, probably in his late thirties. He was disheveled and whiskery but didn't look as bad off as some of the other bums that had been hanging around the old Silver Angel. He was coming at them fast and waving his finger. Gene was used to this. Homeless people approached him all the time asking for change. He didn't mind emptying his nickels onto them. He wasn't a monster.

But now wasn't the time. Gene was in a different world and couldn't deal with this one. "How the hell did he get past security," Gene mumbled to Harvey.

"Not now, buddy!" Harvey shouted at the man.

"The hole," the bum said. He was near tears. "You gotta leave it. I-I-I'm supposed to watch it."

Gene smiled benevolently at the man. "If I give you twenty bucks, will you leave us alone, buddy?" Then under his breath, "Get him outta here, Harvey."

"No no no no," the man said. He rubbed his face on his knuckles. "You can't. You can't. You you you."

"OK partner," Harvey said, trying to grab the bum's shoulders.

"Look," the bum said. "A message." He shoved his finger under Gene's nose.

Gene looked at the digit and on it saw the message: *This one ain't for you, kitten.*

"Harvey," Gene said, becoming annoyed. Harvey grabbed the man again, but he struggled free with strength that belied his frame.

"Look!" the man said, his finger still extended.

On the finger, Gene saw the writing change. This time it read: *And be nice to Kirby, would ya?*

"What the fuck is wrong with your finger?" he asked, stumbling back.

"What?" Harvey asked. "What is it?"

"His finger," Gene stuttered. "It's . . . it's . . ."

"I stick it in," Kirby said.

"Stick it in what?" Gene asked, befuddled.

"The hole."

Gene and Harvey looked at each other.

"I did it lots of times," Kirby continued, his face down. He stood there, his arm still extended, finger still erect.

"Did you ever . . ." Gene paused, thinking so fast his mind was almost numb. "Did you ever go in further?" Gene asked him.

"I wanted to plenty of times," Kirby said, dropping his arm to the side. "But the hole isn't big enough. And Bruce doesn't think it's a good idea."

"Who's Bruce?" Gene asked.

Kirby shrugged. "He lives inside."

"Inside the portal?"

"Yup."

Gene looked at Harvey again. Until then no one had said anything about actually going into the portal. Gene sure as hell wasn't going in. He didn't know why it was there or what it was for. All Gene knew was that he didn't want any bad press. But if someone had already passed through the gate once and nothing terrible had happened . . .

"Kirby," he said. He put his arm around Kirby's shoulders and angled him so he wasn't facing the sun. "What if I told you that you *could* go all the way in?"

"In the hole?" Kirby looked up at Gene.

"Yes, sir." Gene smiled. "And I'm going to help you."

♥ The media was all over it. Gene Banks was sending a man into Hell. The publicity stunt of the century. Every eye in the world was glued to the TV in fear and fascination. The Catholics railed against the blatant idolatry. The *Watchtower* rapidly calculated dates to see if they had, in fact, been predicting this all along. Cults sprang up all over the country, while the Mormons turned their ruddy faces to the skies. It would be the end of the world as we know it, or at least the biggest party of the century.

"My brave friend, Kirby, here, has offered to go into the depths of the portal"—Gene's voice played on the TV, a recording from a recent press conference—"to see what lies beyond and report it to you and me."

The crowd clapped and cheered.

"Then as we celebrate the grand opening of the Inferno Hotel & Casino, we'll celebrate everything on earth we enjoy and deserve: pleasure, indulgence, extravagance, sin. We will celebrate life!"

Before the electrified crowd, there they stood, the fiercely happy face of Gene Banks and his new partner, adventurer, Kirby, a schlumpylooking fellow with a crooked sort of grin and a forever extended right index finger.

Molly watched the news coverage from bed and turned the TV off. She poked the sleeping lump next to her. "I can't believe you're actually sending that poor boy into Hell."

The lump groaned. "He wants to. He wants to see his buddy. Bruce the demon."

"Gene, you're an asshole."

Molly rolled out of bed and straightened the duvet on her side. She looked out the window at the orange egg-yolk sunset. A fire in the sky, every night. What were these idiot people thinking? Vegas was bad enough as it was.

"There's people dying around it, Gene. You know it ain't coincidence. Ain't nothing good coming out of that thing." She chose a pair of pink lacy panties for the night. "C'mon, you gotta get going. I'm going to the club early tonight." She pressed her foot against the comforter and nudged him again.

"What? God," he said. He sat up and rubbed his eyes. "They were security guards. Sometimes they die. It's their job. To *guard*." He swung his legs out of the bed and reached to the nightstand for his watch. He looked blearily at her. "When can I come over again?" he asked.

"Security guards with guns don't just die for no reason while they're guarding the portal to Hell. You know?"

Gene stared at her blankly.

"I'm off Tuesday night," Molly sighed. She turned and looked into the mirror. She pulled the skin under her eyes and wondered how many more years she could take this town. She watched Gene's reflection as he stretched and got out of her bed. She loved him, most of the time. He was all right to her and always wanted to give her things. But Molly had never tricked in her life, and she wasn't going to start just because the most powerful man in Vegas happened to take a shine to her. They'd met years ago at Cheetah's, where she'd been known as Bountiful Betty. Gene had a reputation for liking the dark-skinned girls, and he certainly had a fetish for nice round asses like hers. He was the only white man she'd ever dated. Didn't know why she liked him. Didn't want his money. Didn't particularly care for the taste of his dick. Maybe it was knowing that this man who could buy any woman in town came sniffing up her tree. Maybe she just liked the power to turn him down, if she felt like it.

"Can I come by the club?"

"I told you, you mess up my business when you do that."

"Ahhhh."

"Baby." She turned and sat on the bed next to him, putting her hands on his cheeks. "I don't think you should be sending that fellow into the portal. It just doesn't feel right."

Gene ran his fingers through his hair. "I can't call it off. Not now."

"You don't know what you're doing." She whipped around, not used to not getting her way with Gene. "You ain't nobody special," she said.

♥ The two security guards they found dead weren't the last. Bodies were appearing almost nightly at the construction sight, near the portal. No marks on the body, but often guns had been drawn. Then the media coverage on the deaths stopped suddenly. Molly knew that Gene had something to do with it. Anyone that mattered in Las Vegas was on his payroll.

But it wasn't hard for Molly to pick up stories about what was going on either. Her boyfriend may have all the powerful men in Las Vegas on his payroll, but these same men were spending their paychecks on Molly. With a face and body like hers, she was arguably more connected than Gene.

Rubbing her ass against the face of the police chief, she learned that in total there had been sixteen deaths at the construction site in the three weeks since the groundbreaking. All people in charge of guarding the portal.

Shaking her tits for the head of Mercy Ambulances, she found out that not one mark had been found on the bodies. Autopsies uncovered nothing unusual.

Dangling upside down from a pole, a detective told her that other people were dying, too. Sometimes women, sometimes men, all along the Strip. Mostly in the vicinity of a 7-Eleven or other type of convenience store. Candy wrappers were often found at the scenes.

Spreading her cunt along the leg of the construction manager, she found out that people were refusing to work for the security company and, coincidentally, the portal was going unguarded at night.

Then one day someone she'd been expecting to make his way into the club finally showed up. It was Kirby.

He walked three feet into the darkly lit bar before looking up. Once he did, he froze solid. He was dressed a little better, shaved, looked more normal, even a little less fidgety. A lot better than the first time she saw him at the groundbreaking. She knew Gene had been keeping him in one of his hotel rooms while they waited for the grand opening of Inferno, but she was surprised to see Kirby by himself. Gene was one to protect his investments. As soon as the song ended, Molly grabbed her robe and approached him.

Kirby shook out of his stare. "I'm sorry. Sorry sorry."

"Don't worry, sweetie. You ain't the first boy to walk in here and be blinded by all the titties."

Kirby smiled.

"You want to talk with me?" Molly asked.

Kirby nodded

"C'mon," she said.

Moments later they were sitting in the empty dressing room and Molly was pouring two cups of coffee. "What are you here for?"

"I gotta show you something," Kirby said, stroking a large pink feather that lay on the makeup table.

Molly came over and handed him a cup of coffee. "What is it?" she asked.

Kirby took the coffee. Then he held out his finger for Molly to see.

On it she saw the marks: *Molly, could you watch Kirby? He has a hard time keeping his hands to himself.*

"What's this mean?" Molly asked. She felt herself start to panic, but panic wasn't really her style. This message, directed to her? She didn't want to be any more involved with this shit than she had to be. She took a breath. "Why you showing me this?"

Kirby shook his hand like an Etch A Sketch and a new message appeared. *It would also be better for everyone if you could keep him out of the portal.*

Molly stared at the finger. Then she stared at Kirby. "This is what happens when you stick your finger in that portal, ain't it? You get messages."

"Bruce wants you to watch me."

Molly nodded slowly. "Why me?"

Kirby shrugged. "'Cause you're the one I wanted. And Bruce said OK."

Molly didn't know what to think. She wasn't a religious person and, if you had asked her a month before all this had happened, she would have said the only hell she believed in was the one right here on Earth. But here was this fellow sitting before her who'd been dinking around with the portal to Hell and now he needed her help. Watch Kirby? What the hell did that mean?

He actually didn't seem that bad. Something wrong with his head, that was for sure, but realistically what man did she know that didn't have something wrong with his head? They were all a bunch of thieving, lying bastards in this town. At least Kirby seemed like he had a little bit of nice somewhere under his brand of crazy.

She didn't notice at first, but Kirby's finger was slowly, hypnotically coming closer to her. She watched this man, curious about what was going on in his head and wondering about how everything got so strange all of a sudden. Kirby's finger moved closer and closer toward her face, and she realized that this finger was the reason Kirby needed someone to watch him. This finger that had been to Hell and back. It was going to cause everyone a lot of trouble, especially her.

It was only inches from her face, then less. As it moved closer, she could feel the heat pouring off his body. His eyes dilated, and he stopped breathing. It was ecstasy. She knew that reaction in a man. She loved causing it, but she was always professional and never let their passion get inside of her. But this swelling connection was even more intense, looping her up as that finger drew her lips down to meet it. Her body started reacting, and she wanted it in her mouth. She wanted to swallow it whole and for it to dissolve inside and become a part of her forever.

But at the same time that rapture was taking hold of her, making her forget where she was, there was another feeling beating up her back. Like something even she had never known before. Worse than when her only child died inside of her, or that night she was caught alone in the back alley. Still, it was a small sensation compared to the paradise the finger was offering. If she could just ignore that pinprick of pain, maybe it would go away. The finger was almost to her mouth. If she could just close her eyes.

But Molly always knew a scam when she saw one.

"Baby," she whispered. "You don't touch unless you're asked to."

Kirby pulled his hand back and dunked his finger into the coffee.

"So I guess it's up to me to keep that finger in its place, huh?"

♥   When Gene opened the door to the hotel room where he was keeping Kirby stashed, he did not expect to see Molly come railing at him.

"He's going into the portal, Molly," Gene said. His voice was shaky. He couldn't yell at Molly, and they both knew it. But this time he would have to stand his ground. He'd give her anything she ever wanted, if she ever wanted anything. This time, though, he couldn't. Inferno, the town, the people, he decided, everyone depended on Kirby going through that portal.

"It's bad. It's bad bad *bad*! Seal it up or something, because I got a message on his finger that said *not to go!*" she screamed. She whipped a plate at his head.

Kirby sat on the bed in the next room with his hands between his knees listening to the two of them fight. He only wanted to put his finger in the portal. He missed it. But all three times he tried to turn that direction, Molly stopped him and turned him back toward the hotel where his room was. He couldn't even enjoy the room that Gene had given him. He had a place to sleep and everything and a refrigerator with lots of pudding and peaches and a bathroom with lotion and all kinds of things. All he could think about was the portal, but now there were always people around it, guarding it, keeping him from it. He would ask politely to go up and see it, but no one would let him. Then he'd get the feeling like he wanted to stick his finger into their mouths, and they'd seem to agree about it. After that, he could go to the hole easy.

The screaming stopped, and a few moments later Molly opened the door. She came in the room and sat next to Kirby. She put her arm around him and handed him a pudding cup. Kirby accepted it and slid his finger inside.

"I don't want you going into the portal, but Gene is a powerful fellow. And right now I don't think you really got a choice."

"I won't go all the way in if you tell me not to," he said. "Just my finger."

"Baby, better men than you have said the same thing. And it never worked for them either."

♥ In the days leading up to the grand opening of Inferno, there was a strange hush over the town of Las Vegas. Electricity ran through the lights and the people. Everyone and everything was ready to burst from the anticipation. Locals chatted proudly about their portal, flexing their muscles, saying that they weren't scared of whatever Hell had to offer. The rest of the country emptied into the desert waiting to see what would happen when the little man went through the gateway from one den of sin to another.

When the grand opening finally came, people packed onto the Strip in numbers never before seen. Inferno was truly glorious. Gene Banks had spared no expense to make this the most spectacular hotel in this or any other universe. Done in reds and golds, there were three brilliant towers reaching, ironically, toward the sky. Flames burst out of the fountains, licking the golden walls at the entrance. 666 Fine Dining Restaurant. Vixen's Nightclub. Hades Café. The casino glittered, a palace in the desert. An island in the lake of fire. Spotlights washed the black sky, welcoming the world to the world of Hell.

And there at the entrance to the casino was the portal. Gene Banks stood on a podium next to it, proud of his accomplishments and eager to give the people, once again, the spectacle they craved. The entire police force had their guns sighted on the portal just in case, but Gene really just wanted them there to heighten the sense of danger. He didn't know what to expect, but whatever happened, whether Kirby lived or came out a bloody stump, the people would be mesmerized and forever proclaim him the greatest ruler of all time.

Molly watched from the crowd as Kirby was led to the portal. He wore a white leather pantsuit. The closet thing Vegas had to an actual angel. She had done her job and kept Kirby away from the portal, though every day she could see the pull in him grow stronger, like that portal was calling to the boy, doing something nasty to his brain. Tonight, though, it was out of her hands. She could only hope Kirby didn't go sticking things where they didn't belong. But she knew better. She always did.

Kirby stood nervously in front of the portal. He'd only ever wanted to put his finger into it. And that's what he planned to do. He'd stick his finger in one more time, then run over to Gene and stick it in his mouth. Then he could have Molly forever, forever, all to himself. He moved closer to the portal and heard the cheering die away. He hadn't seen the hole in months. Molly wouldn't let him anywhere near it. The portal was much bigger now. It stretched over his head, and he could feel the thick gravity coming from its center, pulling him closer. As the hypnotic colors swirled before him, Kirby felt his arm moving toward them. All the months of separation came charging back through him, an addict sniffing a glass of scotch. He had to touch it. To claim it. To enter. Now.

Once his finger was inside he was overcome with sensation. The warmth. The union. His mind went weak and all his good intentions were lost. Colors wrapped up his arm and he felt himself melting away like butter. Then his hand was in, too. It was impossible, the pleasure, on the edge of explosion. Vaguely he knew he was going too far, but now he was up to his elbow, then his shoulder. Kirby moaned out loud, and his eyes rattled in his head. Only his promise to Molly was keeping him from experiencing pure bliss, but nothing could matter more than letting himself fall into the colors. With one last strangled breath, Kirby let go and slipped easily inside the portal.

The crowd waited expectantly. They wanted blood. They wanted carnage. They wanted Hell to live up to their expectations. But nothing happened. Fifteen minutes passed and breaths started to be exhaled. People started conversations. Some booed. Of everything Gene had prepared for, he hadn't prepared for nothing.

Suddenly someone screamed. People turned their heads to see a finger poking out of the portal. It wiggled. It was followed by an arm. Then the rest of Kirby's small frame. He seemed the same except he couldn't shake the blue and red from the portal. Molly clasped her hands and jumped while the rest of the crowd cooed and clapped at the sight. Into the microphone, Gene said, "Welcome back, Kirby, my friend."

Kirby stood dazed on the platform. Swaying a little.

"Can you tell us a little about what you saw?" Gene asked.

"Molly?" Kirby called.

"Torture?" Gene continued. "Rape? Sodomy? Bad sitcoms?" he laughed nervously. "Kirby. Tell us. Is Hell ready for Las Vegas?"

But before Kirby could say a word, something else began to emerge from the portal. It was long and thin at first, spearlike, leathery black. A leg. It stretched out and hit the ground next to Kirby, at least three times as tall as him. Another leg followed by squeezing out of the hole. This bore into the ground on Kirby's other side. The rest of the body poked out of the portal, and soon an onyx stick figure with fire for eyes stood two stories above Kirby. The creature squealed a piercing note and in that instant shook itself into full form. Fire exploded down its back and shards of black spun robotically, clapping joints into place, while its limbs opened like bat wings, extending nearly as high as the three towers of the Inferno.

No one said a word as the creature breathed heavily and stared fire into everyone's soul.

"Molly!" Kirby shouted. "Look! You know who it is?"

Without moving Molly responded from the silent crowd: "Hi, Bruce."

Bruce stood up straighter and a pair of black wings oozed out of his back. He opened his mouth and squealed again. Everyone covered their ears.

"Goddammit!" he said. His voiced boomed down the Strip. "We were just playing *cards*! Do you know how hard it is to find a nice, quiet spot to play a little rummy with a couple of buddies in *Hell*?" He flapped his wings. "You!" he said, pointing a bony knuckle at Gene Banks. "You kept at it. I told you to stop and you went and threw Kirby into Hell anyway. And now I'm pissed."

"Heh," Gene stammered. "I just wanted to give the people what they had been asking for. This is what you wanted, right, Las Vegas?" He shook out of Bruce's glare and turned to the crowd. "Tonight, at the grand opening of Inferno we've blurred the line between Las Vegas and Hell. Now they are one. They are synonymous!"

The crowd cheered again, and the thundering applause was felt around the world.

"Oh, c'mon," Bruce said rolling his eyes. "Vegas isn't that bad. Promises of sex and money don't make you *evil*." Bruce leaned against one of the Inferno towers. "Now Tulsa. There's a place you don't want to go."

"You suck!" someone called from the crowd.

"Yeah!" another person shouted. "We want to see a real demon!"

Bruce leaned forward and cracked his knuckles. "Well, the rest of the world has another five years left, but we can go ahead and do a little cleanup here if you're all going to be bastards." Bruce nodded. "Kirby."

Kirby smiled and drew in a huge breath. Then he extended his arm. With a flash of blinding blue and red light, Kirby's finger suddenly filled the mouths of every human in Las Vegas. There were no sulfurous screams of agony. There were no wails of torture. Hell came silently and stealthily as everyone in Vegas dropped dead to the ground.

Everyone except Molly.

She tried to push the panic down inside her, but this time Molly was losing. Then Kirby's eyes fixed on her. He moved toward her, gliding over bodies and floating past debris, arm extended. She heaved and cried, clutching her belly and trying to rip out the terror. But through it all, she felt that pull again and the desire to have his finger inside her mouth, to share his rapture as he penetrated her. The finger came closer and closer. She felt her jaw loosening. She felt her fear fading away.

"I want you to come back with me," Kirby said. "You can come with me."

His finger reached her lips.

"I want you all to myself. Forever forever. Bruce said OK." He gazed into her terrified eyes, then pushed his finger past her lips and inside her wet mouth.

They stared at each other. Kirby's head went back ready to accept the ultimate pleasure, but nothing happened. Kirby wiggled his finger in her mouth a little, but still her soul didn't reach out to join him.

Then he felt shocking pain in his finger. He looked at Molly as blood ran out of her lips. He retracted his hand, but his finger, *his finger!* was gone.

Molly spat the lump onto the ground. "You know what?" she said, putting her hands on her hips. "I'm a stripper in a club in downtown Las Vegas. I pucker my pussy for dollar bills every night. If you think some bum with a wonky finger is gonna tell me what to do, you got another thing coming."

She turned on her heels and started stepping over bodies. She had to get the hell out of Vegas. It was long overdue.

FELICIA CAMPBELL

Cities built on sand are by nature ephemeral. Vegas was no different. It was always a kind of mirage that you could move into. The hotels played it up big in the old days before the town got uppity and became one of the world's "great" cities. Think about it. Before Wynn was the Mirage, before Excalibur was the Dunes, before Paris was the Sahara, before Monte Carlo was the Desert Inn, before Venetian was the Sands. Anyway, you get the idea. The town knew it was in the desert. Then it got greedy, and so noisy it didn't hear the desert winds blowing their warning. It forgot who was boss.

Moving two and a half million people into a mirage is probably a bad idea. When there are only four major highways in and out of that mirage, it's probably a worse idea. Add to that railroad trains carrying hazardous wastes running behind the Strip hotels and the whole thing is a really lousy idea. Then, of course, there's the problem of water. Just for kicks add a nuclear test site nearby and whole thing becomes even goofier than Dubai's building islands in the ocean. They didn't listen to the ocean's voice any more than Vegas listened to the desert. But that's another story.

Yet, insane as it seems, it worked until the butterfly that flaps its wings in China and causes a tornado in Kansas went into overdrive and the lights and everything else went out in Vegas. Talk about the butterfly effect!

The butterfly's name was Hank, which is, I realize, a strange name for a butterfly, but it was Hank who set off the chain of circumstances that left so few to listen to the winds blowing through the canyons of the empty city.

Once he had been a colorful, if minor, character around town. When the color faded, what was left of Hank was pretty dismal. A small-time gambler who had outlived both his pals and his environment, he combed his few remaining strands of reddish hair across his patch in an effort to conceal his baldness when shaving his head would have been the cool thing to do. His grizzled stubble was far from cool. His shoulders stooped, his sports jacket rode up in back, so far out of style that it was almost back again, and he incessantly moved his jaw back and forth. He peered at the world through giant glasses that made him look like a fly. The streets in which he'd felt like a conquering hero when the glasses were new now made him feel like a fly, the gigantic high rises looming, ready to swat him. He was pissed, royally pissed.

There wasn't a joint left on the Strip or downtown that he could walk into as though he owned it. He had gradually been edged out to the run-down casinos on Boulder Highway, but even there the old faces in the pit had been replaced by hip young ones who looked right through him. He had become invisible, which, he dimly realized, could be one hell of an advantage if you plan to bring down a mighty city.

In the afternoons, he read the morning newspapers that he scrounged in the coffee shops where he ate his late breakfast and began to formulate a plan. He knew the tourists had stayed away in droves after 9/11. The town had been weird. With almost no air or ground traffic, the silence had been palpable. The parking towers at the hotels were empty of all but a few of the employees' cars. You could have fired a gun through the casino pits and not hit anybody but a fake-tanned pit boss, a whey-faced dealer, or a bored hooker carrying her stiletto heels in her hand. What he needed was to create something like that but better, different, something that would last forever. It would be his revenge, his monument.

He finally remembered stories told by his buddy JC that scientists at the test site or the university or somewhere years ago had worked on creating germs or microbes or something like that that were impervious to radiation and could neatly wipe out any of the population left after a nuclear attack or make nuking unnecessary by killing just the people, leaving the buildings intact. That still left the problem of the corpses. I mean, think what a mess it would be to have to deal with a half-million pounds of rotting human flesh, assuming the carcasses averaged out at only a hundred pounds each. Then there would be all the dogs, cats, birds, rats, mice, and other living things that presumably would be affected and add to the decay, not to mention the flies, which would, of course, not only be attracted to the site, but multiply insanely in the rotting flesh, all on a day when the temperature reached 114 degrees. JC had said that the research was abandoned when funding ran out, because they couldn't figure out how to dispose of the bodies. There are advantages to decay. Worms and flies do have their place, but Hank didn't much care what the results were. He just wanted to get even.

I guess I forgot to mention that I had more or less known Hank for the last forty years. He'd been a buddy of my ex back when a lot of Vegas men tried to emulate the Rat Pack. None of that crowd, including the Rat Pack, had any idea what horse's asses they were, and they danced through life, all presuming that they had been born knowing everything that the rest of us spent years studying to grasp. They didn't hold conversations as much as outshouted each other, which didn't matter because none of them listened to the others. They knew the answers to everything. Even when they were sober, they failed to notice the glazing over of the eyes of their conversational victims. Without empathy, they were like an out-of-control horde of Asperger's patients. After my divorce, I pretty well managed to avoid them, except when one would register for one of my classes. Finally even that stopped, and I was free until Hank resurfaced.

If I had thought of him at all in the years since I had last seen him, it was to suppose, with no sadness, that he was dead. At first I had no idea who he was when he appeared in my office door wanting to know if I could help him find his old buddy JC who had been a kind of universal genius in the early days of the campus and had spent some time working at the test site. Wanting to get rid of him, I surfed the Internet a bit and made a couple of phone calls, finally tracking JC to Pioche. While I felt a bit guilty that I had done this to old JC, whom I had always rather liked, I certainly had no idea that I was accelerating the speed of the butterfly's wings and the death of the city. I guess you would have to say that I was the strange attractor that caused the shift by letting these two idiots get together in their dotage.

I did remember that JC had carried *The Anarchist Cookbook* around with him in the seventies and used to plot ways to blow up the humanities building, but I'd never taken him seriously, thinking it was just a macho pose, something hard for a fat-thighed man to sustain.

The long and the short of it is that they hit it off, and the more they thought about bringing the glittery new city to its knees, the better idea it seemed. The city that thrived on youth was about to get its comeuppance from a couple of old dudes. It happened while I was on vacation, so I didn't get the letter they sent thanking me and suggesting I stay away on 4/18 until after the Event had occurred. I'll leave that letter with this account in my effects in case anyone ever has time to be interested.

The letter didn't give the details of the mechanism by which they planned to introduce the agent or how they managed to get it into every huge property on the Strip and downtown at the same time, but manage they did. My guess is that they rounded up a number of similarly disaffected old coots who, invisible among the Paris Hiltons and boomers, managed to introduce it into the ventilation systems.

The effects must have been instantaneous. At 11:00 p.m. on Saturday, 4/18, every living thing in every major casino in Las Vegas froze in the posture it was in. They didn't turn to ice, but into something hard and nonperishable, as if they had all been playing a game of statues and someone said: "Freeze!" There was no pain, no blood, no screaming, no panic, and absolutely no property damage. The agent must have dissipated almost immediately, because those who entered after it happened weren't affected.

The upside was that the corpses weren't nasty, smelly, rotting things that had to be disposed of immediately. The downside was that the corpses weren't nasty, smelly, rotting things that had to be disposed of immediately. Hotels that had been filled to capacity were now filled with what amounted to thousands of statues, every nook and cranny a diorama of life on the Vegas strip. The rest of the city was unaffected.

Consider the buffets. The lines of people still stood stretching into the casinos; at least those still stood who were in a solid stance when it hit. If they were off balance, they toppled, sometimes taking others with them. In the serving lines, people hunched over their partially filled plates landed facedown in their mashed potatoes or mac and cheese. In the kitchen areas, cockroaches, rodents, and flies froze in whatever foul act they were performing, no longer venomous or germ filled, just tiny monuments to the reality behind the buffet lines.

The casinos were eerily silent, craps players frozen between the come and don't come, slot players poised in front of their screens, pit bosses stonily vigilant, and the ever-present watchers still staring at the action that was no longer action. People entering the casino after it happened bumped into the statues, causing them to topple, before they fled screaming, the first sound in the whole affair.

Thousands of hotel rooms were, as you can imagine, filled with people caught in the act, doing everything from the comic to the obscene that one can do in a hotel room.

The showrooms, too, froze. In one, the chorus line had toppled like dominoes before its eternally attentive audience.

Looters who rushed in before the cops arrived managed to grab the loose cash, but most were too freaked out to hang around for a big payoff.

Why the university escaped, I don't know. Old JC used to proclaim that he wouldn't blow up the humanities building with me in it, so maybe that's why they didn't bother with the campus. Of course, the school as well as the rest of the town was dead anyway. With the economic base gone, the living fled, by and large abandoning their homes and possessions to the desert. Vegas had become nothing but a symbol.

The fundamentalists liked to proclaim that it was God's vengeance, a twenty-first-century version of Sodom and Gomorrah with people turned to plastic. In fact, the whole thing was so weird that it sobered the entire world. If it was a terrorist attack, then why did no one claim responsibility? Where had it come from? Was London or Dubai next?

Everyone was thrown off base by the lack of blood and guts. None of the victims had suffered. There was no room for heroism and nothing that grandstanding politicians could take credit for in this world of giant mannequins. All had been achieved without bloodshed or destroying a single building.

Amazingly, the tragedy has brought the world to its senses. No one knew from whence it had come or where it would strike again. The world united. Weapons were destroyed, with those who wished to deploy them largely driven from power. Giant steps are being taken to restore ecological balance. 4/18 has caused 9/11 to be consigned to history. The earth is still far from paradise, but nearer than it was before.

Like the pyramids of Egypt, Vegas has become a giant mausoleum in the desert, monument to hope and hype, dream and nightmare. It will take eons before the sand covers it.

Only Hank, JC, and I have any idea what happened. I have no idea what happened to them. I like to think they got a whiff of their own medicine, so they can't emerge to take credit for 4/18.

For my part, I am content. Perhaps centuries from now this account will be found, hopefully too late to undo the good that was inadvertently done.

JAQ GREENSPON

Mirrors and Infinity

Steve looked through the chain link of the fence with longing. He knew the way home was there, sitting on the black asphalt. All he had to do was get there and they would take care of him. He was in pain. Hurt shot through his lung every time he breathed. Maybe he was dying. He remembered a few days before when he had stared with anxious anticipation at a different runway.

♠   The heat radiated off the tarmac in waves as he looked through highly ineffective sunglasses toward the horizon, waiting for Janet to arrive. Steve had never seen Janet, but was told she was a beauty. Sarge had told him. "Steve," Sarge had said, "just wait until you see her. She's white and beautiful and she'll take you from hell to heaven on earth and all points in between." Steve had smiled, or at least his mouth had crinkled in an impression of what he had seen Sarge do when Sarge was happy. Now that he thought about it, Steve wondered if his crinkly smile would be seen when he was wearing the suit. He had reminded himself to look before he came outside, but he had forgotten and now he didn't want to go back inside to check. He had waited to see Janet long enough, and now that it was his turn he wasn't about to miss any of it.

Suddenly his vision grew dark. His mask had slipped and he couldn't see, so he reached around, trying to be gentle, but his fingers were big and clumsy in the gloves and grabbed at the neck of his suit. He pulled down, and the holes in front of his eyes lifted back into place. He should probably tell Sarge about that, see if maybe Sarge could fix it before they left, but if he hadn't remembered to look in the mirror, he was pretty sure he wouldn't remember this. But then, if he couldn't see and walked into the wall, Sarge would probably figure out something was wrong. And then Sarge would laugh at him while everything was being fixed. Sarge often laughed at him, but that was OK, that was how Steve learned about how to smile.

Steve wasn't his actual name. It was just what the guys at the base called him. They couldn't pronounce his real name. He'd tried to teach them, but their palates just couldn't handle the sounds, so they called him Steve after the first thing he seemed to recognize: film of a spaceship crashing at the front of an old TV show from the seventies. It reminded him of how he'd first gotten to the base, his own crash. He pointed at the screen and tried out the new words he was learning.

"Me."

Sarge had looked up. "You?"

Another Sarge joined in. "I guess it is." He stood up and, with a finger pointing, waved his arm in a plus sign pattern and intoned: "I hereby dub you 'Steve,' Visitor from Another Planet." It was the first time Steve had seen a Sarge smile. He tried it himself.

"Christ, that's a scary sight, Steve-O," said Sarge.

"No wonder they keep 'em locked up here. Imagine a smile like that showing up on *Oprah*." Then they both laughed and went back to watching the TV.

Steve played with the new word. He rolled it around inside his mouth before he tried it out. "Seeevve," he said.

"Almost," said Sarge. "St-St-Steee-vvvv."

"Steeevv."

"Keep working on it."

"Steve."

Steve turned slowly to see Sarge coming toward him. This was a newer Sarge. Steve knew this Sarge wasn't the one who had given him the great name Steve and wasn't the Sarge who had hurt him and called him an abomination and wasn't the Sarge who liked to play Boggle. This Sarge was the one who asked him questions about numbers and said it was OK for him to go with Janet. Steve liked this Sarge a lot.

"Hi, Sarge." Steve waved.

"How long you been standing out here?"

Steve looked at his bare wrist, where a watch would be if he wore a watch. "Four years."

"Hours. Four hours."

"Hours, yes."

"You shouldn't stay out here that long. The heat's not good for the suit. I wouldn't let Janet leave without you. Not on your twenty-first."

Steve shrugged and shrunk down in embarrassment. Inside the suit, things got a little looser and his eyeholes moved again. He readjusted.

"Steve-O, you can't do that when we hit Vegas. The tourists don't take kindly to strangers who move their faces around until their eyes line up."

Steve nodded. He understood and concentrated very hard on keeping everything lined up. "Should I go inside and wait?" he asked, slowly and deliberately to make sure his mask's lips were moving along with his own.

"No need now," laughed Sarge. "Janet's almost here." He pointed toward a shining speck on the horizon.

Steve's eyes were better than Sarge's. They had run enough tests on him to figure that much out. Steve could see the plane clearly, as well as the heat signature and the radio waves. Something that showed up on a radar screen as no bigger than a breadbox looked like a flying battleship to Steve, and this was a normal airliner with none of the special shielding his eyes had helped develop.

"That's Janet?"

"That's her: Just Another Non-Existent Transport." He emphasized each word, pointing out the acronym. "She's making a special trip just for you."

For a moment, panic struck. "But you are going?"

"Of course I'm going. Not gonna let you loose on the good citizens of Las Vegas without someone to make sure you're OK. Me and Captain Dexter'll be taking good care of you." He clapped Steve on the shoulder, squeezing just tight enough to feel the synthetic skin give under the pressure.

♠ Inside the airplane, Steve was rummaging around like a kid at Christmas. Aside from some brief trips into the desert, this was the first time Steve had been off the base. He went from seat to seat, trying to find the best one, testing the bottoms and resting his costumed head against the rests. Before the trip, Sarge had explained everything to him, how he had to sit when the light was on and that even though it was a private plane he still couldn't smoke. Sarge had laughed when he said that, but Steve didn't get the joke. He knew what smoking was, at least in concept. There were pictures on the TV, but Steve didn't know how to go about even starting the process.

The light went on and Steve found *his* seat. It was perfect, just the right squishiness for sitting and it was next to a window. Steve looked out over the arid Nevada landscape as the plane took off.

"See your house?" asked Sarge.

Steve could make out the buildings of the base, but from this angle he couldn't tell which ones were his and which belonged to the rest of his friends, both the ones like him and the ones like Sarge. Steve looked but couldn't pinpoint anything. It all looked so different from this angle, and, just when he thought he was getting an idea, a way to navigate himself toward his own place, the plane would move in some way, either up or to the left or right. He started to make the noise he made when he got frustrated, pushing air through the upper palate, the same palate that let Steve pronounce his own name in his own language.

"That's OK," said Sarge. "There's plenty to see as we get closer to town." Sarge rubbed Steve's neck, hard enough to separate synthetic skin from real, just like the other Sarge had done, and sat down in *his* seat.

Steve sighed and rested his forehead against the window as he looked out over the almost endless expanse of desert. Sarge would never understand and Steve didn't have the words to explain it. It wasn't that he couldn't find his particular metal shack amid the hundreds of nondescript metal shacks. Rather, it was that he used to fly this high all the time, looking down on planets instead of military structures. He had been young then. He had forgotten what it was like, this perspective, and, he realized suddenly, he missed it.

♠   As Steve watched, the scene outside the window shifted. First there was desert, a dry scrub, featureless and, from this height, without any sense of scale. The ground changed, turning red and orange as it passed below, then there was water spreading out underneath the plane. Steve watched it all, a bit wistfully. So far, this wasn't what he was expecting. He was hoping for excitement and adventure, new and different, but the ground looked the same, really, as it was back at Groom Lake. Truth be told, he wasn't impressed. He began to look around the plane again, fiddling with the controls to make his seat back move up and down. He found a quarter deep in the recesses of the pocket of the seat in front of him and used it to practice picking up thin objects with his gloves on. Using his bare hands, he could have accomplished this easily, but with the human gloves, it wasn't quite as simple. He had to be careful; if he squeezed too hard, he would bend the coin, but not hard enough and it would stay on the tray table.

It didn't take long before Steve was able to pick up the quarter every time with just a little concentration. It focused him, kept his thoughts away from the fact he was riding in the back of the plane as opposed to sitting in the cockpit. It had been a while since he crashed, and while he still enjoyed the relative newness of Earth, was still energized by learning new things, being back in the sky affected him much more than he would have thought. He wondered if they knew that. If that was why the first Sarge had told him to get used to walking, that flying was not in the cards, whatever that meant. Sarge knew Steve would feel this way and was trying to protect him, to make sure he didn't feel bad. Sarge was a good guy, at least the first one was.

"Stevie," the new Sarge shouted from the back of the plane. "How you doin' up there?" Sarge was talking to the girl who had helped Steve with his safety belt. Steve liked the new Sarge, even if he did laugh too often at Steve's expense.

"I can pick up a quarter!" Steve yelled back.

"Where'd you get a quarter?" And then, before Steve could respond, Sarge continued: "And how do you know what a quarter is?"

"I asked Sarge when the Franklin Mint was selling them on TV. He told me all about money."

"Excellent," said Sarge. He walked up the aisle and took the seat directly across from Steve on the nearly empty plane. "That means I don't have to explain it to you. And money is gonna come in very handy when we land there." He pointed out the window, and Steve turned to see the buildings of Las Vegas appearing ahead of them. The sun, which had been in his eyes back on the runway, had fallen behind a mountain, and the lights of the city were just starting to twinkle on. Steve felt his hearts begin to pump faster.

When Janet landed, Sarge led Steve into the private terminal and past the security checkpoint. The other Sarge stopped to talk to the camouflage-wearing guards, pointed to Steve, nods and secret handshakes were exchanged, Steve waved, and all was right with the world: Las Vegas awaited.

♠   Steve thought he knew the city from TV, but the reality was so much better and so much worse. Sarge gave him a present, a baseball cap with the logo of the local AAA team on the front. "Hiding in plain sight, the only way to go," he said as he adjusted the band around Steve's head, making for a snug fit. "Let's get a picture to commemorate the occasion." He pulled the beige sedan over in front of the Welcome to Fabulous Las Vegas Nevada sign and made Steve pose underneath it. The other Sarge questioned the wisdom of "photographic evidence," but Sarge just laughed and said no one would ever know. Steve thought it was nice that Sarge laughed at everyone, even another Sarge.

The lights of the Strip made Steve happy, even if he didn't understand why. The fake buildings and huge statues with swords all seemed to be smiling down directly at him. For Steve, the whole world was a big grin and he liked it that way. He grinned himself as they passed by the dancing waters and the Eiffel Tower. When the nondescript four door pulled in toward the front of the high-tech Metropolis, Steve's eyes, behind his mask, went wide. The gleaming chrome and reflective glass of the three towers multiplied the lights of the city like a mirror to infinity. Steve could get lost staring up at where he assumed their room would be.

♠ Inside the hotel, Steve was amazed at how big everything was. He walked up to a table and pushed his head up over the lip so he could see what was going on. Cards were flying across the table, and from his vantage Steve could see the pictures and diagrams. He didn't understand the game, but the patterns made sense. In his mind, there were equations being thrown about. The rectangles with numbers and the images, common symbols for equations. The complete randomness of it explained why the humans had never been able to figure out interplanetary travel. If they couldn't see that the cards were defining a gravity generator, there would be no way for them to figure out how to escape the sun's pull.

The next hand explained invisibility in a way Steve had never seen before, and yet, there it was—so simple. He was about to say something when Sarge tapped him on the shoulder: "We got our room. Let's go."

Sarge had explained the idea of a hotel room, a place to stay away from his room back at the base, when they were still trying to make this trip happen. Steve had to promise to be good, to not break anything. And not eat anything from the fridge in the room. That had been the hardest concept for him to grasp, that the food in the fridge was not his to eat, even though he was living in the room. At the base, his room also had a fridge, and whatever was inside was his, so he didn't understand what was different. But he agreed to not eat anything, just so he could make the trip.

Sarge led them across the casino floor to a row of doors—"elevators" he called them, but Steve already knew that. He'd seen them on TV enough to know what they were, even if he'd never been inside one. Inside, mirrors were everywhere, making the tiny room look much larger than it was. Steve looked up at the many reflections of the two Sarges and the little boy wearing the hat. Steve reached up to touch his hat and the little boy did the same. "That's Steve," he thought. When the doors opened again, Steve followed the Sarges down a door-filled hall. Sarge stopped in front of one and placed a card in front of the handle. A red light turned green and Sarge opened the door. Inside was nothing like Steve was expecting. It was like his house at the base, only all in one room. And there was a window. A big, glorious window that looked out over the whole world. Steve smiled inside his mask. Not the whole world, he knew what that looked like, but this window did look down the Strip toward the giant pyramid. Sarge told him the light on top was for signaling spaceships. Steve joined Sarge in laughing at the ridiculousness of that.

♠ Over the course of the next few days, the Sarges took Steve around town, mostly at night, when he wouldn't attract as much attention with his almost human look. During the day, they saw the sights from the window of the car or hidden behind Elvis sunglasses, complete with sideburns. No one noticed them. The only problem Steve encountered was that the heat of the day, even in April, was hard on the suit. His skin itched and there was no way to get underneath to scratch it. Sarge said it reminded him of the time he had broken an arm and used an unbent coat hanger to get under the plaster, but that option wasn't open to Steve. He couldn't get past the skin without the tools back at the base, not unless he wanted to destroy his façade, and Sarge had warned him of the extreme danger in exposing himself. Sarge had chuckled when he said it.

By the third night, the advertising had done its work. Sarge wanted to go to a nightclub. Both Sarges did. Politely, they invited Steve to go along, but their effort to drag him along was so half-hearted Steve didn't find any reason to accept. He could stay in the room and watch TV, what he wanted to watch, until they came back. At worst, he could sleep and in the morning they would go to the dam, like Sarge promised.

♠ The next morning, Steve woke up ready for the dam adventure. He was alone. Neither Sarge had made it back to the room. Steve wondered where they were, how long they'd be gone. He spent the day inside, waiting. By the time the sun went down, he was hungry. He opened the fridge and stared at the food he was forbidden to eat. He wondered how bad it would be if he had some of the peanuts? He waited until he couldn't take it anymore and then waited a little while longer. He knew as soon as he opened the nuts that Sarge would walk through the door and yell at him for breaking the rules. Steve didn't like it when Sarge yelled. It had only happened twice, and Steve was not eager for a third time, so he just held the nuts in his hand, waiting. Outside, the dark sky got lighter and still Steve sat there, staring at the door, holding the blue and silver packet of nuts. He knew if he didn't eat something soon, he would get sick, and he knew he couldn't leave. So, slowly and carefully, he ripped opened the packet.

No one rushed through the door; the world didn't end. Steve tasted the salty protein and felt revitalized. He rationed his peanuts so he didn't need to get more anytime soon. He watched the TV until he knew everything that was going on in the hotel, then he switched to the news. The news told him the bad things happening in the city, including people killing other people, people robbing other people, people just doing horrible things to other people. Steve didn't understand people at all. That was when he saw Sarge on TV.

He didn't look well. He had his eyes closed, and Steve could tell, even through the screen, that something was wrong. Sarge had a certain energy Steve could see, and it wasn't there on the screen. Not that he could see the normal people energy when he watched TV, but this was different. This was Sarge and he was still. The voice on the TV said they couldn't identify the face on the screen. "It's Sarge!" yelled Steve. The voice continued as if it hadn't heard him. It said the person was dead, killed along with a companion, in a car accident. The identifications they were carrying were fake.

Steve stared at the screen. It was definitely Sarge. But if he was dead, then Sarge wasn't coming back. Steve was alone. He could leave the room. He could explore the city. He didn't have to go back to the base.

He was free.

Steve thought about that idea. Ever since he had crashed, he had existed at the whim of one Sarge or the next. They had treated him well, certainly, mostly, but the option had been theirs alone. Even his name, his *real* name, unpronounceable to the people who sheltered and fed him, had been changed to make it easier for them to say. But now he was free of that. He could walk out of the room and down the street and anywhere without having to ask Sarge for permission. He went to the fridge and looked inside. There was a can of soda and a chocolate bar that screamed his name, his real name. Steve ripped open the candy and put as much of it into his mouth as he could. It tasted wonderful. Only one Sarge had ever let him eat chocolate and never very much. He ate the rest of the sweet and drank the soda and let himself out of the room, remembering to put on his glasses and baseball cap first. As the door clicked shut behind him, he realized he didn't know how to get back inside. Sarge had waved a magic card and the door had opened. They hadn't given Steve one.

He was stuck. The door wouldn't open. The red light stared at him every time he shook the handle. He stared back. It was a machine, and he was good with machines. He could see inside it, see how it worked, but couldn't make it do what he wanted. A bell rang behind him. The elevator. Steve tried to hide in the doorway, making himself blend into the woodwork. Sarge had explained what would happen to him if he was found out, if he was caught. The elevator's doors opened and a young boy rushed out, followed by two adults, each wheeling a suitcase. Steve remained perfectly still. The boy walked directly up to him and looked him in the eye.

"Hi," the boy said. Steve said nothing. "I'm from Kentucky." Steve nodded. He smiled slowly, feeling his lips inside the mask and hoping everything was moving properly. He could not remember ever having been more scared in his entire life. The crash, meeting Sarge, even his first time flying to this planet, nothing scared him more than this little boy from somewhere called Kentucky.

"Come on, Josh," said the woman. "You can play with your new friend after we've unpacked."

"Bye," said Josh. Steve timidly raised his hand and waved as the family disappeared down the hall and into a room. They must have a magic card. Steve knew there was no way to get back into the room without the card, and he didn't look old enough for them to give him one. And staying out in the hallway waiting for Josh from Kentucky to return wasn't an option. Steve knew he had to leave. He turned for the elevator and made his way downstairs.

♠ Outside, Steve experienced freedom for the first time since he had landed on this planet. The world was a big place with big things and no one was looking at him. How could they? There was too much else to see. Steve wandered down the Strip, walking past the things he and the Sarges had driven by over the past few days. He could look closely at the metal construction of the Eiffel Tower and could see the wear and metal fatigue and knew it would only last another forty years before one of the legs gave way. He looked at the men and women holding hands in front of the artificial lake across the street and drifted in his memory. The fountains reminded him of something from his youth, from before he ever learned how to fly. There were fountains like this once, bigger fountains. And hands being held. He watched the water spray into the air again and again, reading into the patterns a beauty the human mind could not conceive, until the light started to fade and the air around the lake became cool and still no one noticed him.

He heard names being called, but none of them were his. He kept looking around for Sarge to spring up, to yell "Gotcha!" and take him back to the room and not really yell at him for eating all the chocolate. Steve was getting cold, and the thing they had called his stomach hurt. He looked for the car but knew it wasn't going to come. He had seen it on the TV, angry and smashed, worse looking than his ship had been when he crashed, and that had taken minutes—years, he corrected himself—to fix. There was no car, no Sarge, no going to the dam. He truly was alone, and he wasn't sure he liked it.

As it got darker, more people appeared. In the evening, his Elvis glasses drew attention; adults pointed at him and told him he looked cute. Every now and again someone would look around and ask Steve where his parents were. He was afraid to answer. "That's good, you shouldn't talk to strangers," they'd say and then walk away, leaving him wandering along in front of the huge hotels. He looked back. He was getting farther and farther away from the Metropolis and he was getting tired. And hungry. He hadn't eaten anything since his candy bar.

Steve walked slower. Inside the suit, his feet were heavy. He just wanted to sit and rest. He looked up and discovered he had made it to the pyramid. The light shooting out the top made him smile behind the mask. It was a quick smile, coming alongside the memory of Sarge their first night here. It was a fast smile, too fast. He knew his mask hadn't moved with his lips. The suit was fading. They were supposed to have been going home by now. That was the plan: see the dam and then go home. Steve had complained they hadn't had enough time, and Sarge just laughed, saying there'd be other times. They had to get home to get him out of the suit. His body wasn't built to last long being completely covered. He didn't breath like a human, not exactly. And with his body completely covered, he wasn't going to get enough nitrogen into his system. He pulled it from the air through the pores under his arms and behind his legs and through his mouth. Right now, he was only getting that fuel through his mouth, and even that was limited, coming in through the mask.

Steve turned as a loud roar shot overhead. An airplane. Janet! Janet would take him home. That's what Sarge had said: Janet would take him to hell and back again. Back home. Steve had to find Janet. He thought about resting inside the pyramid, thought about going in and enjoying the filtered cigarette smoke, something that would give him a boost of needed energy, but he couldn't do it. Now that he had a plan, to find Janet, he knew he couldn't stop until he found her. He had to retrace his steps. He kept walking.

Slowly.

The sun caught him in front of the Welcome to Fabulous Las Vegas Nevada sign, sleeping. He had collapsed and rolled behind the small mound of green-colored dirt the city council had put there to make taking pictures easier. He remembered standing there, getting his new hat and posing for Sarge. He was tired. He had to find Janet. He woke up as another plane passed overhead. He was close. He hurt. He looked up and followed the plane's heat trail backward. He crossed the street toward it, with a single vision of purpose, not seeing the fence until it stopped him.

Steve knew the way home was there, sitting on the black asphalt. He just had to get to it. He was hurt. Pain shot through his lung every time he breathed in. Maybe he was dying. He followed the fence around to the building. He needed to get past the fence and back to Janet.

He staggered into the building certain he looked bad, dirty. The skin of the mask wouldn't show how tired he really was. It didn't sweat or get bags under the eyes, but the way he shuffled up to the counter betrayed his healthy look.

"Can I help you?" asked the blonde woman sitting behind the desk.

"Janet," Steve gasped. "I need Janet."

"I'm afraid there's no one here named Janet," she said kindly but firmly. "Where are your parents?"

Steve shook his head.

"I'm afraid I'm going to have to ask you to leave then."

"Sarge," Steve shook his head. "Sarge said Janet would take me home."

The girl's eyes went wide. Scared. Steve looked around. There was no one there besides him. He looked back at the woman. "Janet brought me here," he said quickly.

She screamed. Steve's lips didn't move. His mask was failing. And she was screaming. The frequency pierced Steve's ears harder than it did a human's, like the humans who ran into the room, summoned by the screaming, to see what was wrong. Steve couldn't breathe. He wanted to scream as well but he couldn't. He didn't have the breath.

They surrounded him. Three, four, five Sarges. They were all there, all around him. His eyes went wide, but nothing changed on his face.

"Sarge," he managed, quietly. He dropped to his knees.

"His mouth! His mouth didn't move!" the woman was still screaming. "He asked for Janet!"

"Janet?" asked Sarge.

"Janet!" said Steve. "Take me home."

"Who's Janet?"

"Janet . . . transport." Steve gasped. He fell backward. Sarge tried to catch him but grabbed the suit instead. It came loose, slightly, like the skin boiled off an apple. Sarge dropped the suit immediately, letting Steve fall to the ground.

"He's . . . he's not . . ."

"No, he's not," said a male voice. Steve couldn't see who said it, but he could smell him. He was calm, ready. He knew Steve. Knew who he was. He could help. Everyone else stopped talking. Steve wanted to see him, but he couldn't see anything. Had the mask slipped over his eyes? Steve tried to talk, but there was no breath left behind the words. The man spoke for him. "Janet's coming. She'll take you home."

Behind the mask, Steve smiled. He closed his useless eyes.

BRYAN D. DIETRICH

Gray Matters

I.

Deep in the valley of night, between its rising walls and falling edges, toward dawn, but not yet so close as to be anything but dark still, they come. Sometimes you hear them first, the sound of the ship that isn't a ship like the sound of thunder that isn't thunder. And under that, a feeling, like the first few tremblings only your bones know when the sky is green and the clouds are curdled and the tornado sirens are making up their minds to wail.

Other times, the light arrives before the sound, like the woodcutter off at the woods' petticoats, bringing down his axe. You see the cutter, the cut, see his oiled arms cargoed with ash and gleam rise again, but all of this before your ears can open their eyes. Yes, it's often like that. Light, all the light of night's stertorous suns, axing its way into the bedroom. Your eyes, lidded and leaden from so many times of having been led before, open, and you watch, terrified not of what you don't know, but of what you do. You know that first the light will creep in through the doorframe, out and around the walls, walking its way along wallpaper the way corn rows run and stretch and move beside a car, a car you will wish you were in, driving away, away from this place, this Las Vegas, to another town in another state in another country, somewhere where the light comes, yes, but not for you. Alaska, say, where nearly a year can pass before you have to chew on another sunrise, where the colored lights may be magnetic, may be magic, but not, though they look it, alive, hungry for that bit of darkness, that sweet meat you make swaddled between bedsheets, sweat, and skin.

Still, you will know this isn't Alaska, isn't Anchorage, isn't anchored at all except for the ones who have come to have their way with you again. You will think of Earhart and Armstrong, of Devils Tower and potato mounds, of Menzies' *Invaders from Mars*. You will think of space-food sticks. And while you think, the light will continue to come, moving, not like Gilman's wallpaper woman, not behind the design, no, nor like that other Gilman's otherworld witch, not from between the in-between. No, the thing is, it always seems natural. A passing car. A mad-man with a lamp.

You will see this and fear this. The light not nearly alive as it seems, not coming from inside you. The doctors (and there have been so many, haven't there?), the doctors might say so, might lay your plight at the foot of the womb, of birth memory, early trauma, the way we see so darkly through infant eyes, but you know, have always known the light can't be yours or your doctor's or the operating room's where blood brought you in just to take you back. There will be a room. There will be blood and large, mutant, operating utensils. There will be more light, more thunder, more cold than in all of Alaska. You will be naked and alone. But the aurora of your screams, the feeling of being lifted by what force lies behind, will take you beyond any pattern, any imagined room, all the walls you have ever known.

The door. This is the worst part. The door will open.

II.

Some nights, they are gray. Others, green, eyes as big as fried pies. Some say they are short, little people, leprechaun leftovers, memory loiter lingering from some other "when," some "back then," when the race itself was green. Perhaps. Perhaps that race of mini-men, the island where they hunted tiny rhinos, elementary elephants with the smallest of spears . . . Or maybe your instinctual fear of dolls, the one where you're trapped in a tiny town, a village of identical . . . But no, you've seen them change, grow. They are always only as big as they need to be.

Their hands? Their feet? What use, have they, of these? And cocks and cunts, balls and boobs? They are all mind. As much mind as we are not. We with hormone poisoning, we with mouthwash and Botox, tummy tucks and bobby socks. Lovecraft would have called them hideous and red, left the rest to what little mind might remain when they come to show you theirs. And, finally, this is what they do. Once they have you, once they have taken you in and fed you and cleaned you and stripped you down to the only skin you know, once they have finished fiddling with your parts, delighted and confused as children, they will let you lie down on the cold metal of the only bed there is.

It looks like a necropsy table, blood gutters gleaming and empty in the jaded light. There appear to be implements. A clutter of dissecting boards, various sizes, laid out like giant magician's cards, some blank, some stained. Rows of rictic Metzenbaum scissors, Adson forceps, what may be a Gigli saw freshly washed and hung from an organic hook. Skull hammers, all kinds of shears, serrated, straight, curved. One long and wet and obscene as the abdominal cavity it was meant for. Lastly, packing tape, spray lube. Nothing could prepare you for such fear.

In the long dark between Neanderthal and now, from those first faint fumblings in caverns where we raised up bear skulls, prayed them onto platforms, paved our passages with bones and bits of teeth, painted each dead infant ocher, tied our elders into squat sausages and dumped them back into the mother's open sex, lining her inner earthen lips with crocus and goat's rue—from that one savanna summer when both brain and beauty began to burden us with the weight of all that matter, when woman started screaming, as afraid of what was coming out of her as the knowledge of its getting in, from our first inklings of what might not be, of the possibility of the possible, we have imagined what lives in the cave, what wanders both in and out of where it is we worship still. No matter what shape it takes, what club we make to fit its terrible brow, what crown we carve to call it god and kill it before it makes us imagine more, it is always the same fear, the same monster. It wants us. It has come for us. And we—after a hundred thousand years of art, after eons of imagination—all we can imagine is it wants us as dead as we want it. We want it dead because we still believe.

So here you are. In a room. On a table. And they come. Here you are, imagining all the best parts, the funniest parts of the Inquisition, every hatchet and hair-pie horror flick you've ever seen, and when they touch you—this is all they do—when they touch you, you scream. Not because of what they do to you. Remember, all you will remember is the light, the tools, the sound of their soft skin, a single finger against your temple. No, you scream because in that instant they show you all you've done, all you, all we, have killed in the name of love, of art, of bearskin and brick and baby Jesus. And you scream, scream long and hard, hardest when at last you recognize this room. It isn't for you. It never was. It is only a replica, a reminder, a memory of their own.

This is where what you imagined they would do to you, we have already done to them. This is where we took their infants and their elders. This is where we opened them and read them and bound their secrets into little blue books. This is where we started to believe. This is the open earth, a place we call The Works, an area often known by numbers alone—51, 18. We buried a grail here, we killed animals here, we made up maps and hid them here. Here, where something was afraid, where something died, where we left no flowers.

PETER MAGLIOCCO

Monsieur Dombo in Glitter Town

I lived then in downtown Vegas near a small tattoo parlor. Those weren't exactly palmy days, and I was trying to make ends meet as a security guard. Monsieur Dombo (as he was called then) owned the parlor, and never failed to acknowledge me whenever I passed his place on my nightly rounds.

At first he was a garish figure to me. Built like a great albino ape rolling in body fat with long tentacles of electric hair and a grandfather's beard, Monsieur Dombo would peer out through his shop's neon-lit picture window. I hated the sight of him, and even when he confessed to me he was God, it didn't favorably change my attitude toward him.

"You should let me give you a fine tattoo, Lorin," he would say, standing in (or occupying) the doorway. "First-time customers always get a good discount, and you look like a young man who could use a flaming snake on his abdomen. It brings luck, you know, among other things."

Each time I laughed, telling Dombo no. A tattoo would be a novelty to a guy like me, and I wanted deeper things in life.

One of Dombo's workers was a good-looking blonde woman who apparently did some of his secret digital engraving. Because of her I was almost tempted to make Dombo happy, but always thought better of it. Until, that is, the night I was so dead drunk that saying yes or no didn't seem to matter.

Her name was "Emelia," and Monsieur Dombo said she gave the best tattoos in the business. He didn't tell me then she was *a wired holy woman,* but that also mattered little.

"She will fix you up, Lorin, believe me," Dombo gushed in his intolerably irritating way, and I could smell his halitosis through the dry August Vegas heat (which crippled my senses more than any prescription drug no doctor would prescribe). "She has such a marvelous talent, my dear Emelia, that anything she does with her needle will astound you."

It took very little to astound me in those days, so I suppose she had a head start. Her summer uniform was a U2 T-shirt and frayed jean cutoffs that looked sticky with what might have been work resins or Dombo's bloodied sperm. (Well, maybe not quite that bad-looking, but remember I was pretty drunk at the moment.) Her breasts were fully there, nipple marks and all, and I had the feeling she was the best doctor available at that time of night. On the back of her shirt was the motto: *I Sing the Body Cybernetic.*

"I'm gonna give you some kind of symbolic markings," she announced matter-of-factly. "Things that resemble the ankh symbol, so I hope you don't mind. Your design will be like a beautiful Mayan glyph."

"I am your disciple."

"You're a human icon to me," she told me, almost crossly. "That and nothin' else."

Beats being a limp penis in a never-quite-good-enough shower, I consoled myself. Noting too that such observations, though private, were probably highly irrelevant. So get on with the tawdry "designing" on my abdominal muscles, I told her, and get off the damn cell phone already.

Create she did, this Emelia, spinning the myriad lines of some privileged vision only true artists must see. Through it I was dodging consciousness like people do jaywalkers on the Strip. I was a fermenting relic, brand-named J&B, dedicated to inertia. My mind slept with false gods throughout the tattooing, my bladder felt permanently overloaded. Somewhere the dead dreams of childhood kept beckoning like ghosts in a fairy tale.

"You're probably tired of this radio jazz," Dombo said, decreasing the volume on a battered cassette recorder that, iconic-like, occupied the center of a musty desk. "By god, music cannot soothe the deeper problems plaguing our race. It is not the answer to our social ills—only another mass opiate for escapism. I'm sure you agree. I could tell that by observing the way you've passed by here every night on your aimless wandering through town. No earphones! Truly a remarkable thing for any two-legged pedestrian around here. Because of that, though you look lost, you're really on your way to being found. Don't you agree, Emelia?"

The tattoo artist neither agreed nor disagreed with her boss's questioning. She was at work, and what her work produced was enough of any answer.

Something odd happened while she worked that sent me into a rather cold spasm. It was Dombo's face, which slowly—yet irrevocably—metamorphosed into that of actor John Candy's, a popular movie star at one time. Unbelievingly I stared at this face, which I knew really belonged to the late Mr. Candy, yet was just as surely inhabited by the spiritual essence of Monsieur Dombo. It was a tellingly disastrous moment for me, and I nearly got sick all over the expanding tattoo Emelia kept obliviously making with her strange electric tools.

"Anything wrong, Lorin?" Dombo asked. He *was* John Candy all right—I would bet my last paycheck on it—yet I knew it would be dangerous to ask him about this sudden transformation. In playing along with the baffling fates that were, I had to feign ignorance of what I took to be the truth.

"Wow! That tattoo is really starting to look sensational!" Dombo laughed. It was John Candy's laugh, right down to the last chuckle. A machine measuring voice patterns would confirm this unmistakably, just as in fingerprint matching.

"No problem," I answered Dombo, yet I felt as if he looked right through me, Great Film Director-like. He laughed again.

"You're loving this!" he exclaimed. "What a makeover. I knew you were right for this! I just knew it."

I didn't say anything for a long while. I felt that it was my very heart that alluring Emelia was cutting into with her needle.

Later I even began to have disturbing dreams about Monsieur Dombo. This taunted me nightly, posing archetypal riddles I knew I needed more time to unravel. Yet how much time did I really have before that "awful something" the dreams portended befell me? My unconscious mind was like that great silver screen at the drive-in movie theater, which awed me as a boy. And Monsieur Dombo, of course, was the leading actor in a picture I'd seen too many times, yet still couldn't figure out.

If anyone could help me get my act together, I told myself, it would be Emelia. The very act of her engraving my skin had filled me with a kind of calm well-being. She would be the start of my attempt to separate the illusions in life from the elusive reality.

"No more escapism for you," she told me. "You're on that desert path to the big mountain."

Where the hell in all of southern Nevada would there be such a mountain? I wanted to ask her during the digitally high-tech engraving, but lapsed into a soft-edged fever out of which there was no complete emerging. I wanted more than ever to go to the jazz concert at Mount Charleston.

Then, in the shallow and harsh spaces of my apartment, Emelia appeared one night to give a sensual direction to my plight. Almost over-whelming me with select surprises, she seemed out to prove that the exclusive delights I knew existed in the hotel-casinos of this city could be mine for a moment—or even all of eternity—if only I played my cards right.

"You want love, don't you?" she asked me. "You want something to bring back to life that flesh of yours, don't you, instead of letting it waste away on a diet of pain. Lorin, if only you would open up and try and trust Dombo."

"But just who the hell *is* that guy?" I demanded, waving the beer in my hand. "He's just another con artist with a thing for trying to be your *Uncle Buck* (one of John Candy's roles), that's all. Actually he's closer to all the fat goons with nonspeaking roles in bad horror movies."

"You're the one imagining such a thing, and when you get that bullshit out of your head maybe we'll be ready to begin."

"Oh, I hope the hell so," I told her. "My tattoo's starting to itch already."

All this was becoming an excruciatingly long foreplay that never really got to the meat of the matter.

"What you really have to do," she told me with bitchy evasiveness, "is to find a way to please Dombo. And to become really worthy of what he can give you, Lorin. Right now you're suffering because of it, something that can become an absolute disability if you let it. I hope you understand this! All your life you've been reverting, because of it."

And I thought I was suffering because of too many John Candy mov-ies. What this mysterious Emelia was telling me somehow took root, in a way, since I resolved from that moment to do whatever it took to become worthy of Dombo. No longer would I just be a nondescript figure in everyday old cowboy attire.

Under old Dombo's spell, I quit my job as a schlock security guard and spent most of the summer driving around town in my decrepit Datsun. I felt freer than I had at any time in my life. If I could just arrive at my pur-pose, everything would be all right.

On the highway I became a roving guardian patrol—a police force of one. If someone needed a ride, I would stop and give it. Dead battery? Out would come my cables. Traffic accident? I'd be on the scene to render assistance until the real police arrived. Whatever the need or situation, I saw it as my duty to help out.

Unfortunately such behavior soon got me in trouble with a speeding motorist who nearly ran me off the road. Believing me a smoke-spewing obstruction, the teenage driver of a red Dodge had all but forced me into an accident and horned me belligerently while passing. Angrily I flipped off the teen as he passed, which proved to be a pivotal mistake. The bastard came to a skidding halt on the dirt shoulder of East Sahara—some fifty yards ahead of me—then began backing up toward me at greater speed than ever.

In the glove compartment of my car was a long-barreled .357 Magnum you've probably seen used in many a cop movie for more than target practice. Instantly I grabbed the pistol as the red Dodge neared me, while with my other hand I spun the steering wheel like a casino wheel of fortune, and with a sudden burst of acceleration gunned my car into a swerving arc around the approaching menace.

It was a daring maneuver, and while doing it I nearly clipped off the red Dodge's left headlight. Luckily we were on a long stretch of road not traffic-busy at that early morning hour, or collisions with other vehicles might have occurred. Instead we were free to race around a private slice of beautiful, dry-hot, southwestern desert with nothing but a vast panoply of majestic and jagged-topped distant hills as backdrop.

"I'll kill you, motherfucker!" shouted the teen dust devil in the red Dodge as I skidded dangerously around him. I was a marauding Indian circling a covered wagon. Dreams of good deeds had given way to bad.

A high-speed cat-and-mouse game with the red Dodge ensued. He chased me. I chased him. At one point we drove off the road into a dusty field of scrub growth, and together our vehicles stirred up great columns of floating dust that lingered lazily in the dry, barren air like plumes of some dancing Indian spirit. And to think it had just been a typical weekday morning with both of us on the way to work. Add to this of course the sight of me waving the sun-glinting pistol in the air now and then—as if about to shoot up some distant cloud—and you get an idea of what truly became a ludicrous scene.

The waving pistol must have been the clincher, for my adversary finally quit the chase and sped madly back toward the highway, leaving me a semi-basket case stewing in a perspiring mess all over my breakfast burrito wrappers. I couldn't believe how quickly I'd reverted to a savage, nor how I'd been ready to revel in the smell of blood—even my own.

There was nothing left for me to do now but the inevitable. I had to find Monsieur Dombo immediately and beg for his protection. I felt like a lab rat, and if I waited any longer, I'd either be dead or in a similar condition.

♥ To complicate matters, at about this time Dombo had all but disappeared, and the ill-washed Emelia was loath to offer any clues. Listlessly I began walking around town at night as I'd done frequently in my pre-tattoo days. The increasing summer heat began to drain all the real and meaningful energy out of me. I began to blame the accursed, solitary tattoo. The longer I wore it, the more something was dissolving in my body. This "something" surely had to be important, I wagered. Linking it to a decaying libido, I realized one night that my sexual identity had diminished. I no longer thought of myself as a man wanting to have sex with Emelia. Now, on the contrary, I was a being for whom identifying gender meant very little.

A void had taken the place of my sexual identity, the way a shadow overtakes a dusk-filled scene.

My emotional reactions to women had also changed. Whatever male prejudices I once held for women were burned away. This became graphically clear to me the night I encountered a woman who appeared to be fighting off a rape in a parked car just off Fremont Street, in a district packed with seedy, fly-by-night motels.

The woman—a teenage girl, really, with lovely blonde hair—was struggling to escape through the half-open door of a blue Honda. What struck me all but immediately was the stark beauty of her almost naked form, which resembled a wild creature's, perhaps due to the poorly lit street. A very muscular young black man appeared to be holding onto the woman against her will. He kept physically trying to continue his violent act of transgression as the woman fought back.

I could almost have reached out and touched her body myself had I wanted. One of her large breasts had become dislodged and jiggled erotically underneath a fashion-printed bikini top. Once I would have reached out, trying to contain that handful of vulnerable flesh. Now, however, I felt no such desire, regarding this scene with a startled but basically unresponsive demeanor. For some reason the young woman could not scream despite the intensity of her resistance. Perhaps she was too scared. She looked at me dead-on for an instant, with a kind of quizzical disbelief in her eyes, as if what were happening became something so surreal even my presence could have been altogether different from what it appeared. I might well have been the man in the moon.

Eventually I made my way back toward the tattoo parlor, hoping to find it open despite the lateness of this weekday night. It had been virtually closed down during Monsieur Dombo's absence, a true stroke of bad luck for me at the moment. When you really need something at a certain point in your life, sometimes it's just not there. And if it is there, it turns out to be something totally different.

What I wanted to tell Emelia or Dombo was: "I have found something. I have experienced something truly paranormal in the apparently normal. And it hurts."

I tried, somehow, to reason with Emelia. It was almost like she was expecting my return, as if an appointment had been made that I'd forgotten.

"You or Dombo have to help me," I told her. "This tattoo you put on me is slowly burning a hole into my gut. It's like acid. Can you take it off? Can you do *anything*?"

Emelia shook her head, disturbing the lay of her munificent blonde curls. "A Dombo tattoo is something special," she claimed. "It's very extraordinary having one removed. Monsieur is always against that. And of course something unpleasant seems to befall the person from whom it's removed."

"Great. Just goddamn great."

Emelia remained unconcernedly smoking a cheroot and watching the flickering blue vision on a laptop screen secreted in a desk corner. Her watchful radiance? In the parlor's dim light, the smoke curling upward gave her an eerie appearance. She looked very tired, perhaps even hungover, with a mask of boredom for a face. We weren't communicating that well, I suppose. I asked her about Dombo, and her answer surprised me.

"You're ready to go out to his house in the desert. That's where he's at. That's where everybody goes after a while. Don't you want to go there?"

I looked at her dully. The electric window sign fizzed noisily, casting a blue-red fuzziness into the room's darkened interior. Sure, I wanted to go. It was a solution begging to solve my problem.

♥   We drove to Dombo's place in a sleek red Corvette, which the speeding tattoo artist handled with bravado. An Aerosmith CD riveted the air with guitar play. Sighing almost happily, despite the abdominal pain, I wanted to leave this great gambling oasis of a city behind forever, for it had become an alien landscape. Dombo's ranch, as Emelia called it, would become my last refuge. There I'd be safe from what Dombo called the enticing pull of chance sins.

Dombo's place was too beautiful to be a desert monastery, however. It was a sprawling hacienda built dangerously on a cliff rim adjacent to the sandstone-red mountainsides. Truly on the edge of things, the view from that ridge was magnificent, with an air of bracing purity. I wanted to shout down at the bucolic hills beyond, speckled by light here and there.

"Are you in much pain?" asked Emelia. "I'll ask if Monsieur can see you now, if possible."

I thanked her as she ushered me into the great house's foyer. The transition from Dombo's rundown parlor to this was staggering, yet Emelia looked used to it. Taking in the glittering ornate detail of the place's interior staggered me even more. Native American Indian artifacts decorated every niche and wall space, giving what looked originally like a living room the air of a tribal tabernacle with technologically enhanced panels containing vibrating, multicolored visions of an unspeakable spirit world and its chanting otherworldly voices.

That wasn't all. There was a motley collection of guests scattered about the living room as well. They obviously had been there awhile, like movie extras waiting for the shooting to restart.

"These are his *real* people," Emelia told me. "They never leave here. They watch over this place, listening to the voices."

The sight of them was too disturbing to believe. Most of the eternal guests were disfigured or deformed, victims of appalling accidents. All of them had tattoos similar to mine. For a moment I hoped it was only Halloween and they were all dressing for the part. They wore the garb of street people mostly, yet were not unaccustomed to being around such sumptuous and rare furnishings.

"They won't bother you. Some of them are even blind. They are lost people from a desert commune some ranchers disbanded."

I couldn't say anything more to Emelia. Something feral inhabited the air the way maggots do a piece of rotting meat.

When Monsieur Dombo arrived, his appearance was certainly not anticlimactic. All decked out in Native American garb, looking every inch the mammoth chief of the place, he even sported a beautifully feathered headdress, which at first glance startled me. All he needed was a three-foot-long peace pipe, which Emelia soon dutifully provided him. The piquant smoke smelled similar to good old marijuana. As he puffed away with an upraised hand in greeting, Dombo's red-streaked cheeks outrageously ballooned the way Dizzy G.'s got when horn-blowing. I wanted to scream.

"Glad you made it here, Lorin," said the Monsieur through a wheezing smoke exhalation, his eyes widening at the sight of me. "I really thought you might not. What you see me smoking here, by the way, is not what you think it is, boy. It's an exotic herb tobacco once used in the ceremonies of a tribe indigenous to these parts."

I nodded, indicating age-old understanding.

"You look in a pretty bad way, Lorin, like you could use a hot bath and a good night's sleep in something resembling a bed. Afraid that I'm going to have you spend the night here, now that you're on your way to becoming an acolyte of sorts." Dombo laughed his hearty Uncle Buck laugh, for his utterances were a rich stand-up humor. "Besides, not many of those who come here ever want to leave, did you know that?"

"I just want to know what the hell it is with these markings your lady burned into my belly, Monsieur." "Nothing to get worried about. Your imprint's just having a little difficulty settling in is all. Therefore its configuration will keep changing until it finally arrives at its final form. When it does, you'll know it by the bliss and absolute confidence you will feel. Truly, I'm sorry if it's hurting you so much now. I'll have Emelia try to do everything she can to make you comfortable. We had a hunch you'd come. But, well, one never knows."

Looking at him more directly, I tried to keep a dog's look of gratitude from my lined features. If I could learn the imprint's meaning by joining his astral circus, I was ready to somersault into another galaxy.

"Perhaps you'd like to meet our guests, several of whom survived the adverse effects of our government's testing of nuclear weapons in the 1950s. You can see that they've also carried quite a bit of pain around in their lifetimes."

I turned, suddenly sweating and very apprehensive. I'd been ill-prepared for anything like this.

"Do you need a drink, Lorin? Or are you ready to swear off the stuff?"

What I needed was to take five and wash the desert dust out of my pores. Dombo agreed readily enough and instructed Emelia to show me the way upstairs. Since I'd been under such obvious stress, Monsieur wondered out loud about calling in his personal physician later.

Lead-footed. Now I'd become lead-footed in Dombo's residence, a man trying to lift his booted feet from underwater. An infinity of stair climbing passed (with the reverberating sound of my own footfalls), and finally I was on the landing where I should have been all along.

Emelia opened the door to my room and promptly disappeared before I could beg her further assistance. For an unpleasant moment I was alone, feeling the gut-wrenching pain of my ankh tattoo growing like a fierce cancer. They had as much as branded me like cattle before the brutal prairie drive. Inside the room I stumbled, holding my side, and found a wall mirror near a divan. Ripping away my shirt afforded me a full-frontal view of the red-welted imprint I'd been carrying around so long. It was a disfigurement now, hardly resembling its original contours, at the moment only a beer-can image with a serpentine form curling around it endlessly.

Laughing so hard out loud caused me to bang my shins against the nearby divan. The endless curling! At that instant I knew a brave new world was at hand, with myself another unfortunate visitor.

Sweat rivulets salted across my lips and stung the contours of my portable design. I had reached a goal of sorts, yet knew that to escape would require a more rational plan, even a sober one. From a nearby room a strange animal mewling accosted my ears with obscene dissonance.

Dombo, I told myself, *if my life's a joke to you—if I'm only another painted clown in your "living" theater—then give me the right to terminate things on my own accord.*

Inside the bedroom a nearly naked woman languorously reposed on a large bed covered by rippling blue sheets. The woman wore a baby-doll mask and a pair of expensive high-heel shoes. My intrusion affected her motionless posture not one way or another. Sitting on the floor next to the woman was a large collie with drooping tongue and a habitually contented look. The collie was no more surprised to see me than the masked girl with the sumptuous young figure, but I detected something expectant in the collie's nearly welcoming expression.

The almost naked woman on the bed leaned forward a bit and eventually parted her legs to reveal shaved genitalia of pink dampness. It was a scene that aroused neither lust nor distaste, but only a kind of pity in me. Directly above the woman's head a vision of desert night could be seen through (or even captured within) the large rectangle of an open window, and the smell of dust-laden spaces was evident. *Am I in an Anasazi bordello?* As I leaned closer to the woman's parted legs, here in the room's beatific stillness, I felt the large collie's eyes follow me with their encouraging wet sadness. The woman said something in Spanish, obviously a lascivious invitation, her voice husky with yearning. I bowed down, eyes closed, and pressed my face closer to her pulsing center, deep with a rainbow panel of intoxicating musk.

Monsieur Dombo, this is the Indian Spirit Woman you promised me in dreams. Let her lay hands on my abdomen and take away the burden of this pain and suffering.

Somewhere distantly I heard drums and the sound of chanting. Though caught inside a mixture of fear and horror, I felt a calm resolution overtake me, despite all the crippling weakness that had bedeviled my life for so long.

For a moment I truly belonged to something, redeemed by this ongoing contiguity with *the source,* and didn't care if I was doing something a beast had done before me. A flash of tears erupted like night fire across my face, and I succumbed to this disembodied sexual essence wielding true power and the liquid necessary to douse an unnaturally fiery pain. Then I staggered from the bedside, again and again, feeling the weight leave my body as air does a balloon.

In the days and nights that follow I will have plenty of chances to leave Dombo and his colony, yet the disfigurement within me is stronger than any force I tell myself not to believe in.

At least the tattoo is gone. There is nothing left on my skin but its faint glow of blinding whiteness.

C. J. MOSHER

A Girl and Her Cat

Dear Mr. Teacher Fella—

A bang and a whimper. And fire and ice. That is how the world ended. Then came the cockroches and canibals. Mr. Teacher Fella—Your talking cat Mr. Henry Miller wanted me to tell you what happened. Yes he is still alive!!! Me too! But you're dead. Unless you're reading this. If you are reading this that means this letter went back in time. To reach you. Like Mr. Miller said it would. But I doubt that. Cuz things cannot go back in time. No matter how hard I wish they could.

♦ Ouch! Ouch! (Yes that's me screaming. A canibal is hurting me bad right now. He snuck up and snatched me minutes ago. And tied me up. Now he's punching me. And poking me with a big knife.) Ouch! (He wants to know where my food stash is. He twitches a lot. His voice sounds broken. Soon he will find out I am a girl. And hurt me worser. Then drag me into the tunnels under Old Vegas. To eat me. I am writing this in my head. To forget the pain. By sending my thoughts back in time. To you. Even if you are dead.) Ouch! Ouch!

♦ My name is Jinx. I am 13 or 14 years old. I was 7 when the world died. I was at school giving a book report. About tadpoles. When a bright light flashed. And my teacher jumped. To cover me with her body. Her name was Miss Hampton. One minute she smelled clean like soap and shampoo. The next minute she smelled dead like meat on a grill. She got fried. All the other kids in my class got fried too. Everyone at Joseph Smith Elementary School got fried. And smelled dead like meat on a grill. Except me.

♦ Stop! Ouch! Please! (I hate canibals. To stop thinking about this awful pain let me tell you. About your cat Mr. Henry Miller's History Of The World After The Bombs.)

♦ Mr. Miller says the world was going to hell in a hand baskit. Before the bombs went off. Even before Presdent Obama became Presdent. But after Presdent Obama became Presdent things got worser. Much worser. So the Mormans killed Presdent Obama and his friends. And Presdent Romnee became Presdent. And the Mormans got all the bombs in America. At the same time the Muslams got all the bombs in Russha. Then the Mormans and Muslams killed anybody who was not Morman or Muslam. So most people decided to become Morman or Muslam. Then the Mormans thought everybody in the world should be Morman. And the Muslams thought everybody in the world should be Muslam. That's when all the bombs went off. And most people got fried like meat on a grill. And everything else turned dark and gray. And cold.

♦ Ow! Dumb canibal! (I shout at him. Then I say.) You better kill me now! Or there will be hell to pay for you! (But he just growls. In his broken way. And twitches. He wants me to tell him where the goodies are.)

♦ Back to Mr. Henry Miller's History Of The World. Well. After the bombs went off there was only one casino. Left standing in Old Vegas. So the rich casino owners got the police to protect it. All the other people that was not police or casino owners. Who did not get fried. Gambolled at this one casino. Most people just kept gambolling and gambolling. To win THE BIG JACKPOT. Cuz if they won THE BIG JACKPOT. They would be saved. Cuz then they could live with the rich casino owners and the police. Down in the tunnels. Where it was safe with clean water and lots of food. People really wanted to win THE BIG JACKPOT. To live in the safe tunnels. So they gambolled away all their canned food. Then they gambolled all their dogs and cats and cockroches. Which was the only food left after all their canned food disappeered. But when their dogs and cats and cockroches was gone. People started gambolling away their children to the rich casino owners. And when their children was all gone. People gambolled themselfs away! To win THE BIG JACKPOT. But Mr. Miller says nobody ever won THE BIG JACKPOT. And those folks that gambolled themselfs away. Just got taken away. In the end. On food trucks. To be turned into people jerky. For the canibals in the tunnels. Who was the rich casino owners and the police.

♦ That's how your cat and me met. Somebody gambolled us away. We was food on a truck. Headed for the tunnels. Under Old Vegas. The truck turned over. People and dogs and cats excaped. Mr. Henry Miller jumped on me. He told me not to run. Or I would die. I never heard a cat talk before. So I just froze up. And did what he said. Police chased and killed everybody running away. I buried Mr. Miller and me. In the ground. Next to the truck. With weeds to breethe thru. For two days. And we have been together. All these years since.

Stop! That hurts! (I am screaming at the canibal. Begging him to stop. But I also say.) I will never tell you! Where the food is! (He pulls out a smaller. Sharper. Cutting. Knife.) Please! Please!

♦ Mr. Teacher Fella—Your cat Mr. Miller told me how you found him. In the road. Alone. With a broken leg. He had got hit by a car. And you stopped to take him home. And fix him up. Then you named him after a famus writer. He also told me how you split his tongue. With a razor. So he could talk. And you had his front claws cut off. And his boy toy newtered. Which did not make him happy. But he says. You gave him whisky and cigeretes. And all the best food a cat could ever want. Real chicken. Real fish. And gormay cat food. He really misses all that. Espeshly the whisky and cigeretes. When I ask him if he is still angry. About you getting his boy toy cut off. He always says this. "Naw. Nobody is perfect." When I ask him if he is angry. About all the bombs going off. And the world going dark and gray. And cold. He says this. "Naw. It was the human race. What did we expect?" And every night. After a long day hunting and trapping food. Mr. Miller always snuggles up to me. And purrs and purrs. And keeps me warm. Which makes me feel loved. He is my gardian angel. One night he told me where he was when the bombs went off. He said he was snuggled up. On the floor. By hisself. In a beam of sunlight. Warm and cozy. While you were at school. Teaching. Then everything turned brighter and hotter. Than that beam of sunlight. Then the world went dark and gray. And cold. Forever. And he said that. Except for you. He misses that last beam of sunlight. More than anything.

♦ Mr. Teacher Fella—There is not much to say about me. My dad got killed in a car wreck. When I was a baby. And my grandfather who I liked a lot. Died of old age. When I was in kindergardin. He always smelled good. And gave me warm hugs. He died before my mom and older brother went crazy with the religion. They went crazy after Presdent Romnee became Presdent. And his Mormans got the bombs. If I was a bad girl back then. My crazy mom and older brother would lock me inside a closet. In the basement. Sometimes for days. With only a bottle of water. And a tin can to pee in. To teach me about the religion. But I must not have been a good religion student. Cuz my mom and older brother started locking me in that closet every night when I got home from school too. They yelled at me a bunch about me getting them in trouble. With their religion bosses. And that I needed to behave more. Like the religion said to. But even now. After all these years later. Sometimes I still have dreams about my crazy mom and older brother and that dark closet in the basement. And about the day the bombs went off. But instead of being at school giving my book report about tadpoles when the bombs go off. In these dreams I am instead at home down in the basement. Locked inside that closet. Learning about the religion. With my crazy mom and older brother upstairs in these dreams when the bombs go off. And they get fried like meat on a grill. And the bombs crack open the closet in the basement. Where Mr. Henry Miller finds me all alone there. And saves me from the canibals! But those is just my silly dreams. The truth is I was really at school. Really giving a book report about tadpoles. Then after the bombs went off I was really all by myself for a while. Until I was grabbed by the evil gipsies. The same evil gipsies that grabbed Mr. Miller and gambolled us away to the canibal casino owners and police. Who put us together on that food truck that turned over. When Mr. Miller first spoke to me. But I never really did know what happened to my crazy mom. Or my older brother. They just disappeered after the bombs. And even though the world went all dark and gray. And cold. I really did like the world much better after the bombs went off. Cuz before the bombs went off I was always locked inside that stupid closet. In the basement. And I was really lonely. And not learning nothing about religion. But today. After all the bombs. Although I don't have much stuff that belongs to me in this gray world. I am the happiest girl alive! Cuz of Mr. Henry Miller. The greatest and sweetest and best talking cat. In the whole wide world! Who snuggles and purrs and makes me feel like the luckiest girl. In the whole wide world! So—Mr. Teacher Fella—I want to thank you.

For stopping. And picking up Mr. Miller. By the side of the road. When he was alone. And hurting with a broken leg. Cuz you saved my life. When you saved his.

♦ Ow! Ow! Ow! (This canibal just found out. That I am a girl. His hand touched me. Down there. The look on his face changed. From nasty to something different. Like he's going to get a treat. Before he eats his dinner. Now is the time for me to act. If I acted any different any sooner. The canibal would smell the trap. So I scream out.) There is food! In a backpack! Buried there! Next to your foot! Don't hurt me no more! (And he holds my throat with one hand. While he starts digging with the other. In a short time he finds the backpack. And pulls it out of the gray dirt. He unzips the backpack. And opens it up. To find a dead cat inside. A delishus looking pretend dead cat. The canibal pulls out the pretend dead cat and holds it up high. And for a small moment. The canibal looks at me. But by now the pretend dead Mr. Henry Miller has his back claws out. And he scratches out both the canibal's eyes. All the way out. They pop out like two bloody toy balls on strings. And the canibal starts screaming. And screaming. And screaming. He will scream. And moan. And cry. And beg. For three. Or four days. Then die. Then Mr. Miller and me will chop up the canibal's stinky body. And turn it into jerky. For cockroche bait. Mr. Miller and me never eat canibals. If we did we would turn into canibals ourselfs. And start twitching a lot. And acting goofy. Instead we take the jerky we make from the stinky canibal body. To a place where cockroches hide. When the cockroches come out to eat the dead canibal meat. We catch them. For food. Mr. Miller likes to joke when eating his dinner. He says what does not kill and eat you. Makes you stronger.)

♦ Anyway. Mr Teacher Fella—We hope this letter gets to you. Mr. Miller says if we put it in the special place. At the right moment. It will go back in time to you. But I think Mr. Miller is tricking me. Like my grandfather did. At Christmas. When I put cookies and milk out for Santa Claus. And woke up the next morning. To find the cookies and milk gone. Cuz whenever I check for these letters after we put them in that special place. To send back to you. They are always gone. By the next morning. And when I ask Mr. Miller what happened to the letters. He just looks at me. And purrs and purrs. Well. Mr. Teacher Fella— If you do get this letter maybe you can do something. To help Presdent Obama not get killed. So he can keep the world from going crazy. With the religion. Also please feed Mr. Miller lots more gormay cat food back in time. And whisky! And cigeretes! Cuz there is no gormay cat food. Or whisky. Or cigeretes. At the end of the world. And open your window curtains! To let beams of sunlight in. For Mr. Henry Miller to be warm and cozy. The happiest cat alive!

♦   Your friends here—Jinx Marie Tanner and Mr. Henry Miller. After all the bombs went off.

P MOSS

Time Machine

Five a.m. The casino bar was busy with regulars as the night was over and the new day had yet to unfold, a time to decompress for many in this 24/7 town. Strippers, cocktail waitresses, and craps dealers blowing off steam after a long night grinding out the gratuities upon which Las Vegas is powered. There were off-duty hookers. Vampires. Lingerers who refused to go home. And then there was Stoney, who haunted the graveyard shift as a means to escape the nothingness that had become his life.

Stoney was seventy but looked every bit of ninety. White hair and scraggly beard, with skin so anemically pale you could practically see through it. Walked with a cane. He was likable and kept the barflies entertained with bizarre stories that had presumably been rooted in truth somewhere along the line. Tales of when Stoney had been a marine sniper in Vietnam. Had ridden with the Hells Angels before they were called the Hells Angels. Been a boxer and a cattle rancher. A high school physics teacher. All before failing health had robbed him of everything but his personality. And his regret of lost love. A haunting sorrow he often confessed to Harry after one too many beers.

Harry was an average sort of fellow around forty, who in any other setting would be as indistinct as the wallpaper. But here he was the graveyard bartender. Front and center. Delighting in his duty as ringmaster to this nightly carnival of characters, especially his conversations with Stoney that made the hours between midnight and eight pass by a little faster. Not that Harry was ever in any great hurry to get home to a wife who bored the shit out of him.

Stoney coughed. Coughed again loudly, then lit a cigarette. Preoccupied with the eternal question, if you could invite any three historical figures to dinner, whom would you choose? For an hour, Stoney and Harry had been deliberating the pros and cons of various combinations. Hitler, Christ, and Sinatra? Einstein, Elvis, and Picasso? Socrates, Lincoln, and Al Capone? Stoney all of a sudden felt a bit light-headed and leaned forward, elbows on the bar to brace himself. "I can't decide. Who would you pick, Harry?"

Harry glanced down the bar to see if anybody needed a refill, then put his foot up on the well and got comfortable. "Oscar Wilde, Oscar Levant, and Oscar Madison."

"Oscar Madison wasn't a real person."

"Doesn't matter. Even if it were possible to conjure these guys up from the past, my wife would never allow them in the dining room. The only time she lets me in there is when her rich uncle comes for dinner."

"No bullshit, Harry." Stoney looked him square in the eye. "What if I could make it happen?"

"If you can do that, I'll buy you a watch that gives milk." But all kidding aside, Harry was definitely intrigued by the fantasy of having dinner with Oscar Wilde, Oscar Levant, and Oscar Madison. Though he found no comfort in the irony that tonight he would be seated across the table from Oscar Shultz, his wife's very rich and very judgmental uncle.

There would be no whimsical repartee, no sardonic wit, no commiserating near-miss exactas at Aqueduct. Tonight Harry would laugh politely at tired jokes, agree with contrary political opinions, and keep his elbows off his own dining room table. The very least he could do, his wife said, in order to preserve her place in Uncle Oscar's will. For all Harry cared, he would rather eat hot dogs in his underwear with Oscar Mayer. But Harry would not eat hot dogs in his underwear. He would wear a tie in his own home and be subjected to tag-team ridicule about how he would never amount to anything more than just a graveyard bartender. But the joke was on them: Harry loved being a graveyard bartender. He felt safe playing ringmaster to the denizens of the night, and there he would remain for the simple reason that his schedule conflicted with his wife's. And Harry liked that. Liked it a lot.

It had not always been that way. Harry was a romantic at heart, and had always dreamed of finding his one true love. But along the way he knocked up a girl and got married, only to find out after the fact that she hadn't been knocked up at all. And try as he might to cultivate love from a stubborn circumstance, it was not to be. By the time he realized that the futility was absolute, he was too emotionally deflated to move ahead with his life and try again. So he worked odd hours, lived vicariously through books and movies, and endured domesticity with a woman who kicked him under the table whenever he did not show proper respect for her rich uncle.

When his shift ended at 8:00 a.m., Harry went downstairs, turned in his cash drawer, and clocked out. Then as he always did, came back to the bar to unwind and have a few drinks. Play a little video poker if he felt lucky. Maybe go upstairs and see a movie or bowl a few frames. Locals casinos were self-contained amusement parks that made it very easy not to go home.

As Harry sat with Stoney shooting the breeze about this and that, they noticed a pretty girl with fire engine red hair and a tight blue dress walk past the bar. Stoney's jaw dropped, and he could not take his eyes off of her as she continued toward the sports book and finally disappeared from sight. He quickly downed a double shot of whiskey and in a quivering voice told Harry that the girl was a dead ringer for Debby, his first love. After another double shot he convinced himself that it was Debby.

Flushed with liquor, Stoney told the emotional tale of a night when he and Debby were teenagers. It was a story Harry had heard often when the booze made Stoney sad, but out of respect he listened as if for the first time. Of how one night at a drive-in movie their make-out session had not ended with the usual frustration. How Debby had given him his first blowjob. And then somehow Stoney said the wrong thing and she got out of the car and walked home, never speaking to him again. It had been the defining moment in his life. It was the reason he drank, so he could forget. Yet it was the liquor that made him remember. And now seeing Debby in the casino, his grief was too much to bear. Self-pity infused with more whiskey had Stoney coming apart at the seams, so instead of killing time at the movies, Harry drove him home as he sometimes did. This particular morning, Stoney insisted that Harry come inside. The messy apartment was cluttered with dusty books, piles of science magazines, and years of an old man's junk. Yet the dining area was pristine. Set up as a laboratory, and on the table some sort of gizmo. A crude contraption of wires and gauges, held together in a plastic casing. Looked to Harry like some seventh-grade science project.

Stoney poured them each a drink, mustering the courage to explain his gizmo. He coughed a lot. And not the throat-clearing kind, giving Harry pause to look at the dozens of empty prescription bottles strewn about the slobbish apartment and wonder just how sick Stoney was.

Stoney gestured proudly at his gizmo. Slugged down another shot of whiskey that settled his nerves just enough so he could say the words. "It's a time machine."

Harry did not laugh. Did not call the men in white coats. Just smiled and said in the most noncondescending way he could, "Interesting."

"I know you think it's crazy, that I'm crazy. But trust me, this machine works." Harry again glanced at the prescription bottles. If it worked, he thought, why not transport himself into the future where there is a cure?

Stoney was impassioned. "I just need to fine-tune the chemical compound which will act as the catalyst, then the machine will be operational. I won't bore you with the systematic whys and wherefores, but trust me when I tell you I know science. I taught it for twenty-two years."

Indeed he had. This Harry knew. He also knew that when the whiskey had finally gotten the better of him, the school board suggested he take an early retirement. All on account of Debby. Every aspect of his life had been a consequence of that night with Debby. The blowjob. How Stoney had said the wrong thing.

Harry indulged the old man as, in great detail and with great pride, Stoney did explain the systematic whys and wherefores of his invention. How it would transport him back to that night at the drive-in where he would get a second chance to say the right thing to Debby. But first, as a gift of friendship, he would send Harry back in time to fetch dinner guests Oscar Wilde, Oscar Levant, and Oscar Madison.

A few days passed. Graveyard shift attracted the usual cast of characters. A limo driver hit video poker for six grand. Tipped fat and bought a round of drinks for everybody in sight, prompting a couple of bar tarts to work their magic in an effort to separate him from the rest of the jackpot. Odds were they would. People laughed and drank. Gambled and argued. It was business as usual.

Stoney showed up in particularly good spirits. No shots of whiskey. No stories, woeful or otherwise. Nursed a beer while waiting patiently, then after a while not so patiently, to catch Harry for a private word. Bend his ear with the hot flash he was bursting to share. That his invention was complete. That he had finally mastered the catalytic compound and the time machine was operational, ready to transport Harry back to round up the three Oscars. And more importantly, to send Stoney back to the drive-in to be with Debby. No man had ever been this happy.

Then he collapsed and fell to the floor.

Paramedics took Stoney to the hospital. When Harry was finally allowed to visit, the doctor told him that Stoney would not live out the week, and that if there were anyone to notify, now would be the time. The following day Harry again visited the hospital, this time carrying a large shopping bag as he was admitted into the intensive care unit.

Stoney was groggy and loopy from medication, but not so out of it that he did not understand the stark reality that his life would very soon be over. His voice feeble, Stoney begged Harry to pull the plug and cut to the chase of what was inevitable. Seeing his friend suffer the degradation of staring down his ultimate moment helplessly attached to tubes and monitors, Harry could hardly blame him for wanting a quick exit. But Harry had something else in mind. He reached into the shopping bag and removed the time machine. Placed it on the bed table for Stoney to see, then asked if he was ready to see Debby. The mere mention of her name gave the dying man a spark of hope.

"Close your eyes, and I'll switch on the machine." Harry's tone was steady and assuring. "When you open them again, you'll be with Debby."

Stoney closed his eyes as tightly as he could manage, then opened them as he heard a soft voice say his name. Smiled through tears as he saw Debby sitting on the edge of the bed. The girl who had shaped every day of his past fifty years reached her hand beneath the blanket. Pulled up his hospital gown and reenacted the blowjob from that night at the drive-in.

Stoney had gone back in time. This time he would be sure to say the right thing.

Harry paid the hooker he had recruited from the bar to dress up in a fire engine red wig and tight blue dress. Sent her on her way. Then looked at Stoney who lay frail and dying. Envious of his friend who had been given a second chance at love.

Then Harry left and went home. Late for dinner with Oscar Shultz.

K. W. JETER

Bones

The worst of it had been over for some time. The noises had died away—the screaming and shouting, the clang of metal against metal, the racking back and forth of the steel-barred doors. Eventually, like the slow digging out from under a dream, there had been silence again, through all the long cement-block corridors.

But different noises outside. They had been able to watch what was going on by dragging a table from the wing's day-room area into one of the cells and climbing on top of it. They had taken turns peering out the narrow slot of a window. Out in the yard, long lines of men, stripped to the skin, hands clasped on top of their heads, had shuffled through the sparkling bits of broken glass. Other men, in uniforms with badges, rifles slung easily at their sides, had prodded them along.

"Just stay here," one of the others had told him. "We don't have to go anywhere. They'll be coming inside soon and doing a sweep, and they'll find us. So it's cool."

He had climbed down from the table and gone over to the transport wing's main door. Through the worst of the storm, the angry shouting and crazy laughter and the screaming that had gone on and on, all of them had huddled there in the darkness, listening and wondering when the door would pop open. They had been able to listen, holding their breath in darkness, and hear whole cellblocks of doors racking open, as the rioters had swarmed over one control module after another. If the guards had still been there, so much the worse for them; if they were lucky, they became hostages, and if not—if there were some long-simmering grudges to be worked out—then something else went down.

More shouting and screaming, with silence at the end. In the transport wing, they had listened and known just what was happening.

Scores had been settled all through the long gray corridors. "They won't bother us," one of the other guys in the transport wing had whispered. "Why should they? They don't know us." Which had been crap, of course, and even the guy who had said it knew that it was. When the storm begins, it doesn't stop at anyone's doorstep. There had been six of them in the transport wing, five of them waiting for the van with the barred windows that would have taken them upstate to the minimum security facility in the morning, if all this other stuff hadn't happened instead. The sixth guy had been scheduled to go to the pre-release unit downtown; that was how close he had been to putting all of this behind him, the steel doors clanging at his back for good. Just one day away; nobody found that particularly funny.

So when the door had popped, even though the long night's noises had died away, even though they could climb up to the day room's narrow slot of a window and look out at the general population stripped and lined up in the yard, under the watch of the guns and police and state troopers, back in control at last—nobody had thought that was a good thing. They had all snapped alert, spines rigid, eyes widened, at the sound of metal sliding against metal, the lock mechanism retracting into the main door's steel frame. Then silence again, broken only by the drawn-out squeak of the door turning on its hinges, pushed by nothing but its own weight . . .

"Don't go out there."

He had known it wouldn't be a good idea.

"The guards will come and find us." One of the others' hands had clutched at his sleeve. "We're okay here. Just be cool."

There could still be others out there who hadn't been teargassed out of the cellblocks and out into the yard. Others, lifers and hardcore badasses, who had hunkered down where they were, damp T-shirts and jackets pulled over their heads so they could breathe, who would just love to have a little more fun before the police swept through, rounded them up, and dragged them off to the supermax wing. Those guys were never going anywhere—this was their home, their world, for which they had been born, day one to eternity. So taking it out on some fool from the transport unit and getting another life sentence stacked on their two-inch-thick files—that wouldn't have meant squat to any of them. Just the end of the party, that would have been all.

"Don't—"

But he had pulled the heavy steel door the rest of the way open, and had stepped outside. He hadn't even known why he was doing it. But he had known he would find out.

He had found a lot of things as he walked farther down the corridors, pushing open one unit door after another. The storm had passed, leaving its wreckage behind. There had been whole cellblocks where everything had been set on fire, the thin mattresses now smoldering heaps, the steel bed frames shoved back against the walls. The cement floors had been ankle-deep in water from the overhead sprinklers, the wet seeping into the cuffs of the faded orange jumpsuit he had been issued when he arrived on the county lockup's transport van. Broken glass had crackled beneath each slow step he took.

He had known—had been able to imagine—what he would find in the protective custody unit. Heavy payback. As bad as it had been way over in the transport unit, listening and waiting, it must have been a thousand times worse for the snitches and molesters and the femmy queers, all the ones who wouldn't have lasted two minutes if they had been thrown out in the general population. In the PC unit—Punk City, as the badasses called it—they would have known that the eye of the storm was headed straight for them.

He had walked past one cell after another, touching the cold steel bars of each one. Like walking through some museum of natural history's diorama displays—he had seen things that might have been alive once, but were no more. Some of the punks and snitches had piled everything—mattress, bed frame, tattered books, radio, hotplate, cache of soup packets and candy bars, anything—up against the cell doors, barricades that might have slowed down the ones outside for a few seconds. All that crap had been yanked out into the corridor—he had stepped over the sodden tangles of clothing and wet cardboard as he passed by. In some of the cells there had been nothing but a single body, facedown in the pink water, brighter red smeared across the naked buttocks and ravaged thighs, a blood mask over the concave pulp of what had been face and mouth. The ones whose screams had been cut short were huddled against the cells' farthest walls, sharpened steel in their guts or the filed and pointed handle of a toothbrush sunk crosswise in their throats.

Those had been the good ones. The bad dioramas had been the ones where infinite loving patience had guided the hands of those who had come and pulled open the cell doors, tossed aside the rags and books and cereal boxes, and stepped inside. All the electricity had been shut off by then, but there had still been enough light seeping through the window bars, from the moon and the police searchlights outside the walls, for the work to be done. A litter of blackened wires and razor blades, burnt-out disposable lighters and knotted cords, floated on top of the shallow water. Things that were still human in shape—torso, legs, arms, bound at wrist and ankle—crouched unmoving in the corners of the cells. But the faces, what had been left of them—their screams had choked on the rags of their own flesh. Too much fun; too much long dreaming of what would go down when the chance finally came. And it had.

He had seen enough. More than enough. But he had still walked farther through the corridors, his shoes mired in the clotted tide.

He had stopped, listening. Somebody—something—was whispering to him. He had been able to hear it, but he hadn't been able to make out what was being said. Close enough to his ear, almost a kiss, that he had turned about, to catch whoever had crept up beside him. But there had been no one. He had stood in the middle of the corridor, looking down the way he had come, past the open cell doors. The indistinct voice, whoever it had been, had gone on whispering to him. He had closed his eyes and listened harder, trying to tell if it was one voice or many, and what they were trying to say to him, all secretive and sly.

The noises outside had faded even farther away. His gut had tightened, squeezing the sour taste of vomit to the back of his mouth. He hadn't wanted to go any farther down the corridor; he had wanted to go back to the transport wing, run back to where the other ones, the smarter ones, had hunkered down, waiting patiently for their rescuers. But the way back there led past the open steel-barred doors and the things inside the cells. The certainty had come over him, the sourness in his throat curdling on his tongue, that if he went back that way, those things wouldn't be huddled in the cells' corners, motionless and silent, but would have crept out to the edge of the corridor. Where they would be able to snare his ankle as he passed by, pull themselves up with their ragged, blackened hands, and gaze into his face with their knowing eyes. They wouldn't whisper then; they would speak aloud, of all they had learned at the square point of a razor blade turned in the teardrop flame of a Bic lighter.

Everything in this world had wanted to tell him something. The gray cinder-block walls had trembled with urgency, drawing nearer with each breath he had taken. At his ear, the whisper had grown louder, its smile entangled with each syllable, but he had still been unable to tell what it said.

The words had touched the walls of little rooms inside his head. As he had turned and listened, to silence and the whispering, their doors had opened all by themselves, one after another. Just as the gray steel doors all around him had opened, one after another, the buttons were pushed on a control panel far from here, unseen.

He had looked down and seen that the shallow water had changed. Other things floated in it, nudging against his damp shoes. Unspooled elastic bandages trailed like white seaweed; little orange bottles and their plastic caps bobbed and sank as he took one slow step after another. The paler, emptier hands of doctors' latex gloves touched him, then drifted on by.

The medical unit, or the hospital or the infirmary—he didn't know what they called it in this facility. It hadn't mattered; he had peered in through a narrow opening, its door ripped off its hinges, and looked across the ransacked cupboards and drawers. It had probably been one of the first places targeted when the storm had broken. All those goodies inside—and they had been found quickly enough. One of the badasses, three hundred pounds of muscle and anger, had laid facedown in the muck, his tattooed bicep tied off with the rubber cord from a nurse's blood-pressure kit. Two hypodermics, wine-red with the badass's blood, sprouted from a pulseless vein like glass hummingbirds.

He had stepped over the badass; the whisper had grown louder, from somewhere farther into the dark. *You've come this far,* he had told himself. *Why stop now?*

Then—at last—he had found where the soft, smiling words were coming from. The janitor's closet, way at the back, past the examination tables and the toppled-over X-ray machine. It held a mop and a bucket, shelves stacked with paper towels and ammonia, folded wheelchairs . . . and one corpse.

The poor bastard must have dragged himself back into this last little hiding place. He had knelt down and touched the body, turning it onto its back. Just enough light had seeped in from the corridor outside that he was able to see that the fun had continued, even back here in this narrow hole. White had glinted through the raw face, what was left of it. Stuff that might have been red, knotted string—but he knew it wasn't that— had thickened the shallow water around his knees.

Nothing had looked back at him in the closet's dark. Nothing looked into him. There had been nothing inside the places where the eyes had been. Hollow and dark, rimmed with clotted red. He had been able to see all the way to the back of the skull.

It had smiled at him, and whispered, soft but close enough that he was able to hear what it said. The closet walls had pressed against his shoulders and there had been no door, no way to go back the route he had taken to that narrow place. There had been no other place but this one.

It had smiled, and whispered, and told him all that he needed to hear, all that he never wanted to hear, all that he had come so far to find out.

♣   "What's there to get into a sweat about, pal? You already know what's going to happen." The click of the yellowed teeth, the whisper of sand through the empty eye sockets. "As I am, you will be. You can take that to the bank."

He ignored the smiling words. Which nobody else could hear, anyway. Which, he knew, only sounded inside his own head. He leaned over the motorcycle's handlebars, chest down closer to the tank, racer-style, getting himself into the little zone of calmer air behind the dark-tinted windscreen.

The bones were up ahead, waiting for him. Enough to just roll the throttle on. To twist the black, ridged rubber his leather glove surrounded—right hand—while the left gathered the clutch in one quick smooth grab, the toe of his boot goosing the bike's gear up from fourth to fifth. Then fifth to sixth, edging it to the top on a nice long straight stretch that he knew well enough to chance without screwing up. Still dark enough to see the headlight beam brushing across the construction gravel scattered across the asphalt, the skid traps that he flicked the bike around with an easy push on either grip. The hidden sun etched the mountains red, out beyond Henderson and the glittering foothills. Clouds covered just enough of the sky overhead to catch the lights of the casinos at the south end of the Strip, MGM Grand's green velvet smear, like some toxic yet eerily beautiful gas. He rolled the throttle on a little more, ducking his helmet low beneath the unfolding wheels of a jet coming in from California.

"Come on, come on . . ." The bones spoke inside his head again. They were just visible, in their gear of tattered rags and oil-stained dirt, up ahead where the 215 Beltway crossed over the road. The cement embankment, throbbing with the early morning traffic, was the headboard of their bed. "You got plenty of time, sure, but that's no reason to take all day about it."

He would have said something back to them, but against the whine of the bike's engine, redlined at 14k, he wouldn't have been able to hear even his own voice inside his helmet. Another half a tab of what he'd left back home in the kitchen cupboard and the bones would have been silent as well.

He hit the brakes, first checking the left mirror to make sure some overloaded dump truck wasn't hard upon him. He smoked the rear Pirelli, letting up on the stamp-sized pedal just enough to keep the bike in a straight line. Momentum lifted his tailbone off the seat, all his body weight moving up into his fists as he squeezed the clutch and front brake levers. Any less pressure and he would have shot by the spot where the bones half-lay, half-sat waiting for him.

"Good to see you."

Said the bones drily—that was his own joke, edited in his head. How else would bones speak?

"Last night you didn't come by." The empty sockets regarded him with fleshless equanimity. "That made us sad."

"Last night I was running late." He didn't bother putting down the kickstand, but just leaned the bike's weight onto his right leg. A scrap of frayed leather, once black and now gray, flicked near the toe of his boot. "Last night I didn't have time for your crap."

"The way you talk—" The bones smiled. They always smiled. Everything, he knew, was funny to them. "Anybody who heard us, they'd think we weren't friends."

"We're not."

Nobody would hear them. It wasn't that kind of a conversation. A pickup truck loaded with Mexicans and lawnmowers roared past on the road, scattering pebbles like unnumbered dice across the dusty patch of ground. He toed the bike's gearshift up into neutral, so he could take his hand off the clutch, undo the buckle of his helmet, and lift it off his head. Even a couple of minutes without the wind of his forward motion and he was sweating.

The overpass screamed above, the voices of the traffic mingling with the bike's insistent idle, right beneath him. If there were quiet places left in the desert, this wasn't one of them.

Still the bones spoke soft and clear to him.

"But I'm *your* friend," said the bones. "You know that, don't you?"

The yellowed teeth might have clicked a fraction of an inch away from his ear, biting the whispered words into little pieces. He turned his head away and closed his eyes, the hard leather collar of his gear rubbing a dull knife blade against the underside of his chin.

It didn't help. He could still see them, hear them. Once the bones, before he had come to know them as well as he did now, had coyly invited him to sit down beside them. The machinery of his racer boots had creaked as he squatted down halfway between the bones and his bike. He had reached back and laid his glove on the front wheel, not to balance himself but to keep his means of escape close by. Halfway between the bike and the bones, he had leaned forward, close to them, to listen.

But the bones hadn't wanted to talk then; they'd wanted to show him something. Joking with him. He'd never be able to say that they didn't have a sense of humor, such as it was. Sand had gritted in the joints under the leather rags as the yellowed smile had risen up toward his own face. A white fingertip had touched one of the eye sockets, directing his attention. Inside the empty circle, a baby scorpion had nested. They weren't so easy to find anymore, even here in the desert; the new houses and condos and apartment buildings had chased them up into the foothills. A vision had come unbidden to him, of the bones on their hands and rag-clad knees, dry white bits scraping about in a widening circle, searching under moonlight and the edges of occasional high beams zipping past on the road. Searching for some tiny carapaced insect, sickle tail erect, its stinger leaving a futile spot of venom on the white fingers that were already so far beyond pain, picking up the scorpion and depositing it in one of the eye sockets. Keeping it there with a little tap of a skinned fingertip, just the way the living might adjust a contact lens that kept slipping out of place. Just so the bones would have their little joke to show him, laughter held silent in what was left of their segmented throat. If it had been designed to get a reaction from him, it didn't work; he had seen worse. The scorpion had regarded him for a moment with its own dark beads of eyes, then apparently decided he was neither threat or prey, and scuttled back into the skull's dark shelter.

"Your only friend," said the bones. Smiling. "That's why you come to see me, isn't it?"

He didn't answer. He let his gloved hand rest on the throttle grip. One little turn and he could've drowned out the sneering words with the engine's high-pitched shout. Two hundred and fifty cc's, goosed up, was more than enough to do that job. And more than enough, if he kicked the bike into gear, to take him away from this familiar spot, like a full-fairing bullet. Just a matter of power-to-weight ratio—that was what the motorheads had told him when they sold him the bike. Strip off everything that didn't matter, make yourself as close to weightless as possible, and then nothing could hold you back from whatever waited for you at the end of the road. A little acceleration, zero to whatever, and he could put the road blurring under the slender wheels again, his chest suspended nearly horizontal above the tank, his heart straining toward its own rev limit . . .

But he didn't do that. He let the bones talk to him, and made no reply. Because he had no answer to what they said. Or he did, but it wasn't one he wanted to speak aloud.

"Go on," said the bones. "Get out of here." They knew they had him. Every night, without even trying, they won. "You're just wasting time. Ours and yours."

"No . . ." He looked away, off toward the east, where a red fragment of sun leaked through a crack in the hills. "It'll still happen. Just takes time, that's all." A semi rolled by, tires bellowing, eclipsing the light for a moment. "To do it right."

"Oh, it'll happen. We know that." The bones always spoke in the plural, as if the rattling white pieces—the ribs like spider legs under the torn jacket, the pelvis with its edge shoveled into the sand—were a committee that had elected the skull their spokesman. "We made a deal, didn't we? You just need to keep up your end of it."

"You don't need to worry."

"Of course we don't." The bones shifted about in their rags, as though about to push themselves up from the ground. He didn't know if they could or not, if they had that kind of strength. "But maybe *you* should worry. Because we've been pretty light on you up until now. That could change."

He could barely hear what the bones said. Not because the traffic's noise had grown louder overhead, or he had rolled on the motorcycle's throttle. The bones' voice had faded to less than a whisper. That was the risperidone kicking in, he knew. He had taken his usual half a tab this morning, while he had been getting ready to hit the road, but he hadn't washed it down with the glass of milk that he'd poured out. The glass would be waiting there on the kitchen counter when he got home this evening, its contents warmed and sour and fit only for pouring down the sink. So the medication, unbuffered, had come on a little stronger and sooner this morning. He could tell for sure by glancing at his hand: a tremor shook inside the thin black leather.

The bones leaned forward, as though the empty eye sockets were having a hard time discerning him. "All right," they said. "We'll talk some more. Next time."

If he looked from the corner of his eye, he knew he wouldn't see them at all. But just rags, empty, nothing yellowed and whitened inside, that spoke and smiled. If the black tatters moved, it was because of the wind that slid along the desert floor, or the trucks that barreled past on the road. That wasn't a good sign, if that was all he saw. It meant the medicine was still kicking in, some remnant metabolizing into his bloodstream. The tremor in his hand would grow worse, and quickly, bad enough that he would have a hard time keeping the bike on the road and in a straight line.

But he wasn't that far away from where he was headed. *Relax.* He could make it if he didn't screw around here any longer. The bones had nothing new to tell him, anyway. They never did; it wasn't in their nature.

"Fine." He straightened the bike and kicked the stand back up with the heel of his boot. "Next time."

There was always a next time. That was how things worked. How they had come to work. He left the bones in their nest of rags, against the beltway overpass. Where they would be waiting for him again. Always waiting.

♣   Looping back into town, then a straight shot over to the motorheads' place—easy westside suburban streets, no tricky curves or intersections near the off-Strip casinos, with their moron, half-drunk cager clientele, who had all watched *The Fast and the Furious* way too many times, boiling out of the parking lots even this early in the morning. He'd bungeed onto the back of the bike the parcel that the UPS guy had dropped off yesterday.

"Hey, you mook." The motorheads were walking and riding museums of things that nobody but them said anymore. They were too young to have picked it up from anywhere but their grandfathers. The redheaded one wiped his hands on a greasy-black shop rag. "Where you been all this time?"

"What're you talking about?" He switched off the bike just outside the house's open garage. "I was just here last weekend."

"You were? Huh." The motorheads had a loose hold on abstract concepts such as time. If it didn't have an engine attached to it, or could have a welding torch applied to it, it pretty much didn't exist for them. "Now I remember. We were fixing the mounting on the Muzzy. How's it holding up?"

"You tell me." He kept his helmet under his arm as he stepped back from the motorcycle, so the other motorhead could squat down on his heels and poke at the muffler. "You put it on."

Hard to tell what the one with the buzz cut was hunting for as he peered at the scorched-looking weld marks. Both of them went into deep meditative trances, silent as skinny, T-shirted Buddhas in jeans frayed out at the knees, as they clicked into the mechanical world. Then they would emerge later—could be minutes, could be hours—with no announcement of what had been revealed to them there.

That didn't matter to him. The motorheads' front yard was one of the places he most liked to be. He set his helmet down on the driveway's edge, close to the bare dirt—if there had ever been a grass lawn, like those of the surrounding houses in the tract, it had died out long ago, from lack of watering and too many midnight oil changes. He was sure the neighbors all cordially hated the motorheads, the rotten spot in their suburban apple. He had caught a couple of them glaring at him from behind the vertical blinds of their living room windows, as he had come downshifting and easing off the throttle, coasting to a stop at their enemies' trashed-out headquarters.

They think you're one of us, Buzz-cut had explained. *Another goddamn motorhead.* They called themselves that; he had picked it up from them. *Of course that pisses 'em off. It's only natural.*

He had wanted to know if he was one. A motorhead.

Shit. Buzz-cut had smiled sadly and shaken his head, as though the depths of human folly had been once more revealed to him. *If you were a real motorhead, you'd be doing all this work yourself, instead of paying us to do it for you.*

He didn't mind being at the perimeter of their world, in a tight slow orbit about it rather than right on its grease-stained surface. He looked around the yard as the motorhead squinted at the racing exhaust. In the red-tinged morning light, the carcasses of every possible variation on the theme of engines and wheels glinted beneath strata of grease and rust. A bent-framed dirt bike with decaying knobblies leaned against an antique golf cart with a canvas top tattered into pennants; one of the neighborhood's stray cats had littered in the cart's popped-open batteries compartment, and had kept the space for her solo nest after her weaned kittens had scattered and staked out their own lairs under the jacked-up beaters with the police auction numbers still spray-painted on their cracked windshields. No exact count was possible of the Japanese cruisers and sportbikes that had died in the yard and along the alley side of the motorhead house. They had all been stripped and salvaged, parts swapped, disassembled, reassembled, and abandoned so often that what was left, especially at night, looked like the ooze from which the dinosaurs' grandparents might have evolved, if their DNA had been pieced together from tiny metric nuts and bolts.

Something that he liked about the motorheads' yard was that it was one of the few places—maybe the only one—where the bones never came. He never saw them here, never had to listen to the sly words from behind the yellowed teeth, never had to look at some scuttling surprise in the empty sockets. That all happened somewhere else—or everywhere else. Maybe the bones never came here because it was a different sort of graveyard, different from the rest of the world's graves. When machines crapped out and went unburied, they didn't make such a fuss about it.

"Looks okay to me." Red had gone into the house and come back out, letting the screen door slam behind him. Digging the last fries from the bottom of a Burger King sack, he watched the other motorhead inspecting the muffler welds. "What's the problem?"

"Let me do it next time," said Buzz-cut, "and you won't have to get all defensive about it."

"Your ass." Red laid his hand right on the muffler, despite its residual heat, and gave it a tug. "I've seen you put on Muzzys before. Tuna cans're put together better." Another tug. The muffler stayed where it was mounted on the side of the motorcycle. Satisfied, the motorhead stood up. "Should hold you, though." A smile. "Not like you're going to be putting a lot of miles on it, anyway. Is it?"

That was the big reason he liked hanging out with the motorheads. They were in on the plan.

They had been from the beginning. He had spotted the house and its yard collection of decaying machinery long before he had figured out exactly what he wanted to do. So when he did know, they were the first people he wanted to talk to about it.

Yeah, we can probably fix you up. Buzz-cut had stood in the doorway of the garage, wiping his hands on the same rag, and had nodded. *I mean, if it's a sportbike you want.*

Red had cut in: *Because we don't do those dorky freak bikes like you see on those TV chopper shows. That shit's for orthodontists and movie stars.*

All that Jesse Jerk-off crap. Buzz-cut had sounded sullen for a moment, as though from some deep personal resentment. *And those father and son morons, that Doodle family or whatever they're called. What a buncha drama queens.*

Yeah—A smirk from the other. *Who says there's no gay programming on TV?*

So if that's what you're looking for, don't bother around here. Buzz-cut had glared at him. *Performance is what we're talking about, mac. Light and fast—it's all about the power-to-weight ratio.*

So no pigged-out Harley bs, Red had elaborated. *Those lardbutts are for guys who need to keep telling themselves,* This *is my penis and* this *is my bike; they are* not *the same . . . not the same . . .*

That was how his first conversation with the motorheads had gone. Which indicated that he had fallen among true believers. A faith in speed and nothing but. That had suited him—and the plan—just fine.

"This came." He unhooked the bungees and lifted the UPS box off the rack. He handed it to Buzz-cut. "Yesterday."

"Cool. Pods." He held up one of the K&N cartons from the box so it caught more light from the garage. "You even managed to get the right size. Congrats."

"Now those," said the redheaded one, "are a definite good idea." Buzz-cut nodded in agreement. "You'll notice the difference, right off. We should've done these right at the start."

"Yeah, instead of that stupid Muzzy."

"Bite me." The motorheads bickered with each other the way old married couples did, just to keep basic respiratory functions going. "We had the Muzzy in the parts bin already, remember? Dickhead."

"Dickhead yourself, man. Airflow's always more important than exhaust . . ."

Half the time, he had no idea what they were talking about. Except that it would make the bike go faster.

So you got a yen for speed? That was what Buzz-cut had asked him, that first time he had talked with them. *That's why you want a bike?*

When he had told the motorheads—told them about the plan—they had both nodded. *Yeah, that's cool,* Buzz-cut had said. *That's worth doing.* His intent hadn't seemed like a strange idea to them. *Lemme show you something . . .*

They had taken him to the back of the garage. Buzz-cut had pulled a tarp off a motorcycle painted an eye-aching green, with *Kawasaki* lettered slantwise on the sides.

He had asked what the hell it was.

It's a Ninja. Red had straddled the seat, then reached down to point out the word on the lower fairing. *Cut ya a deal on it—only has a couple hundred miles on the odometer. Guy bought it for his wife, she hated it, he sold it to us for cheap.* He had patted the tank with obvious affection. *Two hundred and fifty cc's. Great bike.*

That had seemed a little small to him, engine-wise.

You want a pig, get a pig. But this'll take care of what you're talking about.

Power to weight, Buzz-cut had said. *That's what it's all about. This little sucker'll get you to a hair under a hundred, no problem . . .*

He had brought cash with him, a wad of it stuffed into his jacket pocket. As though he had known he was going to find just what he needed.

That had been then, the start of the plan. But even now, the motorheads bickered on.

"So why're you getting on my case? Now he'll have both airflow *and* exhaust. Same thing, really."

"True." Buzz-cut glanced over at him. "Then you'll be way over a hundred on this puppy."

"Good thing we got the handling sorted out for ya, right off."

Actually, the tires had come before that. Those had really been the beginning, the first items the motorheads had started on. Working from a list scrawled on the back of the handwritten receipt for the bike. *Tires,* Buzz-cut had said, licking the point of a stub pencil. *Either the Pirellis or the Bridgestones . . .*

Pirellis. Red had leaned over the paper from the other side of the bench. *Go with the Sport Demons. Those are killer. Nice sticky rubber, traction like flypaper.*

Mileage is crap on those. Get a lot more with the BT45s.

So? He's not going to need 'em that long.

True. Buzz-cut had kept writing on the scrap of paper. *Plus it's not going to do him any good to take a spill. Those trucks have really got the roads ripped up out there past Durango. He hits some frickin' pothole and winds up in the hospital, that'll just delay the whole process.*

So we're gonna trick out the suspension for him also?

Yeah, he's gotta be able to get around stuff. More scribbling. *Better get some cartridge emulators on those front forks. What's a set of Race Tech Gold Valves going for these days?*

He had asked how much all this was going to cost.

Don't worry. It'll be worth it. You'll see.

We can probably get an EX500 rear shock off eBay. Somebody's always selling one . . .

By the time the motorheads had finished writing stuff down, there had been about a dozen different items on the scrap of paper, things he hadn't had a clue about. Right from the beginning, the plan had started to get more elaborate than he had figured.

"What's going on?"

He looked over to the house's front porch. A girl came out of the house, barefoot and a ratty blanket thrown around her shoulders. There was always a rotating cast of them at the motorhead house, lookers with the resilient breasts that indicated professional employment, either in one of the off-Strip shows or the gentlemen's clubs along Industrial. Their connection with the motorheads was hazy; he was pretty sure that neither Buzz-cut nor Red was sleeping with any of them. Maybe the girls crashed there because it was one of the few places in town where they weren't automatically the center of lustful attention. The motorheads' preoccupation with internal combustion engines was probably a welcome change of pace for them.

"Now what?" She laid a hand on the back of his neck. Together, they watched the motorheads futzing around. "What are they doing for ya this time?"

"Pods," said Buzz-cut. "We're going to get the air intake all fixed up on this bad boy."

"Whatever." One of the showgirl's artificial fingernails drew a smooth, meaningless figure at the top of his spine. "How long's it gonna take?"

"Couple of hours. To do it right."

"Great." She leaned her head a little forward, so she could smile at him. "That means you got enough time to take me for breakfast."

One of the advantages of living in a city without time, where clocks had been banished from the casinos, was that it was always time for breakfast. So you could delude yourself that the whole day still lay ahead of you, filled with bright promise. For a little while, at least.

Though being stuck in a Formica-tabled booth with a beautiful woman wasn't too bad. They all had appetites like army privates after a fifty-mile pack drill—he poked a fork at a Denver omelet and watched her demolish a couple of stacked plates.

"I used to be a vegan." She mopped up maple syrup with a strip of bacon. "When I was at UNLV. But then I noticed all that soy was making my boobs hurt. So I figured, screw it."

"Yeah, that would probably change my mind, too."

"Now something's gotta die for me at every meal." She licked the syrup from her iridescent nails. "So why do you hang out with those guys, anyway? I see you over there all the time."

"The motorheads?"

"That's what you call 'em?" She still had her stage lashes on, long and stiff enough that a bird could have perched on them. The tips of the sweeping dark curves quivered with her laugh. "That's cool. Motorheads. Yeah, them."

He shrugged. "They're helping me with a plan."

"'Plan?' What kind of a plan?" She speared a small sausage and bit it in half on the end of her fork. "You going to race? So that's why you've got 'em hopping up your bike. That's where I met them, out at the speedway. I was an umbrella girl. Just a one-off gig." She swallowed the rest of the sausage and started in on the pancakes again. "You know, with the winners up on the podium, you got the trophies, all that good stuff. But you always got champagne all over you. Seems a waste." The showgirl regarded him with a critical if not unkind eye. "You seem a little old for racing, though. Is there like a senior division?"

His smile was a lot smaller than hers as he shook his head. "I'm not going racing."

"Then why the hot bike? Just a style thing? That's cool. I like the boots."

"These?" He was wearing his Oxtars. He stuck them out from under the booth's table, so they could both admire the silver-and-black Power Ranger-ness of them. "They're just to protect my ankles. I had a low-speed get-off a few months ago, over on Industrial and Twain—you know, just behind Caesars. Didn't break anything, but I twisted my left ankle pretty bad. Kept me off the bike for about six weeks." He reached down and tapped the intricate, machinelike sides of the boots. "See, these've got a torsion control system built into them; they can only twist so far before they lock up. That's why real racers wear them. See, you want to make sure that—"

"Whatever." It was obviously more than she wanted to know. "I still don't get why you have those guys working on your bike all the time. Hopping it up and stuff. I mean, it's a nice bike and all, but still."

He shrugged. "Like I said, I've got a plan going."

"So if it's not racing, what is it?"

He had talked with the motorheads about it before—and of course the bones—but the showgirl would be the first civilian, as it were. So he told her.

"That's what you're going to do?" It didn't seem to faze her. "With the bike?"

He nodded. "Pretty much the idea."

"Cool."

Another advantage, he supposed, of living in this town. You could talk to a beautiful girl about something like this—not joking around, but serious—and she wouldn't freak on you. "Are you going to eat that?" She pointed to his untouched waffle, then forked it over to her own plate before he could reply. She'd probably had enough guys already talk about the same thing, and do it, that it no longer seemed like a big deal to her.

"Why use a motorcycle?" She drizzled syrup across the waffle. "Seems messy."

"I've got my reasons." He wasn't going to tell her about those; he figured that part was kind of a downer. "And it's not like it's a totally original idea. Other people have done it that way."

"Like who? You mean, on purpose? I had a boyfriend who crashed his Road King, out near Mesquite, and he was in the ICU for six days before they pulled the plug on him." She could've been talking about flicking off a light switch. "But he'd been doing crystal and Jack before he hit the road, so it's not as if he'd planned on winding it up that way."

"No, this is more an intentional thing." He pulled his research up from his personal memory bank. "Back in the eighties, there was a fad in Germany—short-lived, so to speak—of these young guys doing the same thing. With motorcycles. Racer bikes. They're big in Europe, you know."

"Um." The waffle was half gone. "What would they do, go over a cliff or something? Or maybe off the top of Mont Blanc—that'd be cool."

"No, they'd slam into something. You hit a brick wall or the side of a bridge, straight on at a hundred miles per hour plus, and you don't have to worry about spending time in intensive care."

"Ohhh . . . I get it. That's why you're getting the bike all hopped up." The showgirl nodded approvingly. "You want to make sure you're going fast enough when it happens."

"It's kinda like insurance." He took another bite of what was left of the omelet. "If you're going to do something like this, you want to make sure you do it right. All the way. You don't want to just wind up all crippled and brain-damaged."

"Yeah . . ." She mulled it over. "That would definitely suck."

"So that's why I've got the guys fixing up the bike." He took the folded sheet of paper, with its black thumbprints all over it, from his shirt pocket and showed it to her. "They figured out a whole list of things I should have on it, to get it going fast as possible." He tucked the paper away. "I mean, if going 105 miles per hour rather than 95 is the difference between getting the job done and just messing myself up real bad—I'd be stupid not to do it."

She nodded. "I guess it's the kind of thing you want to get right the first time."

"Exactly."

"Well, you came to the right place," said the showgirl. "Those are pretty helpful guys. For that sort of thing."

Also true. He wouldn't have been able to pull the plan together without the motorheads. They had even taught him to ride the bike, since he had never even been on one, before coming up with the plan.

Which hadn't gone well at the beginning. Both Buzz-cut and Red had wound up gazing down at him, as he had lain on his back in the middle of the street, breath knocked out of him. He had just toppled over on the Ninja, which had then sputtered dead, its sideways weight trapping his foot.

This isn't going to work. Buzz-cut had pointed to his trembling hand. That was why he had dropped the bike; the tremor had been so pronounced that he hadn't been able to manage the clutch lever. *Are you on something?*

The technical term, he had known for a long time, was iatrogenic choreoathetosis. He had done his research. A lot of antipsychotics besides risperidone caused the spasms and trembling hands. He had been through most of them, starting out with amitriptyline hydrochloride and then perphenazine; this stuff was better than most. The quetiapine had been the worst; he hadn't even been able to use a knife and fork while on that.

He hadn't told the motorheads about the medications. Just that he would be back the next night, to give it another shot. When he had gotten home, he sat for a long time looking at the little orange plastic container on the table in front of him. He knew what the choice was. The shakes, with no voices whispering at his ear, no crazy things crawling right at the corner of his vision, where he could just barely see them. Or his hands nice and steady, tremors gone, and all those bad things coming back to him, out from behind the little doors in his head that the medications were so good at keeping locked up tight.

Then he had decided, and had rolled one of the tabs out of the bottle, and with a paring knife from the kitchen drawer, he had carefully cut it in half . . .

When he had gone back to the motorheads' place, the tremor was light enough that nobody else would notice it. And he had been able to handle the bike, or at least start getting the hang of it. *Just takes practice.* Buzz-cut had watched him doing slow figure eights in the middle of the empty street. *That's all.*

"You're right," he told the showgirl. "They're pretty helpful."

There had been more stuff they had shown him.

You gotta look where you want to go—

That was something else Buzz-cut had told him, back when they had been teaching him to ride the bike. Out in an empty supermarket parking lot, about three in the morning, so there had been more room for him to get up to speed. He had just come close to ramming the Ninja straight into a cinder-block retaining wall, and had barely managed to keep from dropping it again.

It's what they call target fix. Buzz-cut had tapped a finger on the side of the helmet. *Happens up here. Whatever you're looking at, that's where you're gonna go. You're looking at the ground, you're gonna go down. Some cager pulls in front of you, out on the street, you lock on 'em, you're gonna hit 'em.* He mimed holding onto a motorcycle's handlebars. *You're on the highway, some eighteen-wheeler comes up beside you, you look over at those great big wheels spinning at your elbow—they'll suck you right in.*

So where was he supposed to look, he had asked the motorhead.

Where the truck isn't, Buzz-cut had answered patiently. *Just fix on the target you want, your escape route, and you'll be fine. Trust me on this one, pal. It works.*

"You got a place picked out?"

He looked up at the showgirl. "For what?"

"You moron." She said it with a smile. "For where you're going to do it."

He shook his head. Actually, he had one—but it was something else he wanted to keep private. It was right out at the overpass, where he met and conversed with the bones. For now, he wanted to keep it to himself.

"I'll miss you," said the showgirl. She took his arm as they walked across the parking lot, toward her tricked-out Escalade. "I mean it."

He knew she did, in some small but genuine way. The way someone would when they sat down in front of the television and hit the Guide button on the Tivo remote, and couldn't find a favorite program, and went scanning through all the cable channels and still couldn't find it. Not the end of the world—hers, at least—but still a real loss.

"At least you got a reason for all that motorcycle crap. Not like all those other guys who are always hanging around over there. That's important."

He knew what was going to happen next. It had happened before. He stopped and looked around at her. She smiled as he looked into her eyes.

"It's important to have a plan," she said. But it wasn't her who said it. The baby scorpion scuttled inside the hollow eye socket, back to the darkness it held.

He nodded and looked away, as the showgirl pressed the button on the Escalade's remote to unlock the doors. There had been no surprise to what he had seen. Just a trick of the bones, to let him know who he was really talking to. Always the bones; always with him.

He climbed in on the passenger's side, and didn't say anything all the way back to the motorheads' place.

When they got there, she disappeared inside—there was an audition she had to get to, somebody big from Los Angeles was in town, something like that. She left him out in the garage.

"There you go," said Buzz-cut. "Pods are in, plus we re-jetted the carbs." He stood beside the Ninja, twisting the throttle.

The small-displacement engine screamed louder, the sound ripping through the suburban streets, until it was rolled off again. "You'll notice the difference. Mostly at the top end." Buzz-cut wiped a spot of grease off the lower left fairing with a shop rag. "But that's what you want, right?"

"What do I owe you guys?"

"*Nada.* You overpaid when we put the new shock in—so this one's on the house." Buzz-cut started picking up his tools from the black-stained towel he'd spread on the garage's bare cement floor. "Besides, we should probably throw one in for you, by this point."

"Since we're kinda done." The redheaded one stood by the open garage door, working on another beer. "That was the last thing left on the checklist."

He nodded. "I guess so." He fetched his helmet from the workbench where he'd left it and climbed on the bike.

"It's been fun." Buzz-cut reached out and shook his hand. "Hope everything works out the way you want."

He didn't say anything. Just slipped on the helmet, rolled the bike down the driveway to the street, started it up and headed away.

♣ A little movie played out in his head. While he was riding. He didn't need to close his eyes to watch it.

Out on Hacienda, to the west, where the Luxor pyramid was a small black triangle in the distance, its beam of light just a faded, starward chalk scratch. Somebody had dumped an old sofa at the side of the road, in the dirt-and-gravel strip between the edge of the asphalt and the big storm channel, the concrete ditch for the monsoon runoffs from the housing tracts farther on. People did that in this town, just abandoned their old crap right out in the open, instead of dragging it from one cheap apartment to another. Usually the old furniture just decayed away, under the hammer of the sun, until it was the same color and indistinguishable from the dust and rocks around it. But this time, somebody had set fire to the derelict furniture—kids, probably, or maybe some homeless guy who had fallen asleep on it while smoking through the pack of cigarettes that an hour or so of panhandling had earned him. At any rate, there really wasn't an old sofa at the side of the road any longer, but a charred rectangular patch on the ground, with blackened springs and scraps of the ashen framework poking up. The negative image of a sofa, something that had been there but wasn't now.

The movie ran inside his head as he rode by the spot. The movie, the memory, was from back when he was first married, long before all the bad stuff had happened, the tide of troubles—mostly of his own devising —that had washed away his marriage and so much else besides. It was a movie of him and his wife, the wife he had then, making love in the bedroom of the first apartment they'd had together. His apartment, that she had moved into with all her woman's things, the clothes that took up most of the closet and all the little bottles and jars that suddenly appeared around the bathroom sink, and which he didn't mind at all, and later missed with a terrible, heart-empty longing when they disappeared. But that wasn't in this movie; it was just the two of them in bed, in twined motion and release, in every direction that heart and lust suggested, the urgent whispers of lips and tongues brushing against each other's ears . . .

The camera of memory pulled back, rose above, to encompass the whole room and the ones beyond. The apartment building had had thin walls that were more like microphones into their neighbor's lives, rather than barriers keeping them out. He and his new wife had been able to hear people sneezing in the bedroom on the other side of the wall closest to their pillows. And as they made love, every time they had known that the others could hear them as well, the slide of skin against skin, the quickened breaths, the cries and commands. Which was confirmed in that movie's night by the sounds coming back to them through the bedroom wall of the couple on the other side, awakened and inspired in the middle of the cozy night, starting up on their own bout. He and his wife had clung to each other, his arms tight around her naked shoulders, the sweat that made her breasts glow in the moonlight mingling with his. They had held each other and listened, sharing a smile, blessed and able to bless. Their neighbors' lovemaking had grown louder and faster, becoming in turn the soundtrack to that night's movie, as he and his wife had gone silently prideful that their own had tapped through others' dreaming. And another little movie had played inside his head, of the couple in the apartment on the other side of their neighbors, awakened by the sounds coming through their thin bedroom wall. And then they would start in as well—*Why not?*—and they would waken the couple in the apartment beyond them, and on and on, upstairs and downstairs, throughout the entire apartment building, all awakened and inspired in the moonlit night. All making love at the same time, the sounds of breath and friction coming back around to him and his wife, resting up from their own exertions, letting their own breath slow and still again, getting ready for another go at it—they had both been so much younger then. And as he had held his young wife, the movie had continued to play, of the whole apartment building, all the windows dark and everyone inside engaged in the same activity, the beds creaking and swaying like small boats docked at the edge of a swelling ocean. And the sounds, though whispers, loud enough together that the next apartment building over awoke, bedroom by bedroom, and one by one, couple by couple, started in. And then the next building down the street, and the next, until the whole block, everyone who had been asleep and had been awakened by their neighbors and their own dreams, was making love. And then the next block after that, and the next, one by one, bedroom by bedroom, couple by couple . . .

The invisible camera's angle rose upward, through the bedroom's ceiling, into the sky, God-like as the clouds rolling beneath the moon. And he could look down at himself, his arms wrapped tight around his wife, and also—higher, beyond the clouds and moon—at what they had started, not a wave-driven ocean now but a fire sweeping through the streets and the dark apartment buildings, ignited by the spark from the one bedroom in the center of it all. Block by block, the couples oblivious to the flames, until the entire city was ablaze. And then, as the camera rose farther, high enough to glimpse the curvature of the earth, the cities on either side caught fire as well, first at their edges and then through all their awakened and still dreaming streets. Then even higher, the round earth hiding the stars, all its cities and fields burning now, and bright points of fiery islands in the blackness of the seas. The entire world burning in desire and motion, casting flickering shadows across the other planets in their lonely orbits . . .

That was as far as that movie went; it ended there, faded to black before the stars themselves ignited hotter. Leaving him, older and wifeless, riding around in the night, going nowhere, past the charred remains of the burnt-out sofa on the side of the road. The sight of which had triggered all the unreeling memory of that night so long ago, when the whole world had caught fire from a single spark.

The wind and the occasional desert rain would smear the burned sofa's ashes into the gravel, the sun bleaching it to gray, until nothing would be left but a shadow on the ground, a ghost in his remembering. To spool back onto its reel from the projector in that private theater, seal in its round flat film can and stack with the other reels, the archive of all he'd lost.

♣ "So how's the machine?" The bones seemed genuinely interested. But then, the plan was as much theirs as his. "How's it running now?"

"Fine." It had seemed a shame to throttle off the bike, after he'd gotten it up to speed on the long straightaway leading to the overpass, just so he could work back down through the gears and ease to a stop. "Real fast."

"Good. That's good." The eye sockets held the same dark, minus the pinpoint stars, as the night sky. "Glad to hear that. So what's left on the to-do list?"

He didn't answer. At least not yet. There wasn't much he could tell the bones. He sat on the motorcycle, both legs swung over to the left side, the scuffed black heels of his Oxtars dug into the gravel. The night was hot enough that he had on just a T-shirt beneath the Gericke jacket, unzipped to the level of his heart. Slowly, the sensory impressions of getting the motorcycle close to a hundred—the optimistic Ninja speedometer had read one-ten—settled in his head, like birds catching up with his passage through them. He stripped off his sweaty gloves and stuffed them into his helmet. There wasn't much he could tell the bones, because there wasn't anything left on the list.

The pods and the carb re-jetting had done everything the motorheads had promised him. With the air intake opened up, the engine had no problem revving to the max, screaming like a torched cat. Sixth gear and the tach redlined, there was just enough road, from where the streetlights ended to here, for him to approach top speed. Which would mean—if he hadn't pushed down on the postage stamp-sized pedal with his right boot and squeezed his right hand into a fist with the lever inside—he would have been into the triple digits when the side of the overpass popped into view. Just as he and the motorheads, with their scrap of paper and pencil stub, had calculated months ago in their garage. He still had the paper, with their motor oil thumbprints all over it, in his jacket pocket. That and the list of performance mods for the bike were the hard copies for the plan. Everything else had been kept inside his head and the rounded, empty white dome shared by clickety smiles and nesting scorpions.

"Come on," said the bones. "You know the answer as well as I do. Don't you?"

"I guess so." He leaned forward, holding the helmet by its rim. "I'd have to check."

"Don't try to bs me, pal. We don't have that kind of a relationship." There was no smile in the bones' voice. "Screw your list. You were telling me a week ago there was only one thing left on it. The pods, right? And some jackass thing to do with the carburetor. Right?"

"Pretty much."

An eighteen-wheeler rumbled overhead. The bones waited until the noise from the overpass faded, so their insistent whisper could be heard.

"And you were just over at the motorheads' place, weren't you? Which is why you're out here so late. That's the usual drill, isn't it? You get some work done over there by those wrench guys, then you come try it out. Vroom vroom. In your boy racer getup." In their rags, the bones sneered. "And of course, you stop to chat with us. Nice of you to drop in."

Get off my back, he thought. "You know," he said, "I don't have to."

"Wrong, wrong, wrong. You *do* have to. There are no options in your life. You got rid of those a long time ago. The only options you've got are the ones we let you have." The beads of the scorpion's hard gaze glinted at one socket's rim, the baby sting hovering a threat at the darkness's center. "Your little plan—that was amusing. We liked it."

"I'm glad."

"Don't be," said the bones. "You know what we liked about it? You go through all the motions, all the little choices you think you have—gotta have these exact tires on your motorcycle, gotta have the suspension tricked out just this way, gotta do this to the engine, your moronic pods or whatever they are, get the air intake just perfect—you do all that, and guess what? Every step brings you closer to right now. This moment. When you're ours." The rags parted slightly, revealing the white cage of ribs and the knotted spine, the bones stirring from their throne in the dust, as though they were about to rise up and fold him in their dry embrace. "When it's all done—and it will be—you're just as dead at the side of the road, in your vainglorious wreckage, the flames and blood, the whole nine yards of it, as you would have been in that dark little hole you're so scared of. So you might as well quit wasting your time and ours. Fun as it's been. Stop screwing around, pal, and get it over with. Because you really don't have a choice. You never did." The bones leaned forward, the empty gaze peering up into his eyes. "You know that now, don't you?"

"Whatever you say." It didn't matter to him. He had heard as much before, a lot of times, over and over. From the beginning, when he had first figured out the plan and what he was going to do. From when he had cut back on the meds, so his hands wouldn't tremble so badly that he couldn't ride the bike. That was when the little doors had creaked open again, and he had heard the whispers again.

All he would have had to do was take the meds, the full dose of the risperidone. Or any of the others they gave him. They were all good. They all worked just fine. The little doors would have closed again, and he wouldn't have heard the whispers. And the bones, in their rags and darkness, wouldn't have crept out and waited for him, either.

But that was the deal. If he wanted the bike—and the plan; that was what it was all about—then the bones came with it. He knew that.

"I guess it's the way things are," he said aloud. "In this world."

"There isn't any other. So let's go." The bones spoke almost kindly to him. Almost. "Tonight's the night. You don't have to wait 'til morning to unwrap your presents." A white hand, its fleshless segments rattling like dice, pointed from the end of one tattered sleeve. "Just throw your leg over your machine and head back down the road. You know the spot; it's all part of the plan, right? Then turn the machine back around, this way, and punch it."

"You don't punch a bike's throttle," he corrected. "You roll it on."

"Have it your way." The bones spoke with the vast patience of kings. "You know what to do. We've talked this all over before, haven't we? And even when we don't tell you—when you don't come out here to see us—then you tell yourself. Because we're always with you."

That much was true. He looked away from the bones, down the way he had come. In the distance the last of the streetlights shone, pale blue, the frayed edge of the city. The night had grown silent, the rumble of traffic on the overpass thinned to nothing. All that was left out here now was the desert and the road. All he had to do—just as the bones told him—was to head down to the starting point he had already picked out, turn around, and take the straight shot back to where the bones would be waiting for him. Except this time he wouldn't roll off the throttle a couple seconds after he hit sixth gear, smoke the brakes, and snick the left pedal back down to first, coming to a stop a yard away from the bundle of rags and the yellowed smile.

Instead—another movie played inside his head, a shorter one, that was all speed and night until the last hard second—he would roll the throttle to the limit, the acceleration mounting beneath and around him, his unhelmeted gaze fixed on the target in the center of the windscreen. A little to the left of the rags and bones, to the right of the asphalt's course.

The blank concrete wall of the overpass, racing toward him and he to it. Crouching down low, his heart against the motorcycle's tank, pulling himself forward with the grips in his fists, to bring himself that last inch closer, the last second cut even shorter, nothing but the wall filling the headlight beam . . .

There wasn't any movie after that. Looking across the night road, he was grateful he couldn't see anything more. He had already figured that the small wreckage would be spotted and radioed in by some trucker crossing on the overpass above, or maybe by one of the crews heading for an early-morning start at one of the construction sites close by. Or if there were flames—if the bike's split-open gas tank sparked just right—maybe a police helicopter cruising over the Strip would bank over to investigate the smoke and glow.

Or maybe—and sometimes he wondered if this might not be the most likely—nobody would notice what had happened. Why should they? Abandoned things and forgotten—this was the landscape for them. People had been hauling their old junk out to the desert and leaving it there for generations, to rot and weather away, or burn to ashes. A crumpled-up motorcycle, complete with the corpse of its rider—who'd notice? Or if they did, why would they bother about it? He could see himself, or what would be left of him, lying where the bones lay now, in the same tattered rags. The coyotes and feral dogs would strip the bruised and bloodied flesh from his arms. The sun would dry his face to leather, then strip it away in the dust and wind. Leaving the cracked bones behind, his own smile yellowing to greet whoever might stop, the next one . . .

"That's exactly how it'll be." The bones had read his thoughts. Or their own. "You've come this far. Ready to wrap it up. All that screwing around with the machine—that's been fun, and it got you here. To this point. That's great, but now you're just wasting time. Let's get it over with."

"Sure." He nodded as he loosened the buckle on the helmet's strap. "That's what I want, all right. But I've got something else to take care of first."

"What are you talking about?" The bones' whisper rasped harsher. "You don't have anything else to do. That's what this is all about. That's why you're here."

"Maybe." He swivelled the helmet around in his hands, right side up. "No, you're right. I know you are." Everything in his life had brought him to this place, a bare roadside in the middle of the night. "So I'll be back in just a bit."

"And just where do you think you're going?" The bones' fleshless hands knuckled the dust; the emptied shape inside the rags leaned forward, the hollow gaze intent on him, as though strength other than its voice had been found, enough to grab him by the legs and drag him back against the overpass wall. "You can't go anywhere. You're ours now. You've always been."

He had already pulled on the helmet, but the bones' words came shrill at his ear, regardless. "I'll see you." He started up the motorcycle.

"Oh, you will." The tiny scorpion crouched at the rim of a smaller darkness. "You will," promised the bones.

♣ Nothing but powder left in his jacket pockets now. With the throttle rolled on, the highway curving away before him, he'd taken his left hand off the grip and dug inside his jacket, close to his waist. His gloved fingers had found the little orange container, rattling with the tabs inside it. He had grasped it and taken it out, thrown it away. In one of his mirrors he had seen a little sparking explosion behind him, the plastic cylinder splintering on impact, the white lid spinning across the asphalt, the tablets dancing for a moment before they were ground under the wheels of a semi heading east.

He should have been able to spot the approaching lights of Barstow by now. A straight shot, coming from the east on the I-15. Even without checking his watch or the motorcycle's odometer, he knew how long he had been riding. That the highway and the bare landscape on either side still lay under the night's dark—not a good sign.

And that he was all alone on the road—not good, either. There should have been plenty of other traffic, in either direction. But for hours, there had been just his bike's headlight, carving out a little section of asphalt and concrete ahead of him.

What it meant, he knew, was that whatever traces of the meds had been left in his system when he started were all processed out by now. The last leak he had taken, the bike pulled over to the side of the road, left whatever remained of the risperidone in a wet mark on the sand. As he had zipped the riding trousers back up, he had looked up at the stars, trembling in their slow paths. Any moment, they would arrange themselves into words unreadable until now. He had seen them before, a long time back, spelled out in the debris swirling on a flooded concrete floor. The message would have to wait, though. He had gotten back on the bike and started it up, knowing that there would be things he would need to deal with.

Taillights showed up ahead. He straightened his back, bringing his gaze higher over the windscreen, and studied them. At first he figured they were a truck, some eighteen-wheeler; the lights were way up in the air. Then the moon edged out from a patch of clouds, and he could see that the taillights were on the butt of some RV lumbering along, an old-model Winnebago or Coachmen. Big panel-view windows were centered under the taillights and down along the RV's high sides. Through the Ninja's top-gear whine, the sound of the way bigger vehicle's engine could be heard straining against the weight it carried.

Although over in the left lane, the RV wasn't anywhere near the speed limit. Coming up closer, he could see that there was all kinds of junk strapped to it, a couple of dirt bikes on the bumper rack, camping gear and plastic storage bins roped down on top. He wouldn't have to drop down into fifth gear to slide past the RV's right rear corner.

But as soon as the Ninja sped alongside, the RV moved over into his lane, like a horizontal avalanche.

Straight highway—if he had been banked into a curve, he would have been screwed. He grabbed the front brakes and trod hard on the rear brake pedal. That yanked him back quickly enough that the RV's bumper missed his front wheel by a couple of feet. He rode the brakes a little more, letting the bike drop another few yards behind the RV.

He didn't need to glimpse the driver's face, looking back at him from the RV's mirrors. This was an old movie that he had seen before. In the bike's headlight beam, he could see the lumbering box shape more clearly now: the dirt bikes strapped to its rear were rusted and decaying, the rubber shredding off the broken-spoked wheels, the frames bent and useless, ready to snap apart with a finger's touch. Scraps of tattered canvas fluttered from the camping gear above. The plastic bins had split open, the rotted contents leaking in dark stains smeared by the wind along the side panels of the RV.

A child's hand or something like it, but whiter and thinner, twitched aside the ragged curtain in the rear window. He could just see an angle of a child's face—but it wasn't—peering out at him with hollowed eyes. And smiling all yellowed before letting the curtain drop back into place.

The RV slowed down as it drifted back and forth across both lanes, blocking him. A different movie, he knew. He leaned his weight onto the bike's handlebars, watching. The game wouldn't be to run him off the road, or crush him and the bike under the weight of all that rusting steel. But instead, to just creep slower and slower, with him and the crawling bike stuck behind, trapped, until time and this world—their world—came to a stop. The road wouldn't end, the night wouldn't end; nothing would.

Maybe I should've stuck to the plan. That would have been a better deal. With the plan, at least, there would have been an end to all things.

But now it was too late. *You might as well,* he told himself. *Do it.*

He drifted the bike over to the far left edge of the highway, as though he were going to try to sail across the boulder-lined ravine at the asphalt's limit. The RV moved the wall of its tail end in front of him, as he knew it would. He goosed the throttle, coming within a couple feet of the bumper. Then he grabbed the clutch lever and kicked the bike down into fifth, then off the clutch, rolling the throttle all the way on while pushing down hard on the right grip. The Ninja bolted itself into a forty-five-degree turn, nearly clipping the RV's bumper as it shot over to the right lane. He kept the throttle rolled to its limit, shoving down on the left grip, bringing the bike straight and upright before it could fly off into the sharp-edged rocks at the other edge of the highway.

Alongside the RV now, he flattened his chest against the Ninja's tank, the scream of the red-lined engine accelerating his heart. Looking straight through the windscreen rather than over it, he could see the open highway up ahead in the broad swath of the RV's headlights. *Target fix,* he told himself. *That's all you gotta do.*

Towering above, the side of the RV walked past him, one slow measure after another. He could see it in his peripheral vision, blocking half the world. Its engine, twenty times bigger than the Ninja's, coughed and growled, then roared as the unseen driver slammed down the accelerator pedal. Black oily smoke bellowed out from the rust-perforated exhaust beneath the RV, its sharp acrid fumes whipped up in the bike's wheels and hitting him in the face, gagging and blinding him. He let go of the left grip and backhanded the helmet visor, knocking it upward so the wind could scrub his sight clear again. The RV lurched beside him, matching his speed.

Or close to. The bike still had an edge, crawling alongside the RV now.

The speedometer's needle trembled past ninety. He was halfway past the RV's bulk, inching toward the open highway beyond their headlights. He curled into a full tuck behind the windscreen, bootsoles jammed against the pegs. The asphalt below him blurred, the moonlit desert to his right, and the silhouetted mountains in the distance, speeding by.

The RV crossed the center line, rumbling closer to his left elbow. Another couple of feet over and it would bat him flying off the highway, the bike catching on the rock-strewn gravel and tumbling end over end. A push against the right grip edged him a few inches away from the RV and closer to the roadside. The RV teasingly moved over with him, the divider line underneath its smoking underbelly, funneling the lane they shared now into a space barely wider than the bike's handlebars.

They want me to look. He realized that it wouldn't be enough to just shove him off the road at speed; that would be over too fast. If he gave in to the pull of the roaring shape looming inches at his left elbow and glanced up and over at the RV's passenger-side window—he would see past it to what was behind the wheel, see their hollowed eyes and yellowed smile. He would even hear the whispered greeting inside his helmet. That would be all it would take. Enough to draw the bike a degree off its straight-ahead course, enough to suck him right up against the RV's battered, rust-stained wall, one of the bike's handlebars snagging against the corrugated steel and fiberglass. That would be enough contact to whip the bike out of his control and hammer it down on its left side, the rear wheel breaking grip with the asphalt and sailing above him, as he scraped and tumbled himself into blood and rags of leather on the road surface.

Look where you want to go. He could hear the motorhead telling him that. *That's where you'll go.* And his own voice, silent through clenched teeth: *Don't look where you don't want to go.*

The needle centered between the zeroes of the 100 mark. He was close enough to the front of the RV that the notion came to that that he could let go of the left handgrip, reach ahead past the windscreen, grab the rusted chrome rim of the RV's headlight and pull himself and the bike up ahead of it. Ahead, and out into the road beyond, the lane opening up full width, where he could just stay tucked behind the windscreen, kick the bike up into sixth, roll the throttle to its limit and leave the RV behind, his silhouette racing to the far reach of its headlight beams . . .

The asphalt and concrete narrowed another foot, as the RV edged over again. Toying with him; if whatever was behind the wheel had wanted to end it right now, a sharp tug on the steering wheel would have knocked the bike tumbling into the rocks and gravel.

But he knew the bones didn't want that. Because then it would be over. They wanted him to ease off the throttle, maybe a little step on the brake pedal. Just enough to let the bike drift back, the side of the RV rolling past him. Until he was all the way behind it, breathing its heavy exhaust, the gravel kicked up by its tires spattering against the windscreen and his helmet's face shield. The high taillights would glint down at him, pulling far enough way from him to shine like smoky red stars in the darkness. Which would only end when he gave up and turned around, went back and kept his end of the bargain he had made a long time ago.

The RV cut away another slice of the road. The strip of asphalt he had left in front of him was barely wider than the bike's handlebars.

Roll it off now, he told himself. *Or don't.*

He didn't get to decide. Already too late for that—the road suddenly turned underneath him. It wasn't supposed to; in another world, the real one—or at least the one that people who weren't so screwed up lived in—the road was a straight shot, a strip of asphalt and concrete laid out across the desert like a knife blade. But here in this world, the bones' world, he found himself looking into nothing but the darkness beyond the windscreen, as the Ninja's headlight beam swept off the right-hand curve that snapped in front of him. He shoved down on the right grip and the bike heeled over, cutting into the road's sudden arc.

At his left side, inches away, the RV groaned onto its rust-choked suspension. In his mirror, he glimpsed the RV's heavy back end breaking free and fishtailing, the wide bald tires scrubbing S-shaped rubber tracks across the road behind. The RV piled into the curve, its engine still gunned to the max, its high bulk tilting over the bike.

The curve tightened. He couldn't roll off the throttle now, even if he had wanted to. The bike's velocity was all that kept it pinned to the road. He tucked in flat enough on the tank to grind the helmet's chin bar against the gauges. The night sky tilted on its hidden axis, the silhouetted mountains climbing up alongside the stars.

Tighter, higher, vertical—speed erased gravity. Stars wheeled in the headlight's beam. On the bike's tach, the needle had redlined seconds, ages ago. The engine's scream vibrated up through the grips, along his arms and down his hunched, contracted spine. The asphalt wasn't a road anymore, but a curving wall that the bike's centrifugal force hammered him into. Farther above him, the RV's bulk blotted out the stars, the maxed-out engine roaring loud enough to banish all perception other than his heart pounding against the tank.

Look where. The words caught in his clenched teeth. *You want to go.* His tongue bled a salt trickle down his throat. *That's where you'll go.*

Flames mingled with the smoke pouring from beneath the RV. The orange glare flicked across the Ninja's gauges and windscreen. From the corner of his eye, he could just see the side panel of the RV break loose from the frame, the wind peeling it back like a broken wing.

The RV's side window twisted and shattered, sending bright fragments of razor-sharp hail across his face shield and the backs of his gloved hands, tight on the bike's grips. The little storm passed over him before he could even duck his head beneath it.

Don't look. The flames and smoke tugged at the edge of his sight. *You look, you'll crash.* He knew that; he knew that all he had to do was turn his head a couple of degrees and his eyes would lock, beyond will or choice, on the churning vision that sped parallel to his course. It had always been that way. *That's how you got to this place.* Lock, and be sucked under the shoulder-high wheels roaring right next to him. *Don't look where you don't want to go—*

The road curved tighter. He shoved the right grip all the way down, twisting his body to keep his shoulder from catching the asphalt. Sparks shot from the skid plate on one of the Oxtars as it ground against the road.

Above him, the RV's side panel ripped all the way free and scythed spiraling inches above his head. Everything inside exposed now—he kept his eyes locked ahead into the dark, but still could see the flames and smoke at the edge of his vision. And worse. He didn't need to turn his head, lock on to what was inside the flames. A red flood, hissing and steaming, mired with little orange plastic cylinders, spilling out bright capsules and tabs, syringes and empty latex gloves like ghosts' hands, fingering torn-up release forms and divorce papers, scraps of some other life, the debris of fraud and vengeance, everything he had been so stupid about, that had caught him at last, wrapping their thin wet snares about his neck, choking him . . .

And something darker, whipping the shallow tide across the RV's floorboard. A storm that never passed. A storm of screaming and shouting, men's cries of furious rage and glee, trapped inside a small dark place that you crawled bleeding into. The hole where you died. Under the screaming that was your own, under the screaming and shouting, the flames and smoke of the storm that never passed. That roared and tumbled, beside and above you, so close that you sucked it in with each breath. All the way, every second, every mile that the road and the bike screamed beneath you, the storm that never passed, that could never end—

Look where you want to go. He opened his eyes wide to the dark, seeing nothing ahead. *Look where you want to go.*

Somewhere else. Somewhere that wasn't this place. Even if he couldn't see it. *Where you want—*

An explosion beside him, strong enough to send the bike wavering before he could balance out its angled trajectory again. The RV's right front tire shredded apart, whips of worn-through black rubber pinwheeling around the bolted hub. One frayed tip struck him across the face shield, knocking his head back for a moment. He squeezed the grips tighter as the disintegrating tire lashed the spine of his jacket and the bike's rear fender.

The RV lifted away from the asphalt, its velocity and the road's curve launching it into the night sky. Now he couldn't help but look, as the flame-filled mass rotated, turned on its axis, centrifugal force all that kept its smoking wreckage from spilling down upon him. If his hand hadn't been locked on the left grip, he would have instinctively, futilely, tried to shield himself from the weight and fire crashing down on him in frozen time.

Now he closed his eyes. He huddled against the bike's tank, elbow and knees welded to the small machine, curling himself into a sightless ball, sparks grinding out unseen against the road as he tilted the bike farther into the tightening curve.

Something hit the road behind him, hard enough to send a shockwave buckling through the road beneath, the front wheel lifting clear for a fraction of a second. Then hitting hard enough to bottom out the forks. He wrestled the grips, eyes sprung open again, to keep the bike from spinning out from under him. A gust of heat, hard and scorching as a steel furnace, rolled across him from behind, wrapping him in churning smoke.

The road straightened, like a rope snapped taut. He heeled the Ninja back up to vertical and squeezed on the brakes, as the bike shot out into air scrubbed clean by the desert wind.

The speedometer's needle crawled down to sixty, then fifty and forty. He kept it there, downshifting and rolling on the throttle. In the mirrors, past his own shoulders, he could see the flames growing smaller, the wreckage diminishing with each mile. Until it was gone and there was just darkness around him, picked apart by stars, split by the headlight beam racing ahead.

♣ "Buddy, you look like hell."

He glanced up from the coffee cup. "What?"

"You're in bad shape." The guy behind the counter, in a T-shirt and grease-stained apron, pointed. "Right there, you're bleeding."

His fingertips came away red when he touched the side of his face. He had set his helmet down on the counter; he could see now where the transparent shield had been cracked. When the shredded tire had hit him—he hadn't even felt it.

"Lucky you didn't lose an eye." The guy topped up the cup, then replaced the pot on the burner behind him. "Stuff like that happens all the time."

"Yeah." He poked the sore edge running from his temple down to his cheekbone. It seemed to be closing up. "I guess."

"Where you heading?"

"LA." He had left the Ninja parked out by the gas pumps. The station and little convenience store had been the first lights he had come across. If he let his hand rest around the cup for too long, the dark surface trembled. Not from the meds—those were long gone—but from the strain tightening his shoulder muscles.

"You got a long way to go." The guy rested his bare elbows on the counter, bringing his gray-stubbled face close. "A real long way."

He looked up, knowing already what he would see.

"You might," said the guy, "not make it."

"I don't know about that. I got a pretty good start."

The yellowed smile widened. "You can get into all sorts of bad stuff out on the road." A thin hand reached over and idly spun a rack of frayed, dog-eared postcards beside the cash register. Vistas of Death Valley and Zion rolled past. "Shit happens."

"Tell me about it." He looked right back, without blinking, into the dark spaces gazing at him. With a fingertip, he drew a red mark across the mottled counter. "It already has."

"Oh?" Still smiling, the way they always did. "Was there . . . an accident?" A nod toward the police scanner sitting on a shelf. "Funny we didn't hear about it."

"Then I guess there wasn't."

A tiny shape, with black bead eyes and a hooked stinger curving over its back, peered at him as it clung to a ridge of white bone.

"You better go back home, buddy." The bones reached for the pot and topped up the cup again. "Back where you belong. You're not going to make it."

He didn't touch the coffee. Laying a couple of dollars on the counter, he slid off the padded stool. "We'll see about that."

"Look at you." The yellowed smile clicked in place. "You're already shot."

"Yeah, well . . ." He zipped up the jacket. The front of it was covered with road dust, and he saw now that the corner of one pocket was ripped loose. "We do what we can."

"That was nothing." The thin hand pointed out the window, past the neon Budweiser sign and down the unlit road. "There's worse things out there."

"Better hurry, then." He picked up his helmet from the counter, removed his gloves from inside, and pulled them on. "I don't want to keep them waiting."

The bells over the door caught and jingled as he walked out to the bike.

♣ Noon when he pulled into Los Angeles; the heat was nothing compared to where he had come from. He could keep his riding jacket on without being pounded into the sidewalk by the sun. And even though the Pacific was still another half hour away, he could smell it from here, ocean salt on his tongue.

He left the Ninja at the curb. It didn't feel right to park it in the house's driveway; it wasn't his house anymore, and hadn't been for a long time. When he slid the ignition key into his pocket, his hand grazed the shape, an egg with edges, of the bike's left front turn signal, which he had retrieved from the end of a six-foot-long skid mark and tucked inside his jacket. He looked the bike over more closely, surveying the damage: besides losing the signal, the fairing had a nasty crack on that side, running all the way up to the headlight. Bending down, he ran his hand over the rashed front fender. Nothing too bad; nothing that the motorheads couldn't either fix or replace.

There was a scrape on his jacket's left elbow as well, and his arm ached from the fall. That would fade; he could tell that nothing was broken just by clenching his fist. A knee of his trousers was torn, exposing the curved armor underneath, plus one Oxtar was a little beat up. Overall, he had gotten off light. He had gone down right at the end of the freeway off-ramp, taking the curve too hot, from over-confidence and relief at having made it all this way. But even as he had been rolling onto his back, the bike skidding in a half-spiral away from him, he had almost been laughing inside his helmet, knowing that this was no big thing. No traffic on the road that he had spilled onto—he had picked himself up, walked over to the bike and righted it, rolled it out of the way. Waiting for the gas to ebb out of the flooded carburetors, he had spotted the turn signal lying in the road, wire dangling from the stalk, and had strolled back to fetch it before it got flattened. Then the Ninja had started right up. *Nice and easy,* he had told himself, shifting into second. He had gotten this far; the rest would be a piece of cake.

Carrying the helmet by its strap, he walked to the front door, past the split-leaf philodendrons that he had planted so long ago. They had grown large and sprawling enough to brush against anybody who came up the narrow concrete path. Maybe there would be another time he could come out here and trim them back.

Nobody answered the doorbell. He squinted in through the pebbled glass panels and saw nothing. Funny if he had come all this way and she wasn't home.

The trash cans were still behind the side gate, right where they had kept them when he had lived there. He squeezed past and stepped onto the wide concrete slab of the back patio. On a little plastic table—that much was new—a nearly full cup of coffee trailed a wisp of steam into the still air.

He poked his head in the open screen door. "Julie?"

She didn't seem surprised that he was standing there. Maybe a little puzzled. She stepped back from the hallway closet and looked across the kitchen at him. "Hey." And smiled. "Wow. Been a while."

"Yeah. I know." They had never been completely out of touch. There had always been some phone calls, especially when he had first got out. But those had tapered off the last couple of years. "Can I come in?"

"Are you kidding?" She set her stationery box back on the closet's top shelf. "You don't have to ask that."

"Well . . ." He set his helmet down on the counter by the sink. "It's not my house."

"Yeah, right. Technically."

Sitting at the table, he watched as she poured coffee for him, adding the half-and-half from the fridge without asking him. "You remembered."

"What?"

"How I take it."

"Hold that thought." She went out to the patio to fetch her own cup.

For a moment, waiting, he let himself slip back. To that other time, long before. He could close his eyes and not see the things that had changed, not even how she had changed. She had cut her hair shorter, but it didn't matter. When she sat down across from him, real time started up again.

"You came all the way out here on that motorcycle of yours?" The helmet on the counter had finally caught her eye. "God, you must be tired."

More numb than tired; the circulation was just beginning to return to his butt. He shrugged. "It's how I get around."

"So I heard."

He looked away from her, across the kitchen cupboards. Even with them closed, he knew just how the dishes were stacked inside, how the cups hung from the little hooks he had put in. Long ago.

He was glad she had kept the place. That had been the main reason for the divorce. Doing what the lawyers had advised. So she wouldn't get hurt too bad when all the hearings and pleas had finally been over, and he had gone in.

"Did you take the day off or something?" He saw that she had her jeans on.

She shook her head. "I have to go over to Accounting in a couple of hours. And cover for Kathy. Remember Kathy?"

"Sure." He had no idea who she was talking about.

"She just had another baby."

"Oh."

"Otherwise . . . maybe we could've gone and had lunch or something. Since you're here. You should've called me."

"It's okay," he said. "I have to get back, anyway. And it's a long ride."

Silence, and a bit of the time before, as they sat and sipped their coffee. He held the cup in both hands, though he didn't need to.

"So what's the reason? For the visit?"

He didn't know. He had come all this way, and he still didn't know. He hadn't known when he had left. If the bones had asked him, he wouldn't have been able to say why.

"Just to see me?" Her voice was soft, a little sad. Maybe she had felt that other time circle around her as well. She set her cup down and smiled. "You could've done that before now."

"No . . . that's not it."

"Then what is?" She waited for him to answer.

Then he knew. "Look at me," he said.

"You dope. I am looking at you. Right now."

"No—" He shook his head. "I mean really look at me. Real close."

"All right." She made a game out of setting her cup down, folding her arms on the table, and leaning forward. "What do you want me to see?"

He leaned forward as well, close enough to have kissed her. But he didn't. And there was nothing that he wanted her to see in his face; he knew he looked older to her. Probably a lot older. Not that it mattered—he really just wanted to look at her, into her eyes.

He didn't see anything. Or just the dark, at their centers; that was all. That was enough.

"Well . . . you need to start getting ready. To go to work." He leaned back in the chair, turned the coffee cup around with one finger. "I should take off."

"You're heading back? Already?" She looked even more puzzled. "You just got here."

"Yeah, I know. But . . ." He shrugged. "I should get going."

"That's really stupid. Look, why don't you just hang out here until I get back? Then—I don't know—maybe we could go have dinner or something." She reached her hand out and laid it on top of his. "Like the old days."

He smiled. "Old days are gone, baby." *Just as well,* he thought. "Maybe next time."

She watched as he got up and took his helmet from the counter. "Next time," she said quietly.

♣   Outside, a patrol car had pulled up alongside the bike. The cop behind the wheel looked over at him as he came down the house's drive-way. "That's an equipment violation, pal." The cop nodded toward the bike. "You need working turn signals in this state."

He took the broken-off signal from his jacket and held it up. "Just need to get it wired up, officer."

"What happened?"

"No big deal." He swung his leg over the bike. "Took a spill a little while ago. Coming off the freeway. That's all."

The cop's gaze took in the bike's cracked fairing. "How long you been riding?"

"Long enough."

The cop leaned farther out the driver's-side window, looking straight at him. "Think you're pretty smart, don't you?"

He knew who he was talking to, even before the cop pulled off the LAPD-issue sunglasses. He had expected as much, sooner or later. The tiny dry claws, the segmented tail and venomed hook arching over the scaly back, the tinier pinpoint eyes watching from the emptiness inside a rim of white. "Smart enough," he said.

"No, you're not." The yellowed smile showed. "We had a plan. That was the deal."

"I changed it." With his boot heel, he kicked up the bike's side stand. "That was one of the things I learned when I was inside. You have to be able to change your plans as you go along. So I did."

"Nice," snarled the bones. "Real nice. When did this happen?"

"I don't know." He had thought about it before. "Maybe when they put the new tires on." A slow nod. "Yeah, that was probably it. Made a lot more difference, performance-wise, than the engine mods." He tilted his hands in front of himself. "I could really feel the bike then. First curve I took, it was like *tight* on the road, you know? And then, with the new rear shock added on, I started to—"

"Oh, shut up. Just shut up." It wasn't a smile anymore, but yellowed teeth gritted with loathing. The bones put the sunglasses back over the cop's eyes, hiding the baby scorpion. "You didn't change anything. Your ass is still mine. You want to know why?"

"Tell me."

"You want too much," said the bones. "You got your stupid motor-cycle; you should've stopped with that. Something real. *One* thing. That should've been enough. That's way more than most people ever get. But you want more than that, don't you?"

"I guess so." He shrugged. "Maybe I do."

"You want what by nature you cannot have." The cop drew himself back inside the patrol car. "What you lost a long time ago. That's what will break you."

"Okay. We'll see."

"Oh, I promise you. Don't worry about that."

"Well . . ." He couldn't think of anything else. "Like I said. We'll see."

"And then . . ." The bones gazed at him in fury for a moment longer, before the patrol car pulled away.

He watched it disappear down the street. A glance back at the house, its door with panels of pebbled glass, the overgrown greenery, the plates stacked in the kitchen cupboards. Then he started up the bike, swung it around and headed east, back the way the roads had brought him.

CONTRIBUTORS

FELICIA CAMPBELL is professor of English at the University of Nevada, Las Vegas, and perhaps best known for pioneering the study of the positive aspects of gambling behavior. She has been executive director of the Far West Popular Culture and American Culture Associations, since founding them twenty-two years ago, and is editor of *Popular Culture Review.*

BRYAN D. DIETRICH is the author of six books of poems and a book-length study of comics. His poetry has appeared in the *New Yorker, Poetry, Ploughshares,* and many other journals. Winner of the Paris Review Prize and a "Discovery"/*The Nation* award, Dietrich is a professor of English at Newman University.

BLISS ESPOSITO was born and raised in Las Vegas, where she learned the intricacies of the gaming world. She writes about the hidden side of Vegas, the details below the glitzy surface, and often subverts popular ideas about the town. She recently earned an MFA in creative writing from the University of Nevada, Las Vegas.

JAQ GREENSPON lives in Las Vegas and has been writing professionally for over twenty years. He has been read widely on several continents and has had the pleasure of seeing his words mangled by professional actors on a number of TV shows and film sets.

KIM IDOL grew up in Los Angeles. She has a degree in education from Mount Saint Mary's, a degree in literature from California State University, Northridge, and an MFA in creative writing from the University of Nevada, Las Vegas.

As well as his own original and much-acclaimed horror and sci-fi novels, including *In the Land of the Dead, Farewell Horizontal,* and *Dark Seeker,* **K. W. JETER** has also written what many critics cite as the first true cyberpunk novel, *Dr. Adder.*

JARRET KEENE is the author of the poetry collections *Monster Fashion* and *A Boy's Guide to Arson,* and the unauthorized rock-band bio *The Killers: Destiny Is Calling Me.* He has edited several books, including *The Underground Guide to Las Vegas, Las Vegas Noir,* and *Neon Crush: A Celebration of Las Vegas Poetry.* He also curated the noise-rock compilation CD *Desertscraped: New Noise from the Neon Homeland.* His post-apocalyptic black-metal band Dead Neon wreaks sonic havoc in the dive bars of Sin City.

ANDREW KIRALY was born and raised in Las Vegas, and he's still recovering. The former managing editor of an alt-weekly, *Las Vegas CityLife,* he currently edits *Desert Companion,* the city's foremost regional magazine.

LORI KOZLOWSKI was born and raised in Las Vegas. A journalist and fiction writer, she is a graduate of the University of Southern California's Master of Professional Writing Program. She has served as adjunct faculty at Chapman University, teaching literature and composition. Currently, she works for the *Los Angeles Times.*

PETER MAGLIOCCO has edited the lit-zine *ART:MAG* for twenty years in Sin City. His latest novel is *The Burgher of Virtual Eden.* His writing has been Pushcart Prize-nominated in the categories of fiction and poetry.

C. J. MOSHER is a classroom teacher. His education column, "Socrates in Sodom," has appeared in the weekly newspaper *Las Vegas CityLife* for the better part of a decade. He used to hate cats until one actually saved his life. Hence, this Harlan Ellison-influenced satire, "A Girl and Her Cat."

P MOSS is a former screenwriter and founder of the popular Las Vegas nightspots Double Down Saloon and Frankie's Tiki Room. His commentary and short fiction have appeared in several magazines and online literary reviews, and he was co-creator of the local television cult comedy *TV/OD.* His first book, *Blue Vegas,* was published in 2010.

CHRIS NILES is the author of six mystery novels. Her short stories have been published in *Tart Noir* and *Brooklyn Noir.* She lives in New York City, but dreams of Nevada.

A longtime visitor to Las Vegas, **TODD JAMES PIERCE** won the 2006 Drue Heinz Literature Prize for his story collection *Newsworld,* which was selected by Joan Didion. In addition to writing the celebrated novel *The Australia Stories,* he coedited *Behind the Short Story* and *Las Vegas Noir.*

GAIL TRAVIS REGIER's stories and poems have appeared in a variety of publications, including *Harper's, Atlantic Monthly, Amazing Stories, American Scholar, Ploughshares,* and *Poetry.*

VU TRAN was born in Saigon and grew up in Tulsa, Oklahoma. He is a graduate of the Iowa Writers' Workshop and was a Glenn Schaeffer Fellow at the University of Nevada, Las Vegas, where he currently teaches creative writing and literature. He recently won a 2009 Whiting Writers' Award for his short fiction, which has appeared in *The Best American Mystery Stories, The O. Henry Prize Stories, Southern Review, Glimmer Train, Harvard Review,* and many other publications.